TEMPT

TEMPT

NATALIA JASTER

Books by Natalia Jaster

FOOLISH KINGDOMS SERIES
Trick (Book 1)
Dare (Book 2)
Lie (Book 3)
Dream (Book 4)

SELFISH MYTHS SERIES
Touch (Book 1)
Torn (Book 2)
Tempt (Book 3)
Transcend (Book 4)

Copyright © 2019 Natalia Jaster

All rights reserved
ISBN: 978-1695808218

Cover by Covers by Juan, coversbyjuan.com
Interior typesetting by Roman Jaster
Set in Odile, Trajan, and Melany Lane Ornaments

This is a work of fiction. Names, characters, places and incidents either are the product of the author's imagination or are used fictitiously, and any resemblance to any actual persons, living or dead, events, or locales is entirely coincidental.

This book may not be reproduced, scanned, or distributed in any form, or by any means, without written permission from the author.

*To the reader who peers at the night sky,
counts the stars, and thinks,
"What if…"*

PROLOGUE

Now she knows what loss feels like.

Her bare feet sink into the earth, the high grass tickles her ankles, and petals brush her calves. And when a breeze rustles her gown—dyed the green of a calla lily stem—the little pirouette of air billows the material, the hem flapping in a farewell gesture.

Something akin to *Good-bye*.

Of all the forbidden words that she's ever written, she has never penned that one. She's never had a reason to do so. Not until today.

Lupines sprout across the vista, a landscape not of her childhood, nor of adulthood. It's a realm caught somewhere in between, a pasture of budding fruit rather than flowers, of moon beams rather than sun beams. Hence, it's not her place.

No, this is his place. Or this used to be his place, back when she hardly knew him.

Back when she hardly knew herself.

He'd once growled an inquiry at her, demanding a truth that she hadn't been able to grasp.

Who are you?

It has taken a long time, but she knows the answer.

Yet it's too late. He's too far from her, too far away.

What she wouldn't give to have that demon back, to tell

him she wants the lightness and darkness. She yearns for that angel's face and devil's heart. She wishes to tell him the past doesn't matter as much as the present.

She wants to call him by his name and mean it.

But she can't. She cannot even scribe these things on paper for him, because he'll never read those words, never any words from her. Not ever again.

Because he's gone.

He's gone because of her.

And this time, he's not coming back.

1

The demon is wailing again. The sound blazes through the library floor, reaching out to her from the underworld of his lair. It's a brushfire raging fast across the room and has the texture of a blister, which shouldn't be possible, heat being an intangible thing to deities.

But nothing concerning him ever makes sense.

Wonder stiffens, her finger arrested on a book title, the pad of her digit pressed hard against the embossed letters. He always manages to stir the attentive parts of her. Perhaps that's why she cannot stay away. She shouldn't be here at this hour, tucked between the nonfiction shelves, the repository a midnight tomb.

Starlight trickles in from the high windows, illuminating writing desks and reading chairs and strands of ivy in a metallic, secretive sheen. It gives inanimate objects a trembling quality, as if his screams torment them as well.

The cacophony builds to a guttural howl, frayed at the edges. By some force of nature, it stings the scars on her wrists.

Her hands fall to her sides. She has never lied to herself before, and she shouldn't do so now. She knows why she's here. Sneaking into the library at this hour has less to do with research and more to do with those shrieks and the wilted feeling in her heart.

Beneath the ferocious calls, there's grief, and confusion, and delirium.

Beneath all of that, there's madness.

She hates when he does this. She hates *why* he does this.

Wonder brushes the pulp of scars running across her skin. Then she draws in a shaky breath, inhaling the wildflower corsage cinched around her wrist—a bundle of eucalyptus, white stephanotis, and a single purple peony.

She strides from the bookshelves containing tomes about languages, the hem of her forest green gown swishing around her bare feet, a delicate sound compared to the riotous one coming from below. The longbow and quiver of quartz arrows rattle across her back as she vacates the four-hundreds section, steps through a partition at the building's rear, and descends into a pit.

The vault is drafty, a place where rare books should be stored but aren't, because perhaps this room lost its purpose long ago. Perhaps the mortals running this repository have found a different area in which to put them. As a result, humans rarely spend time down here.

Even if they did, they wouldn't see what she sees, since deities and their possessions are invisible to humans. Thus, they wouldn't have the capacity to view the fire pit that produces a curdling funnel of smoke from the fuming logs. Neither would mortals see the rustic telescope in the corner, a model from another century. Nor would they see the rocking chair with the saddlebag draped over its shoulder, nor the crate of sepia stained envelopes on the floor, beside the chair's rockers.

This used to be his domain. Now it's his prison.

And he's her captive.

His howls multiply and radiate down Wonder's spine. In the cavernous vault, she halts on the final step and gulps at the sight before her. Lunar light flashes through the window and leaks across the floor. In the murk, a nimbus of golden hair breaks through, gilded at the roots and coiled with tension at the ends.

Tucked beneath those locks is his face. His countenance of taut cheekbones and square jaw. He sits on the rocking chair, his eyes locked shut, creases burrowing into his flesh. From those twisted lips comes the proof of a nightmare: irritated roars as though he's annoyed more than traumatized, as though he wants to figure out the nightmare, to unpuzzle its secrets rather than recover from it.

The chair's joints creak, bearing the weight of his tirade. His fingers clench, those long fingernails resembling talons. The folds of his leather sweater shift, following his movements as he thrashes.

This often happens at midnight. He shouts through his nightmares, and she catches the sounds.

Two grilles shimmer within the room. Conjured by her classmates, who'd beseeched the stars for assistance, the grates barricade this vault from the stairs and the basement window, thus preventing escape.

Like a cage. Like a dungeon.

Like an asylum.

Wonder steels herself, evicting that cursed notion from her mind. At least the bars provide a compromise, precluding the necessity for shackles. This god may be villainous, but she and her peers refuse to treat any soul like a beast.

They'd even offered to supply a bed for their prisoner, but he'd spat at their attempt. He prefers the rocking chair, though how he stands the lack of comfort, Wonder cannot comprehend.

She swallows, lifts her chin, and hazards through the star-dusted grille. In one swift move, she kneels before him and grasps his arms, alert to the muscles flexing beneath her grip. She digs into the leather sweater and gives a shake.

"Malice," she says, jerking back as he writhes unconsciously.

"Malice," she tries again, fending off his claws.

"Malice!" she demands, only to receive a shove as her reward.

The force of it sends her to the ground, her backside bouncing on the floor, her weapons jostling. It's not a surprise; where he's lean, she's fleshy. Yet Malice is athletic under those clothes, taller and even more robust than Wonder. Therefore, if it's necessary for her to snap him out of it, he can take a measure of aggression.

That fact is enough to leach the guilt out of her. He's not whom she thinks he is, whom she wants—and doesn't want—him to be. He's not good, nor kind.

Moreover, he's a maniac who would kill her if given the chance. The only reason he hasn't yet is because he's unarmed; her classmates took his bow and arrow.

He flails as though invisible restraints strap him down. His fingernails cleave through the seat's arm, those claws peeling a thin layer of wood from the surface. Any more of this, and he's going to hurt himself.

Wonder lurches upright. Grappling his elbows, she hoists him from the rocking chair and slaps him across the face. The crack of her palm splinters through the vault. His head whips sideways, the contact immobilizing him, so that she dumps his weight back into the seat.

Malice slumps. There, he's all right now, spared the rest of the nightmare. She should leave him like this, let him segue into an easier dream, whatever that dream may be.

Yes, she should leave. She should leave now.

She waits until his features relax. Lost in slumber, he resembles...he looks like...looks just like...

Wonder's throat clogs. Squatting to the ground, she plucks an envelope from the crate, the paper yellowed with age—one of many artifacts that remind her of someone else.

Someone who isn't him.

Any resemblance is merely a coincidence. This prisoner is no one to her, nothing but a stranger.

The envelope crinkles in Wonder's grasp. Smoothing out the creases, she tucks the item into his hand. Dormant, he clings to the paper, his claws curling around it and his breaths evening out.

If her peers knew about these escapades and how she dares to step through the veil of bars, they would try to stop her. They would try because they care, and because they're careful.

Malice is not her friend.

At the onset of his captivity, she and her classmates had checked this vault for perilous or devious devices. Confiscating his archery had been indisputable. But they'd shown mercy and permitted him to keep items that posed no threat, including the crate of envelopes that contain letters.

To be on the safe side, her friends had needed reassurance of the content's harmlessness. Wonder had checked the missives, only to discover blank pages, Malice having managed to conceal them from view. Only a particular ink can achieve this, granting the paper illegibility unless read exclusively in the Peaks.

She shakes her head. In any case, in the human realm, the envelopes' contents have been rendered inaccessible. Malice cherishes them for reasons her classmates don't know about, for reasons that invade her consciousness on a regular basis.

Do the missives contain mortal words? Or immortal ones? Do they provide enlightenment? Hidden knowledge that her class would benefit from? Or knowledge about Malice, himself?

Why do the envelopes matter so much to him? What else matters so much to him?

She watches her demon prisoner cradle the envelope like a stuffed animal, and she watches him sleep, and she stays like this until the stars slant. Unbidden, her treacherous hand reaches out, yielding to temptation. One gilded curl links around her finger, softer than she had imagined, so soft for such a harsh being.

Malice would despise Wonder if he caught her doing this. He would mock and spew elegant yet mind-bending insults. He would indulge in his favorite pastime, pushing her buttons, testing how many he can locate.

Looping that curl behind his ear, she lets go, because she has to *let go*. Resigned, resolved, repentant, she stands. Padding across the vault, she resists the urge to glance over her shoulder. He's the enemy, a diabolical deity. Being weaponless hasn't made him an obedient captive—being clever has.

Malice doesn't need a bow to free himself. It's his crafty brain, and his serpentine tongue, that she should be wary of.

And it's only a matter of time before he tries something mutinous.

The next morning, Wonder descends into the vault to find the demon swaying back and forth, the joints of his rocking chair creaking in tandem.

Actually, it sounds more like a cackle.

He's lucid and reading a book. One of his legs balances atop the opposite knee, the tome propped on his lap, the text spread wide open and offering itself to his voracious eyes.

Cinders fill the fire pit, the smoke of yesterday extinguished. Dawn slithers through the basement window, exposing dust motes while the fragrance of pomegranates clings to the walls.

Wonder takes a moment to reflect. So much has happened, in so brief a period.

This mortal world has been ruled for eons by the Fates. Blessed and empowered by the stars, selfish gods and goddesses like Wonder have steered mortal destinies since the beginning—unbeknownst to humanity.

When they're of age, deities become archers that wield human emotions through the strikes of arrows.

Those archers are mentored by Guides.

And the Fate Court reigns over everyone.

Back in the Peaks, the realm of her people, Wonder grew up in an elite class of archers. She and her peers—Love, Anger, Envy, and Sorrow—had been the most promising group in history until they'd grown too close to humanity, developing a forbidden fondness for its inhabitants. Through a chain of unforeseen conflicts, each of them began to question a deity's right to control anyone other than themselves. And through a chain of rebellious acts, they've since become the Fate Court's enemy.

So here they are, in the Celestial City. It's a mortal landscape but also a haven for immortal exiles. Ostracized from the Peaks, Wonder and her peers teeter on the brink of a war with their own people, all on behalf of humanity and in the name of equality.

A battle of fate versus free will has begun to simmer.

In the midst of that, Wonder and her renegade companions must contend with a second nemesis: the lone god in this very room where she stands.

Their prisoner had been expelled from the Peaks long before

Wonder or her friends. Having settled in this metropolis, he'd elected to haunt this library. And since then, he's spent his existence wreaking havoc on fellow outcasts.

So he deserves this confinement. That isn't the quandary.

The quandary is that he reminds Wonder of her past. He reminds her of someone she once knew and has never forgotten. Someone she had cared for.

Someone kind, unlike him.

This conundrum has disrupted her ever since she first beheld the god one year ago, just after she had arrived in this place.

Thinking better of it, Wonder breaks away from these thoughts and returns to the present.

At the slide of her foot across the floor, the rocking chair pauses, and the creaking-cackling stops. A gilded head rises from the page. Ashen eyes prowl toward her, gray scythes that flash with recognition, then gleam with mockery.

The impact ignites across her skin. But how can he achieve this? Is it her imagination? Or is this truly what heat feels like?

Malice's voice slinks into the space between them. "Well, well, well. It's my lucky day. Not only is the sun busy outside—you know, busy being the sun, doing sunny things—but I've got company. Pleasant morning to you, Wildflower."

He's taken to calling her that, lauding the flowers that she dons as accessories. She likes to wear natural symbols of her celestial homeland, even if she isn't welcome in the Peaks anymore. Plus, she loves the perfume and pliability of petals, bred from earth and soil. They're products of aboveground and underground.

Huff. What she doesn't appreciate is the nickname.

Giving him a "nice try" look, she approaches with industry. Her dress swats her legs and snags his attention. To her annoyance, the fact that he's eyeing the lower half of Wonder's body sends blackened fissures up her tailbone.

How deplorable that he provokes such a reaction. She'd been prepared to wear her detachment like armor, when really she should have simply worn pants. They're convenient for discouraging—and for kicking.

Her hands balance a tray laden with refreshment: a fruit bowl, plus a choice of lemonade (from Merry) or tea (from Love). The third option of arsenic (from Anger), Wonder had covertly discarded before heading to the library vault.

Yes, the two rage gods share a recent and bitter history. Nonetheless, the clash between Malice and Anger is getting old, and it's very much getting on everyone's nerves. With their temperaments, neither is to be trifled with, but Fates! Must they act infantile?

Dishes clink as Wonder sets the tray on the fire pit's rim beside the rocking chair, within Malice's reach. He regards the provisions with an impish sneer. "You might want to step back, unless you'd like your frock stained."

"Spit your meal at me again, and I'll wedge the rest down your gullet until you asphyxiate," she warns.

To which he tsks, slapping the book shut with a single hand. "Your upbringing should have taught you the merits of being on the offensive. Otherwise, you'll never win a strategy game."

"I don't play games."

A smirk crooks into his face. "I do. Matter of fact, I invent them." He indicates the provisions. "Feel like dining with me?"

"I'm more partial to cherries and peaches."

"I wouldn't mind tasting what you like."

"Starve, for all I care," she says, flexing her scarred hands.

"For all you do care," he replies, steepling his digits beneath his chin.

His rasp takes on a curious, husky note. With his head casually slumped to the side, Malice possesses a conniving beauty that belongs in a crime scene.

In the beginning, his sinister twist of the mouth had racked her from head to toe. Now the impact has condensed to a few choice spots, unmentionable and unforgivable spots that tighten and chafe deep inside her, causing a tumult of friction.

All he's missing are the horns, curling like cornucopias above his head. But in that case, he'd resemble a satyr instead of a devil.

Malice swipes a pomegranate from the fruit bowl. Balancing the flushed orb between slender fingers, his nails trace delicately. "Pomegranates," he snubs. "This is a bit niche for a nutritional choice. What makes you think I like these?"

Because this antagonist's "home, away from home, away from home"—as he likes to call it—reeks of the fruit.

"Do you?" Wonder asks.

"I think you'd like to find out," Malice intones. "I think you'd like to find out many things, a great many things, and very much so. I think you expect me to savor these plump baubles. Why is that?" Without waiting for an answer, he continues, "I think you're looking for a validation—or proof to the contrary. Against her very nature, I think the Goddess of Wonder is looking for a guarantee, so that she doesn't have to dwell on hypotheses. So that she doesn't have to..." He pretends to contemplate, twirling his free hand. "What's the word?" Then he raises a finger. "So that she doesn't have to wonder."

His canines dig into the rind, biting clear through the pomegranate's shell. With every crunch, she imagines the burgundy kernels bursting in his mouth, juice leaking down his tongue. It would be tart and sweet on the palate.

He swallows. "Tell me: Yes or yes? Am I right? I like being right."

How marvelous it would feel to wedge that pomegranate down his esophagus.

Wonder feigns a grin. "And how often are you actually right?"

He stops chewing. His mouth falls, flattening to a plank.

Flippantly, he tosses the pomegranate into the bowl as if bored by the conversation, the discarded fruit causing the tray to quiver. Reclining in the chair, he switches tactic, brandishing the book cover at her. His current selection is about the myth of Hades and Persephone. "Pomegranates that resemble your cheeks and taste of deceitful shenanigans. Rather symbolic, so I'd bet you knew what I was reading. How thoughtful. But hmm, how did you guess?"

Andrew needs to stop giving Malice the wrong books. Captive or not, the misfit appeals to Andrew's bookish side, which Wonder can't blame since she has this fetish in common with both of them. But something tells her that Malice had specifically requested this title, which can only mean trouble, the likes of which she cannot discern from his selection.

As to his assumption, no. She hadn't known he was reading about that particular myth, because she hadn't been paying attention to his book stash while venturing here last night.

"Have you ever tippy-toed through the library's romance section?" Malice inquires. "This classic tale has merit, but there are some amusingly pretentious mortal retellings of the myth. Christ, it's always about the self-aware, wiser-than-her-age maiden taming her dumbass-but-muscular abductor. The bad boy versus the good girl." He widens his eyes. "Who'll win the battle? Will they fuck before or after the climax?"

Only one word stands out in his diatribe, and it's the last

one that she wants to concentrate on. But when he says that lewd word, flicking it out like a vice, she has a yen to catch it. Therefore, it takes her thighs a second to recover.

Wonder would ask where he's going with this recitation, but one can never guess in which direction his cranium is pointing. It might be random, or it might be very intentional.

"Have you read this myth?" he asks.

"We're not doing this again, dearest," she affirms.

"That means no. I gotta say, that's irresponsible of a deity, even if the human version of Greek mythology is inaccurate. I would have thought—"

"I've read it, Demon."

"Which interpretation, Wildflower? Any risky modernizations or hybrids? Or are you a traditionalist who sticks to what you know?"

There's an obsessive, harassing lilt to his commentary, badgering her to indulge him. And it's not going to work.

Anger and Love get riled up too easily. Envy doesn't care to face off with someone as good-looking as himself. Sorrow gets depressed by this cavern. And Merry and Andrew chatter too much to accomplish quick visits.

Wonder is the only candidate equipped to play Malice's warden, which isn't saying much. A spike of erudite rivalry curls up her throat like a weed, but she refuses to get dragged into another book-a-thon. It's not entertaining or stimulating in the least. Not at all.

Not. At. All.

They stare at one another. Wonder does her utmost to remain taciturn, cementing her features into a mask. For all intents and purposes, he does the same with her, which is better than him throwing another colossal fit when things don't go his way.

At least he's blissfully unaware of last night, ignorant of his spastic grunts and her visit. That's one less thing to fret about.

So, there. He doesn't know everything. Let him spend eternity trying.

On that score, she's got her own buttons to push. "Your envelopes," Wonder demands. "The letters inside. What's written on them?"

His leer vanishes, a snarl building in his mouth, which is probably the only thing left that fits inside it. Out of nowhere, he raises the envelope that she'd placed in his hand last night, the paper poised between his claws. "You mean, letters like this one?"

Checkmate. Her stomach swoops, a tremor sprints across her skin, and her cheeks stain.

He knows that she was down here, tampering with things that don't belong to her.

Had he been awake? Had he felt her take liberties? Had he endured her petting his hair?

What else does he know? Does he know how much he resembles someone else? Someone important to her? Someone she has lost?

Does he know what loss is?

"I...," she falters.

"You," he echoes between his teeth. "Yeah, you. I've got so many ideas about you. How I can pay you back. How I can leap out of this chair right now and demonstrate what I think of you touching what isn't yours. How you don't even see that one of your arrows is tipped toward me, ready for stealing, and how I'm thinking of the best place to use it on you."

Wonder resists reaching for the arrow, to nudge it out of range. If he indeed gets up and tries something hostile, she'll block his effort.

But that would be too simple for either of them. Because when Malice rages with words, it's got a sharper edge than physical retribution.

His voice takes small bites out of her. "On the other hand, I'd rather prolong the inevitable and then take something that matters to you. Something precious. Then I can see what you look like tempted, with your bright—" he swats the pomegranate bowl off the tray, "—spellbound—" then the lemonade, "—eyes—" then the tea, "—full of doubts instead of daydreams."

Ceramic and glass clatter across the floor, and drink spills across the boards. Malice gives Wonder a terrible look, one that promises he'll deliver, and that he'll make her deliver, too.

He was once her target. Now she's his.

And now she knows what that feels like.

2

Once upon a myth, she loved a boy. That boy had blond curls and a charming smile, a benevolent smile, a mortal smile. He was different, and different had attracted Wonder.

That had been her first mistake.

The second mistake had been falling in love.

It had been unconventional, seeing as she'd never had a single physical or verbal interaction with him. Rather, she had cherished him from afar, pining until the distance became intolerable.

And that's when she made her third mistake. And that grave error had earned her scars, a pulp of starbursts carved into her hands.

But those had healed. The boy hadn't. Not after what she did to him, giving in to temptation and causing him pain in the process. For a goddess who'd once steered the destinies of humans, she had sealed the worst kind of fate for a boy who hadn't known she existed, yet who'd suffered because of her.

Once upon a myth, she had overstepped her boundaries. She cannot do that again.

Hopefully, she won't have to. Because Malice isn't that boy. He cannot be that mortal boy from another century, from another era, from another life.

They're identical. They're mirror images.

Having returned to the library's main hall, Wonder stops in her tracks, because this thought always forces her to stop in her tracks. She stalls in between the stacks, under curtains of ivy as the same ceaseless questions orbit her mind.

How is this possible? Can destiny produce such a sequel, such an accurate rendering of the past? Why would fate do that?

Everything about him is the same, yet nothing about him is the same. On the outside, he's a replica. On the inside, he's the opposite.

Are Malice's features a coincidence? Or are they a resurrection?

How to explain his residence in a library? How to explain the items in his vault? The saddlebag, the rocking chair, and the 1800s telescope?

How to explain the envelopes stained with age?

How to explain all these details and objects associated with the past, with that other boy?

None of this makes sense, no matter how many texts she's consulted, no matter how many pages she's rifled through, no matter how many times she's begged the stars for an explanation. And while this mortal library is beautiful, it's also inadequate to provide answers.

Only a forbidden place filled with forbidden texts will yield such information. Only there, in the heart of the Peaks, can one untangle these quandaries.

The problem is, she's banished. Thus, that great landmark of knowledge is off limits unless she finds a way back.

Wonder glances at her surroundings. Throughout the building, human patrons either mill about or sit in cubicles where they type on their laptops. Someone discreetly pries open a plastic bag, the crinkle skittering into the air. Another soul unzips a pencil pouch. Another soul turns a page.

She wants to take a few conciliatory laps around the hall. She wants to stroll and watch them muse and ruminate. She wants to distract herself.

He knows about last night. He'd felt my fingers in his hair.

Five minutes ago, she'd left him in the vault. She'd refused to apologize, instead rising to her feet and marching away as if his revelation had been inconsequential.

Free from the underworld, Wonder takes refuge in sunlight streaming through the windows and ropes of plants swaying overhead. All the same, she projects an image of him sleeping, of him resting in peace, safe from nightmares because she'd been there to stop them.

Picturing his taloned fingers curled around that dainty envelope, she slumps against the nearest bookcase and allows herself the luxury of trembling.

A hand pops into her line of vision. She blinks at the set of masculine digits that presents a hefty book bound in leather, gold embossing the surface. It's a tome about the history of meditation.

Wonder's gaze roams from the title to a pair of broad shoulders, then to a countenance inset with pewter irises and crowned in a froth of messy white hair. The male props himself against the shelf and regards her with a lopsided grin. "This looks like a pile of boring," Andrew says. "But desperate times call for desperate measures."

Wonder laughs. Andrew is good at this, making her peers chortle in spite of themselves. He's also good at finding her, his thirst for narrative matching her own, except he leans toward the fictional. Back when he was a human, he used to work at a small-town bookshop, fancying tales about dragons and time travel.

In contrast, Wonder frequents the factual. They harmonize with each other this way, and they've had plenty of invigorating discussions about it, since they both spend a lot of time here, ever since Andrew became immortal.

It happened five years ago, when he and her peer, Love, met.

Love had been an invisible goddess, and Andrew had been an unsuspecting human, and their friendship had been precarious at best. Yes, mortals don't have the power to see or hear deities—with one exception. Only the purest soul can breach that rule. Hence, Andrew. His ability to see past the myth had rendered him universally dangerous to their kind, therefore essential to vanquish, for the sake of the Fates' preservation.

But when Andrew and Love fell for each other—a forbidden relationship—that bond had rescued them from annihilation. It's a long story, but ultimately, it took another series of events in order for Andrew to become immortal like Love.

Wonder accepts the meditation book. "I'll trade you, dearest," she says, giving him a chastising look as she extends the volume on Hades and Persephone, because again, it's doubtful that Malice had weaseled a specific title from Andrew without an agenda.

That becomes clear when a pink azalea hue rushes up the young man's neck. "Ah, goddammit. He punked me."

"That remains to be seen."

"The douchebag punked me. I swear, his noggin needs its own distorted Dewey Decimal system. Talking with him is like dropping peyote with Satan; it screws with your mind until it's tangled up like a pretzel."

"Oh, your time was coming," she jokes. "You were the only one left."

It's true. Andrew had been the only one whom Malice hadn't

yet manipulated in some way, shape, or form. Up until this point, perhaps Andrew had been immune because he used to be mortal, which somehow empowers him, rendering him a tad resistant to the demon's tongue.

From one former human to another?

It's best not to go there. Besides, Andrew deserves more credit. He's snarky and inquisitive enough to have detracted Malice all this time. Indeed, Andrew had won the heart of Love, which alone proves his abilities to take on a deity.

Also, he's adapting to immortality. Despite the inexplicable retention of his limp, and the fact that he's not actually a god, he has been endowed with tenacious reflexes. He moves as swiftly as any of their rebellious class, able to predict an arrow's direction and evade its strike. Though unfamiliar with weaponry, it's essential for him to prepare himself for a prospective battle. To that end, he has opted for a crossbow granted by the stars and forged of frost because it reminds him of home. With time, he'll prove himself formidable, especially with Love as his instructor.

Back to the subject of Malice. Luckily, Wonder had the presence of mind to confiscate the Greek title before departing his lair.

Andrew is about to swap books with her, but he pauses. "If you're thinking what I'm thinking, you might want to give this a peek. Just in case."

He's right. Wonder should pour through the pages before shelving the title, so she piles it atop the meditation book.

Sunlight seeps into the lane, trickling across green book spines like a path leading someplace pertinent. It's nothing unusual, a mere stream of illumination. Yet the visual is familiar, steering her into the past, to a bygone era when she'd witnessed a similar effect in another repository.

In fact, the illusion is identical.

When Wonder blinks, the trail of light vanishes. How queer.

Anyway, is the book she'd collected from Malice the only mythically themed manuscript worth checking? Or must she be thorough and expand her reading?

What had Malice said about the romance section? About retellings?

Had that been a random inquiry or a duplicitous one?

She would do best not to underestimate the demon god. Whatever he's hunting for within these chapters—some sort of bribe or manipulation—it would behoove Wonder to stay on top of it. Matter of fact, to stay a thousand leagues ahead of him.

The last thing they need is for Malice to play another mind game. Or Fates forbid, plan an escape they never saw coming. They all have more important things to contend with.

Things like plotting a revolution.

⁓

The glass arrow spears past her face. It lances the air, flitting by her navel and stabbing the gullet of an oak tree trimmed in fairy lights.

She swivels while nocking her bow. But it's too late. Wonder's reflexes lag, and the glass projectile rams into her sternum, shoving her into the earth, archery scattering across the hill.

The landing tears her blouse, causing a rift in the material, a slit like an open mouth that's screaming. Her belly pumps with air, her skin inflating from the textile's gash while the glass arrow vanishes and reappears in her opponent's quiver.

A male specimen slides toward Wonder, his knees mowing seamlessly through the grass. He halts beside her, slanting his head in scrutiny. Unlike his usual smarmy features, the god's expression warps with cynicism, the pleats of his almond skin hardly the sum of amusement. At least not today.

It's rare to exhaust Envy's sense of humor. Rarer still for him not to gloat.

Instead of congratulating himself on winning this bout, he flattens his palms on his thighs and regards Wonder. Her consciousness is prone to drift, which is nothing new. But this is a whole different type of meandering, because she's never been this out of sorts during training.

A deity's arrow doesn't have the magic to be fatal, since it's crafted for a different purpose. Its job is to infuse emotions into humans—love, anger, sorrow, envy, and wonder, for instance—thus controlling mortal destiny.

It's a benevolent undertaking, not a violent one. However, that doesn't mean a strike won't hurt, or that given the right velocity, the impact alone can't shatter a bone or two. If a deity gets inventive, he or she can manipulate an arrow's effect, forcing the weapon to be harmful.

Even deadly.

Envy's hit is a reminder of that. He doesn't point out the obvious, but he does reserve the right to judge. He extends his hand to help her rise, a gesture that Wonder claps away before tramping to her feet. In case of a battle, no one will be a gentleman, and no one will be a lady.

It's been hours since her chat with Malice. Evening has descended, the firmament glittering beyond thin sheets of clouds.

From behind Envy, a groan rumbles out of Sorrow, who palms her face in abject misery, aware of what's about to happen.

Once Wonder's upright, Envy swaggers to his own booted feet. As soon as his towering frame straightens, clad in houndstooth trousers and a swanky button-down shirt, he chucks his weaponry to the ground. "Are you kidding me? Or just distracted by my face? Choose your excuse wisely."

Wonder flaps a hand at him. "Don't start. I'm allowed to have a poor day."

"What about yesterday? And the day before?" he jeers. "Far be it from my hunky self not to thrive on keeping score and stealing another archer's thunder, but these easy pickings are getting obscene."

"Would you stop carping," Sorrow says, striding up to him in her vest and shredded skirt. "Easy pickings are exactly your thing."

"What's that supposed to mean?" he blares.

While the pair clucks at one another, Wonder checks the rip in her off-the-shoulder blouse, the garment burdened with dirt and grass streaks. Her harem pants have suffered the same fate, and bits of debris cling to the long blonde—her compatriots call it "marigold"—curls sticking from her ponytail.

What has become of her corsage? Did the wristlet come loose during the fight?

Wonder twists in a full circle, but the blooms are nowhere in sight.

And Envy has a right to be furious. Wonder's precarious ability to focus is compromising his time. Though it's not wholly unusual from her, she always pulls herself together when it counts—when others are relying on her.

"Just let her be," Sorrow lectures Envy. "Since when are you as militant as Anger?"

"Anger's not here," Envy snaps, adjusting his ensemble. "He's either busy yelling at the sky, prowling the city for recruits, or spooning Merry."

The purple-haired goddess snorts and pats his backside. "Is that why you have an attitude? You're spoiling for the same romantic sustenance?"

Envy tosses her a handsome scowl. He jerks away from the intimate touch as if finding her attempt to mollify him repugnant. Surprise clutters Sorrow's face, and the bandage plastered across the bridge of her nose crinkles—purely decorative, she's been wearing that accessory for over a year—as she watches him hunker to collect his bow.

The scene exposes a multitude of phenomena, not the least of which is Envy's cantankerous attitude, Sorrow's efforts to actually tease, and the tension coiling from both.

Envy, not in the mood to flirt? Sorrow, wounded by the rejection?

This is the first time that Wonder has witnessed an entanglement between them. They'd become lust partners shortly before their group had first arrived in this city. Since then, the couple hasn't denied each other once.

Perhaps it's the stress. Their rebel class trains hard while also harvesting allies amidst the outcasts, those who oppose the Fate Court and support the empowerment of humanity. They'd begun hopeful, but it appears the strain of a potential battle with their supreme rulers has caught up to them.

Sorrow shuffles, the folds of her skirt grazing the hill before she recovers, because Sorrow knows how to recover from injuries. With a scoff, she flicks the back of her hand as if to say, *Bah. Good riddance*. She trounces off, stomping down the hill, her glossy hair gleaming beneath the stars.

A muscle ticks in Envy's jaw, but he doesn't stop her.

It could be their first official lust quarrel, though Wonder wouldn't know. She's hardly a virgin, but she's never been involved in such an arrangement as theirs. She's only been with one other person, and that had been an oversight—one she doesn't plan on making again. When next she takes a lover, it will mean something.

Wonder addresses her companion's rigid shoulder blades. "Oh, Envy. You know better."

He belts out an ironic, humorless laugh. "Why don't you stop dabbling in everyone's affairs and deal with your own instead? Oh, wait. You would need an actual mate for that."

He strides away, charging in the opposite direction from Sorrow. Neither of them opts to simply vanish, electing to walk it off instead.

Wonder flinches. Envy is behaving like a mongrel, but he's right. She meddles in everyone's relationships because she has no bond of her own.

Kinships, indeed. Friendships, certainly.

Something more? No.

She stands atop the summit, blinking at nothing, thinking everything. Her surroundings materialize as if she'd forgotten where she is. She orientates herself to the expanse of grass, the central oak tree that stands proud, and the two shimmering telescopes that crane their necks toward the constellations.

The heliotropes, ultramarines, and magentas of an amusement park surround the hill: the Carnival of Stars. It's an urban spectacle of celestial-themed attractions, where ethereal rides laud the galaxy and all its majesty. It's a beautiful place, on a beautiful night. It's a splendor of bulbs, twinkling trees, and pathways lined with sparklers. Elated laughter and joyous shouts spring from the attractions and the mortals who frolic through the area.

Their class selected this bluff as a suitable training ground because it reminds them of home. Growing up in the Peaks, they used to practice on such an incline.

This one is called Stargazer Hill, and it rises from the earth at the nexus of the carnival, while the theme park glows at the very heart of the Celestial City. Beyond the park shines the magical metropolis, a panorama of historical buildings, radiant trees, and rooftop foliage. Since becoming exiles, she and her peers have made their residence here, a mortal landscape where the stars shine the brightest.

The book repository's distant silhouette cuts through the inky sky, a smattering of stars flexing above the roof. Somewhere in that building are more books that Malice will hanker to read, more books that Wonder will yearn to explore, more books that lack the answers she seeks.

Actually, there may be a way to redeem herself, a means to atone for her uselessness of late. Although she'd tucked into that mythology title earlier, there are alternatives to study, as Malice had said. She could station herself in a cubicle and consult additional versions, scouring the retellings for whatever he has in mind.

Soon, midnight will come. Soon, the carnival will close, the bulbs shutting like eyelids. Soon, the library will shut its doors.

But there's no need to rush. If there's one thing she has, it's plenty of time to get there.

The hours pass, dissolving into the firmament. By the time the city retires, the library is all hers.

The repository is a chasm, with six levels of corridors and labyrinthine stacks comprising the building. Though a historical edifice, it's been modernized with three original stories above ground, three contemporary stories below.

Buried underneath all that is the vault.

Wonder toys with garlands of ivy as she wends her way to the second-floor mezzanine, then to the third. This quest would pass more quickly if she were acquainted with the fiction section, with its backlists and new releases. If this were a test of her nonfiction prowess, she would be victorious.

Her saving grace is that the romance quarter sprouts with an abundance of blushing covers and swooning fonts about fantasy royals, highlanders, and billionaires. The cursive words *Duke* and *Scoundrel*, *Cocky* and *Cruel*, *Sword* and *Series*, loop across the spines. Some of the options intrigue her, the dust-jacket designs ranging from seductive to fierce.

Her fingers pause on one of the titles. This isn't the time to curl up and crack open a slow-burn tale.

She scans the paperbacks, the carousels organized by author rather than genre. But she disregards that once she locates a special mythology display based on librarian recommendations. The covers are darker, with a lot more lightning, old world architecture, and imperial-looking characters, though the amount of bare muscles and puckered lips is the same as everywhere else.

Her feet stall at the sight of three books pressed together like shoulders. The first one suggests a retelling of Eros. The second, Icarus.

The third, Hades and Persephone.

The library has divided these recommendations based on corresponding myth. Yet this trio is out of order, mishmashed together.

Wonder plucks the third title from the shelf. With a less lavish cover, its black façade displays shadowed profiles, the title interlaced with wildflowers and pomegranates. The book's plastic crackles when she opens it, the pages stained with coffee. She turns to the prologue—and her hand freezes at the sound of a toxic voice.

A voice that shouldn't be here, that cannot be here.
Because that voice should be locked in the vault.
"My, my," Malice drawls. "Look who got curious."

3

She barely has time to turn around before he's on her. In a flash, Wonder's back slams into the bookshelves. The titles quake. An avalanche of fiction tumbles and hits the floor, while the hardcover slips from her fingers and joins the casualties.

The impact of Malice sucks the air from Wonder's lungs, his forearm jabbing into her throat. His solid body flattens against hers, the muscles beneath his clothes flexing. Those eyes—saturated tones of gray in his face—pierce through her, the makings of a vendetta conspiring to brighten his irises. The chaos of his breath buffets her neck, a thick current making contact with her pulse point.

Pinned together like this, his form inundates hers. And up close, and for an instant, she mourns *that* boy, wants him to be *that* boy.

But despite having the same face, he doesn't possess the same soul and never will. Bereavement morphs into resentment, because this moment is nothing to lament about.

This is something to fight.

Wonder's knee jams in between his thighs. He howls, and she takes that opportunity to ram her flat, upturned palm into his jaw. The force of it sends him flying into the opposite bookcase, the structure tipping like a domino, which hits another domino, which hits another, until the lane of stacks crashes in succession. The ground shakes as paperbacks and hardbacks plummet, the texts striking the floor.

Vaguely, Wonder ponders whether a video camera is catching all of this. To the human eye, the shelves tumble over on their own, lacking points on the Richter scale to explain the phenomenon.

The demon god leaps, throttling her back to the position in which they'd started. However, this particular bookcase stays put, a lone survivor that rattles but doesn't yield.

She should have finished the chore and pounded him when she'd had the chance. Instead, his forearm resumes its task, crooking into her throat and making her wheeze. His gilded curls sweep along Wonder's cheekbone, and his features crinkle with pleasure.

He'd fooled her. This morning, he hadn't been alluding to a secret or clandestine tip. No, he'd merely lured Wonder with the illusion of one, maneuvering her like a chess piece, placing his queen to strategic advantage.

He'd expected her to come here. He'd predicted that she would take the research bait, unable to help herself.

But how did he escape?

"Good girl," Malice sing-songs. "Bad boy."

"How," Wonder chokes. "How…?"

"Smart girl," he answers. "Smarter boy."

That voice slithers, a hum-hiss along the shell of her ear. His lips twist into a smirk, and his free hand pins her wrist overhead, a taloned thumb scraping her flesh. A few more inches, and his hips will wedge between her thighs, though it's hardly a lascivious move on his part.

Wonder squirms, writhing between him and the shelves,

wrestling for an advantage.

"She's restless. It's a wonder—ha!" A demented cackle springs off his tongue, finding the pun uproarious. "It's a wonder that you'd cave so easily. Or it's not a wonder at all. Tell me, Goddess. Is it a wonder? Is it? Hmm?"

"Get off me," she grits through her teeth.

"Come now," he coaxes, resting a digit against her mouth. "Aren't you impressed? Or if you're not going to answer, at least tell me what happened to your hands. Every time I ask, you clam up."

She hacks up phlegm and lobs it in his face. Sniggering, he wipes the glob from his chin.

Then Malice's humor drops like a rock, and his arm hammers her deeper into the shelf. "Don't care for those questions? Then how about this one." He exerts pressure, making her gag. "Where's my fucking bow?"

Malice leans in to hear the answer, like it's a secret.

Close enough. Wonder's teeth lash out, snatch, and sink.

Her body slumps as he releases her, in order to clutch his bloody lobe. Spinning, Wonder whips out an arm, executing a backhanded strike that catches his profile. Malice goes down, crashing atop the books. Doubling over, she braces her hands on her thighs and pants for breath while the rage god keels into himself, cursing and worming across the mound of titles.

Four pairs of feet barrel down the library. Two pairings crash into the scene.

That's how Wonder's class finds her and Malice.

Andrew's shock of white hair glows in the dark. His high-collared black coat hangs off him, gaping open in the same manner as his mouth. "Holy shit," he bleats.

His beloved Love stands beside him, a spritely vision of angular features and black tresses snarled in a lazy bun. Beneath her oversized jacket, a white linen dress drapes to her knees, hovering above motorcycle boots. She grips her bow, an iron arrow nocked, but she lowers her weapon when she spots Malice wailing.

Anger, on the other hand, doesn't lower his bow. He's livid, the planes of his olive skin taut. "What the Fates!" he blusters.

Poised on a skateboard, his lady love brightens the hall with an aurora of pink hair and a frothy sweetheart dress, layers of tulle flaring like a carnation above high-top sneakers. "Kindred!" Merry pipes while hopping off the board, about to make a beeline toward Wonder, which will put her within snatching distance of Malice's claws.

Anger blocks Merry, preventing his girlfriend from achieving more than a step. The protective motion offends her, so that she's about to shove past her lover. But Anger jolts again, shielding her from Malice's growls.

"You're a tad late, dearests," Wonder wheezes at the gawking couples.

No one replies or budges. No one except the demon nursing his crimson ear.

Wonder has two options: joke or weep.

She hates both choices. She hates all of this. She hates that he's locked in that vault. She hates the ash of his eyes, the inferno of his voice, the structure of his face—the familiarity and foreignness of it. She hates that he's deceived her. She hates what his stare does to her heart, her skull, her womb. She hates that he has escaped, that he's imprisoned. She hates that he suffers from nightmares. She hates everything, when she's never hated anything before. She hates that he attacked her, forcing her to injure him, when she doesn't want to injure him—and she hates that, too, because he deserves nothing short of contempt.

She doesn't want to rush him. She won't rush him. She won't rush him.

"Motherfuck!" Malice thrashes to a sitting position. "You scholastic bitch!"

She rushes him.

With a battle cry, Wonder barrels toward the demon. Malice launches to his feet, an anticipatory grin leaping across his countenance, his bloody ear forgotten.

Two pairs of hands snatch Wonder's arms, and she's hauled backward, her heels skidding across the carpet. Merry and Love clamp on to her, the moment slapping Wonder with remorse. She goes limp, her eyes widening at the hideous, heartrending sight of Andrew and Anger restraining Malice, gripping his shoulders while he slings profanities her way.

"Who are you?" he sneers. "Who the fuck are you to me? Where's my bow? Where is it? Don't fucking touch my things ever again! They're mine!"

Merry's hold loosens, and it's all Wonder can do not to dart forward, to pry her peers' hands from Malice, to make them stop.

Stop hurting him! Stop it!

He's unwell. His mind is unwell. He doesn't know any better!

Doesn't he?

Still harnessed, Wonder manages a step. But then, Merry's there, swiveling in Wonder's path and clasping her cheeks, filling her vision with sympathetic eyes.

"Don't look," Merry whispers. "Don't look at him. Just look at me."

Wonder focuses on her friend, who instructs her to breathe, just breathe. Their foreheads press, with Love hugging them both, the females knitting themselves together while Andrew and Anger haul Malice around the corner, his threats tearing down the corridor, marking a path back to the vault.

⁓

"Wonder, get down here," Anger grumbles at the oak branch from which she hangs upside down, her limbs hooked over the bark.

"Leave her alone," Merry peeps, smacking her soul mate's knee. "This is no time to snarl at our kindred, so lost in her time of woe."

The archer mutters to himself while holding Merry close, his limbs clamped around her waist on the grass. She caresses his arm as he makes a crescent around her middle, tucking her into him, her back nestled into the cliff of his torso.

It's an endearing vision, one the lovers have earned. Shortly after Love and Andrew became a couple, Anger had been banished. Having been ordered by the Fate Court to prevent such an indiscretion between the goddess and a mortal, Anger had chosen to protect Love and Andrew instead. And so he'd been punished—ostracized from his people and shunned from the only life he'd ever known.

Four years passed in which he'd roamed the mortal realm alone, until he'd arrived in the Celestial City, the hub of fellow outcasts who'd been expelled from the Peaks either for disobedience or inadequacy. And here, Anger met and gave his heart to Merry, a misfit goddess who inspired him to redefine fate and free will.

That's where Malice comes in.

He'd been exiled here as well, for his own indiscretions in the Peaks. Wanting retribution against his superiors, Malice had tried to manipulate Anger for help. When that hadn't worked, Malice had attempted to kill Merry and Love, in order to get Anger to comply.

Malice had failed, especially when Wonder showed up and helped thwart him. At which point, their group had imprisoned that loose cannon for the sake of everyone's safety.

Wonder gazes at her friends. The sight of Anger and Merry together warms her soul. Another becoming vision is Andrew reclining on the hill, his weight braced on flattened palms while Love straddles him.

What's not a precious vision is the third pairing. Envy and Sorrow have stationed themselves apart from each other, still smarting from their earlier quarrel. It doesn't cease to amaze Wonder how those two became lust partners in the first place. They're polar opposites, with his narcissistic banter and fetish for bespoke suits, and Sorrow's cynicism and frayed attire.

Of everyone here, Sorrow cares the least what others think of her, whereas Envy feeds off admiration, hopping from female beds to male beds.

Imagine the immortal versions of a corporate playboy and a college goth.

Fairy lights entwine the oak tree, the branches glittering around Wonder, this angle flipping the universe on its head. It's a fine place, and a fine perspective, for meditation.

Her locks dangle around her face as she inhales, exhales, inhales.

How dare Malice call her a scholastic bitch! No fiend insults her aptitude!

Yet confusion squats in her gut as she recalls the beating she'd given him. When it comes to that fiend, no reaction to him is ever simple, or singular, or straightforward.

He's back in the vault, quarantined like a monster—like a mad god. And this time, they'd really, truly, permanently shackled him.

Wonder hadn't watched. Needing time alone, she'd retreated shortly after the incident.

Sparklers sizzle along pathways throughout the Carnival of Stars. Embers speckle the picnic lawn where their group huddles, surrounded by dormant attractions. The sun begins to scale the horizon, splashing the sky with light. The archers would have gathered on Stargazer Hill, which is their routine meeting place, but Wonder had already settled in this spot, inverted like a possum when they'd found her.

Each of them knows about Malice, what his face signifies to her, because she hasn't kept it a secret. Consequently, they'd given her space to grieve over the library incident.

At last, Anger's patience has worn thin. His graphite eyes riot in frustration as he drums his fingers against the incline of a toned thigh, while his free arm encloses Merry. Sorrow hunches over and avoids Envy, who's flat on his back, twirling his glass arrow like a baton. From their straddle position, Love and Andrew cast Wonder sideways glances.

How did Malice get out? That's what everyone's thinking.

They're also betting on how long it will take Wonder to get the devil out of her system—and get back on the ground. She doesn't have an answer for either.

There are plenty of questions to broach, plenty of contingency plans to make now that Malice has an inexplicable means of escape. One that he'd refused to share, no matter how many times her classmates had threatened him with ultimatums, trying their utmost to get innovative without resorting to violence.

Deities are not susceptible to illnesses, neither physical nor mental. Back home, their kind would have no trouble abusing Malice. Skewed mind or not, he'd earn little compassion.

But having experience with the execution of torture had restrained Wonder's classmates from going there. They'd all learned not to condone such acts. So thankfully, she hadn't had to intervene on Malice's behalf.

Moreover, there's training to master, tasks to embark on, and knowledge to procure.

How to battle the Fates? How to balance fate and free will?

Wonder has made the most of her limited resources, hunting for bits of wisdom via the stars and exiles, but their class doesn't have enough allies yet, nor enough intel. There are dignified issues to deal with, and there's a plan to revise. This isn't a juncture to get shallow.

Unfortunately, Envy breaks the silence. "You need a release."

"For the last time!" Wonder vents. "I don't need to be plucked!"

"I beg to differ. Having a beautiful prick upon which to ride will do you a *wonder* of good."

Anger groans, and Merry squeaks. Love stares blandly, and Andrew palms his face.

Sorrow grimaces as though questioning how Envy ever succeeded getting her into bed.

Wonder has had enough of the god's incessant mockery, which hasn't ceased in nearly four hundred days. A grain of time, yes. But these days, it takes seconds to nettle her.

She doesn't care that Envy is surly. Whatever collision of ego and angst has transpired between him and Sorrow, that's their problem. He has no right to take it out on Wonder, especially not after she was almost throttled.

And he calls himself a friend? By Fates, deities are selfish!

"Why must you make everything about sex?" Wonder gripes. "This isn't about sex."

"That's because you're the only one not having any," Envy says.

She gnashes her teeth. Unanimously, Sorrow and Love lean over and slap Envy upside the head, causing him to drop the glass arrow.

"What?" he asks, innocent.

"Stop being a jackass," Love grits.

Andrew shakes his head. "Nah, he's not being a jackass."

Envy flashes a smug grin. "Thank you."

"The word for it is dickhead."

The grin vanishes. "Who invited you?"

"Who banished you?" Andrew and Love retort at the same time.

"Gracious, Envy!" Merry snaps, "Have you no compassion—"

"Frankly, I leave that to Pity," he says, petulant.

"Wonder was just attacked by the love of her life!"

That shuts everyone up. Wonder has never confessed to loving Malice. She'd testified to loving a boy from history, the mask of whom Malice wears. There's a galaxy's worth of difference.

Before she can whisk up a proper speech, Envy is striding halfway down a sparkler path. The remaining males stalk after him, Anger bent on anger management, Andrew intending to keep the peace by making a few pacifist quips.

When all the immortal testosterone leaches from the atmosphere, Wonder consents to drop from the oak and join the females. Merry drapes herself across the grass, inviting Love to rest her head atop Merry's lap. Love paws like a needy feline until Merry chuckles, obliging the request by combing through her friend's hair.

Sorrow flops onto her back, landing in a puddle of shredded skirt layers. Absently, she mimics Envy's previous performance, twirling one of her ice arrows.

Wonder is the last to recline as they watch the sky awaken. They form a mesh of color, a pinwheel from Merry's pink layers, to Love's ebony tresses, to Sorrow's purple strands, to Wonder's marigold locks. She muses at the disparity between her peers' personalities, their clothing, and their vocabularies. Some of them have adapted eagerly to a mortal's template of fashion and modern speech, while some of them cling to their roots.

"Don't listen to Envy," Sorrow grouches. "He's nothing but a sexually frustrated harlot blowing hot air. Talk about one for the history books."

There's bafflement in Merry's reply. "Oh, but I thought you were—"

"We are." Sorrow clears her throat and amends, "We *were*, but you know."

"He's Envy," Love translates.

"Wandering eye, wandering cock. It's not a grand arrangement. We've never even kissed—what?" she asks when all three gape at her. "Kissing isn't essential to get the job done; that's what bodies are for. It's hard and fast, without the residue of sap, but obviously, he's grown bored. And what did I expect?" She flips her hair as if it's a trivial matter. "He can do whatever, and whomever, he wants. I don't care."

A sharp nod from Love. "You tell him."

"Brava," Merry echoes.

"So don't worry," Sorrow assures Wonder. "He's just tossing judgements like he tosses his prick—impulsively and stupidly."

"I don't love Malice," Wonder stresses.

No, she doesn't. She loves a person of whom he's merely a

celestial forgery.

If she closes her eyes, she'll see that human boy resting on his back in the middle of a wildflower prairie. He'd had a name. It's a name stamped onto her heart, a name she hasn't permitted herself to say aloud in well over a century.

Not since she lost him. Not since she destroyed him.

Love stares at the firmament. "We worry, is all."

"But we're with you," Merry chimes, abandoning Love's hair and reaching out to clasp Wonder's hands. "Always."

Sorrow windmills her translucent arrow. "We've got to admit: For a nemesis, our prisoner is one erotic asshole. His criminal beauty rivals any thriving God in the Peaks, and don't lie—we've all been subjected to his sleazy mouth. If it weren't intended to harass, it'd be an aphrodisiac. The heckler's pornographic vocabulary would be fodder for every deity who's had their fill of Envy."

Woefully, the appraisal is correct. Among the males, Andrew is boyishly pretty, while Anger is a handsome tempest, and Envy is a spicy rogue.

By contrast, Malice is...provocative.

Whenever he opens his dirty mouth, someplace in the universes a riddle is published, dynamite explodes, and hymens break. To consolidate his delinquency, the stars have anointed him with wily features—an impish countenance and blond waves piled atop his head like a farce. The tyrant possesses a deceitful sort of attractiveness, the kind that makes one second-guess every truth in existence.

Wonder drags her palm across the grass, which reminds her that she's yet to locate her corsage. Perhaps she should hike to Stargazer Hill and search. Hadn't she lost it while training?

On second thought, she doesn't recall wearing the corsage

during practice.

Mentally, she retraces her steps, going back in time, before the training session, before she'd brought their captive pomegranates for breakfast, before...

Her fingers seize the blades of grass, her starburst scars tensing. She had been wearing the corsage when she'd thrust a stopper into his bad dream. The blossoms had been tethered around her wrist as she'd reached out to touch his hair, unaware that he'd been awake.

The deviant must have divested her of the corsage by some sleight of hand.

The significance floods her. Wildflowers and pomegranates, an immaterial combination in this realm, a notable one in another.

When one grinds a petal and seed rooted from the Peak's soil, the sequence fuses and yields a liquid that opens barriers.

It's called Asterra Flora.

Although the Fate Court had buried this information, Wonder is the only one who knows about it. She and one more soul, it seems.

Someplace in the vault, Malice must possess a pomegranate originating from the Peaks. That accounts for the tart scent of fruit down there. And if he'd pinched the spray of blooms gathered from her home, and if he'd combined the two, the result would dismantle blockades.

Hindrances like star-dusted bars within a vault.

That's how he'd escaped. And if he had successfully fled once, he'd do it again.

And oh, he wants her to know this.

I'd rather prolong the inevitable and then take something that matters to you. Something precious.

An alarming notion squats in Wonder's gut. If he hasn't simply used the Asterra Flora to escape for a second time, then he's waiting for a more valuable commodity…an asset that only she can provide in exchange.

An idea of what it is percolates, because he knows what this discovery means to her. He knows why she'll want the mixture.

Inwardly, she festers until her class leaves the carnival. Then she festers all day until midnight. Then she festers her way into the vault, where he reclines in the rocking chair, his ankles and hands bound in chains of starlight, his head angled nonchalantly toward her.

"Where is it?" Wonder demands.

"Where's what?" Malice inquires, guileless.

She nocks a quartz arrow and targets his chest. "I won't ask again."

"Yes, you will. You'll ask three more times. No mates for backup?"

"Where is it?!"

"By all means, go treasure hunting. You won't find it."

True. She and her peers may comb this vault, then this entire library, but they won't find a concoction of petals and pomegranate seeds. Malice has spent a century and a half dwelling in this repository, becoming fluent with every nook and cranny. That means he has stashed the brew someplace inaccessible.

He must have done so before stalking Wonder in the library. He'd hidden the pomegranate and corsage as a precaution. A bargaining chip for later.

For now.

"What do you want?" she demands.

He raises his arms, illustrating the manacles. "You know what I want, Wildflower."

"Don't call me that, Demon."

"Why, I want the same thing as you: for us to make a deal."

"Which is?" she draws out.

His orbs darken, confident and malicious. And then he smiles. "We're going to abduct each other."

4

Wonder has done a few stupid things in her life, not limited to breaking rules, which has led to breaking into restricted places. But the stupid part isn't that she actually took such actions. No, it's that she'd eventually gotten caught.

She would muse, but she doesn't have time to muse. Because this is another stupid moment, and she's really getting tired of those. Her fingers choke the bow, her quartz arrow aimed and tracking his breath, while his gaze tracks the pulsating button at her throat.

He feasts on her expression, on whatever it reveals. It's a window of opportunity that Wonder hustles to close as she hardens her features into stone.

She'd heard him right, about them abducting each other. Though she wouldn't have used such hyperbole. "You've been reading too many Greek myths," she says.

"I've been engrossed," he acknowledges. "I'm a sucker for a page turner, especially if there's a sex scene. Christ, lower your weapon. It's blocking my view of your mouth."

"I should use this arrow to cut out your tongue."

"You'd miss my tongue. You'd miss it so much." Malice erects his pinky, propping it against his lips. "As to my hiding places, shh. It's a surprise."

"I don't want to go anywhere with you."

But she has to. She must.

Apparently, Malice must go with Wonder as well. Whatever his ultimate goal, he requires her company, however much he loathes her. Against their wills, they'll have to do this as a unit, or they'll be at an impasse.

A vision of home swells in her mind. She pictures the Peaks, with its blooming crags, hills of celestial hyacinths beneath a sky buzzing with silver dragonflies. Nestled within the sylvan valley of those bluffs is a repository.

The Archives. The great library of the Fates.

Deep within that immortal repository is a forbidden cellar, a channel of ethereal secrets. That's their destination.

One, trespassing is unlawful. Two, it's dangerous.

Three, this should be a moot subject. As exiles, they've lost the ability to transport themselves there.

But there are two exceptions.

The first is when an exile has immunity. Anger and Love are examples of that. They'd sacrificed certain magical privileges when breaking away from their people, but they've since regained those powers. As a research diva of the Archives, Wonder had uncovered two legends, star-granted loopholes that ended up benefitting her friends in that regard—among other regards having to do with romance.

But thus far, Anger and Love haven't infiltrated hostile terrain because revolution requires foresight and a cool head. Neither can brag about their knack for moderation, and until they learn to curtail their hotheaded impulses, Anger and Love aren't ready to take that gamble. Certainly not without a plan or a solid foundation—advantages crucial to winning this battle.

As Wonder has feared, gaining the upper hand relies on more

than just allies. It relies on additional research, the sort limited to the Archives. If they want to win this fight, the key lies within the repository.

This brings her to the second exception, the other way to breach the Peaks as an outcast. It requires a concoction that opens barriers: Asterra Flora.

Trespassing into enemy lands means certain doom. They'll be recognized within an instant of planting their feet on the soil. Without a contingent behind them, it's suicide.

Not that Wonder can bring her friends into this. Again, they don't have an immediate plan for such a quest, and two infiltrators are quieter than a handful.

Least of all, they don't know the Archives as Wonder does. She's the only one with experience in that place.

She and Malice.

He used to be a frequenter of the Archives, a masterful patron. She has also learned from past events that Malice has been desperate to return to the Peaks since his expulsion, pent up enough to manipulate and endanger anyone in order to succeed.

To what end?

And what precisely is she thinking? In the Peaks, they'll be outnumbered and outarmed. They cannot, simply cannot…can they?

A grin worms across Malice's face. He reclines in the rocking chair, his leather sweater fitted to whipcord muscles and split open at the throat, bearing ivory skin and the shadows of his collarbones.

"No," Wonder forces out.

"Yesssss," Malice coos, reading her mind. "Aren't you the least bit homesick?"

"We won't last three seconds."

"Come, now. At least, five. Long enough for me to spit on the ground."

"We'll be surrounded before I can punch you."

"It's Stellar Worship," he points out.

Wonder goes silent. How has she forgotten?

Every ten years, deities in the Peaks retire for a month of tranquil worship, paying introspective homage to the stars. This cessation includes keepers, librarians, and scribes guarding the Archives, who bar the structure and retreat to their homes by the sea.

Malice's blond locks spill across his forehead. He digs his nails into the chair arm, as he'd done while entombed in nightmares. "You haven't asked me about the pomegranate."

"And spoil your fun?" she retorts. "I wouldn't dare."

"I would. Dares are so daring. I'll give you the abridged version. Even before I was banished, I had a palate for pomegranate seeds." His eyes drift toward the fire pit, an accordion of confusion surfacing between his brows. "For some reason, they tasted nostalgic."

Wonder struggles against the comment, which reminds her of that prairie boy. Is this detail a confirmation or coincidence?

Malice shakes off the recollection. "Let's just say exiles burn a lot of calories. Pre-banishment, I was famished, so I plucked a token of my heydays and brought it with me. Isn't it lovely how long it takes immortal fruit to decay? Mine has an impressive expiration date. To this day, it's only slightly overripe, with plenty of kernels to spare. If you're nice to me, I'll let you try some." His voice darkens. "Won't that be pleasant, tasting my seed?"

If she doesn't step back, she's going to smack that filthy mouth so hard that she'll tear a new hole in his face. She deliberates whether to voice this threat, but juggling the word *hole*—or any such adaptation—for Malice to catch is a terrible idea. He'll chew it up and regurgitate something obscene.

But the worst part is that she'd known all along something like this would happen. She'd known from the beginning that they would need Malice. He has the means to get her to the Peaks, the means to access the Archives. And a book diva she might be, but this demon knows as much as she does, his skill in curating knowledge on par with hers.

She'd get far without him. But with him, she'd get even farther.

Whatever his intention, whatever he's searching for in the Archives, he needs her, too. And oh, she cannot deny it. To smell all those pages again, to walk those endless, magical halls, hunting for a way to empower her class…

Wonder rounds her shoulders. "When do we—"

"Now works for me," he says. "My schedule is wide open. How's yours, Wildflower?"

"Let's get one thing straight."

"Only one? Boo."

"My name is Wonder, not Wildflower."

"Are we finished being tedious? Call me crazy, but your warrior mates are going to arrive any second, high on an adrenaline kick and spoiling for an intervention. Either way, it's this or nothing; we go together, or we don't go at all. See how quickly your lot flounders in their campaign for free will, humanity, etcetera." The veneer of amusement drops. "Now hurry the fuck up."

She can refuse, but she will not. For the battle ahead, she cannot.

Delaying further will cause a Malice conniption, so she straps her bow across her back and squats. A lock secures the starlit manacles. She goes through the motions while questioning her sanity, rummaging for alternate options that she might have bypassed prematurely.

There aren't any.

Thrusting the tip of her arrow into the bolt's chamber, she gives a grudging twist, the mechanism wheezing from his ankles. It shimmers, succumbing to the pressure.

Indeed, there's another way to open barriers. It's called a damned key. In this case, it's the tip of any arrowhead belonging to her peers.

What is she doing? What is she doing? What is she doing?

She's freeing him and condemning herself. She's making a deal with the devil.

That's what she is doing.

Another necessary evil is his proximity, his form hovering while she kneels beside him. The air thickens, forcing her lungs to contract as she moves on to his wrists.

It's no use, for she has to touch his skin. She cannot do this otherwise.

Wonder's knuckles skim his, her pinky bumping into his wrist. He scarcely flinches, but she pretends not to notice one of his claws straining toward her scars, as if to sketch them. But the fingertip pauses just short of her marred skin, his digit curling in on itself.

If he makes contact, what will happen? How will it feel? How long will the effect last?

She picks open the shackles binding his hands. The clamp yields, its croak resounding through the room. She jerks back, needing to be the first one on her feet.

Peering at her, Malice rises. She stands her ground, choking the arrow in her fist. If she's not careful, it's going to snap.

Her gaze drops to where he massages his chafed flesh, the circumference of his wrists larger than she'd noticed. When he drags a thumb along his pulse point, a similar tempo beats in her throat.

"Thank you," he mocks, the undercurrent of wrath sneaking into her hair and pulling on the roots.

"You're not welcome," she says, jamming the arrow into her quiver.

Her response washes the acid from his voice. "Being welcome? Where's the fun in that?"

Naturally.

He moves with stealth, gathering relics of this place, including his saddlebag, which he stuffs with every envelope from his crate. One flutters to the ground by accident. Because she's a glutton for punishment, Wonder bends to pick it up, gasping when his grip fastens around her arm, tightening like a vice.

They're hunkered over, their knees tapping one another. With his free hand, he rescues the envelope. "Come near these again, and I'll slit your scars open with my fingernails."

"Where did you get such old paper?"

"Conjured them in the Peaks, back when I was a strapping young archer-in-training and suffering an identity crisis. Did you hear what I said?"

It's a warning made of silk the color of oxblood.

Glowering, she wrenches her arm backward. Feasting on that glower like it's his last meal, Malice tucks the envelope into the bag. This time, they gain their feet in unison, the movements synchronized with caution.

His answer accounts for the old envelopes as well as his rickety vintage telescope and saddlebag. While she has seen similar objects before, Malice's possessions aren't exact replicas. This fact is a relief as much as a torment.

They abandon the vault, with Malice able to pass through the stardusted bars while accompanied by Wonder. They travel side by side, keeping one another in sight.

At the stair landing, Malice throws back his head and inhales what she imagines is the scent of scholarship. It's a minor indulgence, a moment of relish before he keeps going. For once, she doesn't have to marvel at his impulse, because she understands this type of devoted worship.

Moonlight crashes through the windows, glazing the foliage that dangles from bookshelves. He strides down the corridor with a fiendish jut to his hips. Wonder would resent that attribute, but his tenor vacuums her thoughts into a black hole. A humming melody slides from under his breath, absently delivered and barely audible, but it's enough to shatter her. Her mind fragments, scattering all over the hallway.

It's only when Malice stalls that Wonder realizes she's paralyzed, her boots stapled to the wool carpet. He tosses her a sidelong glance. Whatever her expression reveals, it tightens his jaw with rancor, as if she's just issued an ultimatum.

"You can sing," she says.

"Not on purpose," he discloses. "You have a problem with that?"

Yes, she does. It's too pertinent, too miraculous, too familiar.

Mockingly, he swings his arm, inviting her to join him, and Wonder recovers from her stupor. Navigating the maze of stacks, it takes a while for her stomach to settle. Many people can sing. It's nothing, merely a fluke.

How long will they be gone? Where in the Peaks will they hide?

They'll need time. They'll need a haven.

In the main hall's circulation rotunda, a central globe perches inside glossy wooden brackets. Malice moseys toward the model and slaps it, making the orb spin. He'd been in such a hurry, yet now he tarries!

What is he waiting for? Where is the hidden contraband?

With a snigger, he says, "Are you ready?"

"Are you daft?" she balks. "The Asterra Flora."

"Ah, yes. We can't go without that." He taps his chin. "I could have sworn, I left it someplace."

She's going to scream at him. She'd been under the assumption that he'd been leading them to the mixture's hiding spot.

But no, his hiding spot isn't in the library…per se. This fact becomes a sinful, appalling, scandalous reality the moment his hand disappears into the front of his jeans. Wonder's jaw drops as he plunges and then withdraws a capsule of liquid.

She's positive that her eyes have inflated to the size of balloons. "This whole time. This whole time, you had it in your…"

"It's called a prick," he supplies. "That makes it the perfect hiding spot, since my groin is the only location nobody's ever been keen to explore. And why didn't I just use the blend on the manacles and free myself? I'm sure you've drawn the conclusion that I need you along for the road trip, so why bother rehashing? Also, making you free me was a lot more entertaining."

He uncaps and smears a bead of fluid across his palm, painting a glistening tributary over the lifelines. Then he snatches her hand and repeats the process. Finished, he drops the ampoule into his saddlebag and pats it. "I'll give you the corsage once we get there."

The capsule in his pants, the flowers and pomegranate in his bag. He'd stashed them in plain sight. Like an amateur, her class has underestimated him for the thousandth time.

Wonder throws up her arms. "Then why did we come here?"

Malice flicks his digits at the repository. "I wanted to say good-bye to my home, away from home, away from home, before we left." He points to the carpet. "Besides, I'm thinking this is a prime spot to meet our exit."

"How about meeting your maker, instead?" a stormy voice growls.

Wonder clenches her eyes shut. Dammit.

She cannot decide whether to be relieved or dismayed, to be afraid for their sakes or for the irredeemable dummy causing mayhem beside her. Daring to peek, she finds her class gaping, or glaring, or grimacing, depending on the source.

Anger, Merry, Andrew, Love, Envy, and Sorrow.

The group forms a crescent, a firing squad of arrows targeting Malice, ready to blow him off his haunches. The iron, neon, frost, glass, and ice projectiles aren't bluffing. Though they can't kill, a combined effort will launch him through the building's skeleton, potentially severing load-bearing walls and demolishing the library.

How did her friends know to come here? Does it matter?

Wonder holds up her hands. "Dearests, wait—"

She chokes as a forearm cranks around her jugular, whipping her against a solid body. Malice moves like a snake, pointing one of Wonder's quartz arrows at her temple.

The visual produces a seizure, a unanimous premonition from her peers as they clutch their archery. Wielded by bows, the arrows don't pierce.

Brandished by hand, they do. It's still not powerful enough to kill, but enough to hurt.

At his leisure, Malice can turn Wonder into a pincushion, lacerating her with plenty of tactically placed cuts to make a difference. Her inhalations escalate. She remembers this, the torment of being held down, of being sliced and diced.

Her scars remember this, especially when Malice glides the arrowhead down, down, down to her starburst scars. One flick, and he'll reopen them.

Malice sighs. "Lower them, mates."

"Are you shitting me?" Andrew snaps.

"And by the way, hand over my bow."

"An even exchange," Love says. "Your bow for Wonder."

"And your intestines," Sorrow adds.

"I vote for the testes," Envy says while aiming. "But nobody ever listens to me."

"Let her go, evildoer," Merry shouts.

"I will. Just not here," Malice assures. "Now hand me my fucking bow!"

Of course. Malice has delayed for this reason; it had nothing to do with bidding the library farewell. He wants his archery back, to a kamikaze degree.

"Drop it!" Anger growls.

"Dearest," Wonder gasps. "It's all right. Give it to him."

Anger's on the verge of charging like a rhino. Therefore, she holds each of her classmate's gazes, pleading. *Trust me. I have a plan.*

Indecision precedes a snarl of rage. To everyone's shock, Anger vanishes and then reappears moments later, bulldozing into the rotunda with a hickory longbow and a quiver holding arrows capped in turkey fletching.

Once the quartz tip leaves Wonder's scalp, Anger tosses Malice the weapons, which he manages to catch with his free hand.

The thing is, they had believed Wonder.

But then, her friends register the lie. Plan? She has no plan yet.

"I hate you," she whispers to Malice.

To which, he chuckles. "If you'll excuse us, mates. My perky, perennial partner and I have homework to do."

"No!" Love and Merry squawk while leaping forward, forcing Andrew and Anger to disarm and ensnare them.

Wonder penetrates them with a warning look, especially Anger and Love, who have the power to cross worlds without Asterra Flora. *Don't you dare follow us.*

The request sinks in, pulling her friends' expressions into grimaces.

To shift realms, they need a portal, a shaft of celestial light. Malice jolts Wonder into a beam of starlight crashing through the windows. They have to travel individually, so their arms lift at the same time, extending toward the ray. That's when the glittering fluid of seed and blossom begins to dance across their palms.

Her friends stand by, helpless as she vanishes into another world.

5

There's a flash of light, a spiraling vortex so prismatic that she clenches her eyes shut from the assault. This is new, the sensation of falling and soaring at the same time, as if she's caught between the above world and the underworld, both ends of the cylinder tugging on her. She's a shooting star, moving and not moving at all, plunging and rising.

The whirlwind sucks out the noise. A beautiful silence trails in its wake, so that her inhalations and exhalations flutter like wings. It's akin to meditation, when all consciousness drifts away.

And then she hits the ground.

A flat surface wallops her, from knees to breastbone to nose. She crashes flat onto her face, smacking into soil hard enough for her molars to clatter like castanets.

Needless to say, she has never arrived like this. She's sprawled, her limbs akimbo, her body plastered to the earth. The trip must have aggravated the harness, distributing the archery around her. She deduces as much when her heels trace the quiver, knocking about a few stray arrows.

Her nostrils burrow into the undergrowth, which scrapes her chin and forearms. Dirt and grass clog her mouth, the textures gauzy rather than coarse, with the faint trace of moonlit incense.

It's a fragrance purer and riper than from where she's just come. It's the aroma of starlight: of sharp silver and fresh white.

Wonder flops onto her back, splayed and coughing at the sky pitted with celestial bodies that tinkle. It's a million whistles, a million chimes, a million cymbals shrunken to pinpricks of sound that skip across the canopy. The stars wink, hovering nearer than they ever will over the mortal realm.

Because this isn't the mortal realm.

An adolescent dragonfly—the length of her foot—settles onto her stomach, its platinum, propeller wings fanning in place. The creature dashes off, zipping into the abyss before Wonder can pet it. They're feistier and more evasive when they're young. A long time ago, on the cusp of thirty, she'd made it her mission to trail a dragonfly for an entire day, just to see how it spent its time.

Hyacinths sprout around her, creating a jeweled tapestry. Wonder lurches upright, swatting the hip-length curls from her face as she soaks in the vista. It's akin to an island dangling amidst the galaxy, with moons and planets bobbing in the distance, so small that she can pinch them between her fingers.

Below that, bluffs slope. Farther afield, on the opposite side of the range, one will discover mineral caves and still waters, a placid gloss of dark pools beneath homes on stilts, where her kin live.

But here at the summit, she's overwhelmed. Nestled someplace in the glen stands a structure, a shrine of books. Secluded in a forest thicket exists her happy place.

Her eyes sting, which is silly. If she'd been apart from it for a few hundred years, nostalgia would be justified. But although it's only been a blink of time since her previous visit, she hadn't expected to see the structure for a much longer time.

Actually, she'd been prepared to never see it again, should her class lose this battle.

Wonder collects her archery and then wobbles to stand while hitching the weapons to her back. She knows the muscles of this ridge, the joints of its shoulders; she used to meditate in this very spot. Also, she'd had target practice with her peers on this hilltop. But...

She rotates, her gaze darting across the expanse.

Malice is nowhere in sight.

They'd left in such a hurry, without bothering to agree on a location. The first place she'd thought of had been obvious, though she hadn't arrived as close to the Archives as she should have. She'd been too frazzled to focus.

And who knows what destination Malice had been thinking of? He might be across the range, somewhere along the shoreline. For kicks, he may have landed in Joy's bed, prompting the goddess into a screeching fit. Or by accident, he may have landed in the middle of an archery range, or worse, in the belly of the Fate Court's throne enclave.

Wonder flicks those preposterous scenarios from her mind. Malice is many noxious things, but a nincompoop isn't one of them. Wherever in the Peaks he is, he'd calculated his destination in advance. What he'd neglected to do was inform her where that is!

Using the stars as channels, her mind calls out to him, but he doesn't answer. They're off to a promising start. Suffice it to say, she'll have to get moving before someone sees her.

The overhead swell of violet indicates nighttime. Stellar Worship aside, her people will have retired for contemplation and sleep by now.

It *is* Stellar Worship, right?

Wonder assesses the sky once again, trepidation leaking into her chest.

No matter what, it's best to travel quickly. She winds her hair into a bun, an onslaught of wild tendrils sneaking out. To the matter of clothes, she shuts her eyes and fixates on an alternative. When next she looks, bare feet and a gown of herb green have replaced the boots, harem pants, and blouse, the shade perfect for camouflage during her sojourn. It's a precaution that Wonder tops off with a cloak.

She cannot alter the quartz arrows, but this half-hearted disguise is better than nothing. The woodland canopy will have to do the rest, shielding the details that identify her.

She's going to flay Malice when she finds him. And she will find him, or he'll find her, though she'd rather be the one who does the finding.

At least they're headed for the same place. Hopefully, he shall make himself useful and avoid getting apprehended or maimed. And hopefully, she will stop fretting about that, because outside of this mission, he doesn't warrant her concern.

Wonder descends the precipice. As hyacinths caress her toes, she smiles at the puckered stalks embellished with dew and midnight. When was the last time she did something simple like roam the fields and pick flowers?

She keeps to dense areas, flitting from tree to tree, shrub to shrub. The lower the elevation, the more congested the wild becomes, tangling itself up into knots.

At the cliff's base, beeches arc their heads over an avenue that leads into the sylvan landscape. A human would say it's the border of a faerie dimension, which is a fine guess. This region breathes magic and majesty.

Her unshod heels sink into the ground as she steps into the

woodland. Some things don't change between worlds, such as the twisting arcades of trees, age gnarling the trunks and moss embroidering the boughs, and the sumptuous tufts of grass. Also, the wildflowers—lilac stems and crocus blooms.

Whereas some things do indeed change, such as the lavender toadstools and the mesh of leaves trimmed in amethyst. Likewise, the violet sky—which will shift to hydrangea blue come morning—and its panorama of planets. The Peaks float in the galaxy, an ethereal islet of cliffs, dales, forests, and seas.

Has she missed it? Has she been gone long enough to miss it?

Birds warble from above. The music settles her stomach, slowing her pulse to a normal tempo. Deities can cross long distances instantaneously, but not short ones. With any luck, she'll reach the Archives within a couple of hours, so long as she makes it though this first stretch.

A school of young dragonflies whisks between the foliage, glowing within the murk and much tinier than their elders. As rays filter through the crochet of branches, the insects synchronize, corkscrewing around her. Twisting, she follows the choreography, sweeping her hand amidst the creatures, tickling the air and teasing them.

Nearby, a twig snaps. As the crack ricochets through the brambles, Wonder freezes.

Malice? She wouldn't put it past him to sneak up on her.

But no, he's too agile to abuse so much as an offshoot. She'd concluded that while appraising his pace in the library.

A shadow swims in her periphery. Wonder whips behind a trunk, wedging her back against it. Craning her neck, she glances around the bend.

However precarious, peace still reigns in the Peaks, cleansed of misfits and rebels such as herself. The quandary is, even if she comes across a stroller—perhaps a Guide or an archer-in-training—and even if that wanderer fails to recognize her or the quartz archery within this shrouded atmosphere, they might recognize Wonder's voice. They might step close to her face, far too close for comfort.

Or they might have been following her all along.

Wonder drags her tongue across her teeth, her pulse resuming its pound. Someone malicious will obligate her into a messy conflict. Someone harmless will consider her stance oddly paranoid, which will alert them to a problem. And she doesn't want to harm anyone.

A map of her heart appears in her psyche, with veins and arteries threading through like rivulets in marble, each one representing a moment, an unforgotten pain or desire. A new channel breaches this map, thin as a splinter piercing through sinew, making her wince.

So this is how it feels to become an outsider, banned from one's home.

The footfalls get louder, nearer, louder, nearer. Grass sinks beneath the person's weight as he or she approaches. If innocent, they shall call out or stride forward with trustworthy purpose. If suspicious, they shall do neither.

Wonder staunches her breath. The stranger's pace slows.

Snatching a pebble off the ground, Wonder aims and lobs it as far as she can, targeting the pillar of a trunk. The rock thwacks against the surface, inciting an avalanche of debris, a safe distance from where she stands.

The footfalls halt. After a moment's deliberation, the presence shifts, attending to the disturbance. It backtracks toward the tree, seeking out the noise.

Time slows, prolonging every second. Wonder's heart drums inside her chest until the figure's gait retreats, the sound tapering off and receding farther into the forest. A whoosh spills from Wonder's lungs, her body slumping.

Just in case, she waits an additional pocket of time and then bolts. Light on her feet, she springs into the woodland, electing to stay off the main path. Veering around columns and bushes, the miles extend before her.

Who had it been? Someone she knows? Someone who knows her?

Someone who—

She staggers backward, the pouch of her hood yanked by a hand.

—who had been faking it?

Wonder yelps. She stumbles into a body, and that body clamps onto her, seizing her shoulders. The assailant begins to pivot Wonder, about to get a full, starlit view of renowned, outlawed features, about to make an inconvenient discovery.

It's a female, one advanced in years, by the shape and strength of her.

Wonder's forearm snaps upward. Her elbow connects with the female's face, cranking her head sideways. Grunting in shock, the stranger flails, lashing a hand toward Wonder, who ducks and switches arms, driving the opposite elbow into the attacker.

A shout of offense leaps from the figure. Sadly, it's the prelude to a match.

They fight. This goddess is assuredly older, which accounts for her speed; she's fast, whereas Wonder is nimble. Each time a limb or set of knuckles launches in Wonder's direction, she dodges with a pirouette.

There's something…transparent about the way this adversary maneuvers, as if they've done this before, with Wonder able to predict the female's moves and countermoves.

Perhaps the goddess senses the same thing, because confusion and hesitation impede her actions. But this doesn't stop her altogether, so neither does it stop Wonder. She spins from the goddess's fists and rams the flat of her palm against the goddess's lower back, shoving her into the barrel of a tree.

The figure recovers, steering around with her arrow nocked, the material of which Wonder cannot identify. Plausibly, that means the wild shadows Wonder's own archery.

The sound of a hiss skates into her ears. A javelin of movement cuts into the forest.

From a spot behind Wonder, an arrow strikes past her cheek and toward the stranger.

The arrow stabs its mark, impaling the trunk between the attacker's thighs. Even in the dappled light, Wonder can tell the shot has unhinged the female's jaw.

Wonder squints to make out the new arrow's component. But it's too far, too narrow, and again, too dark. On the other hand, she has a hunch.

The stranger unleashes a gruff sound, as though her dignity and honor have been called into question. The linen texture of it causes Wonder's flesh to prickle with renewed familiarity.

The twang of the female's bowstring gives Wonder a single warning. Her eyes lift and meet the incoming point of a flying tip. It slices toward her while she's immobilized, with a beech at her rear. In that second, she visualizes herself surging backward, the impact of the blow thrusting her into the pillar, which is solid enough to crack her spine.

The arrow is too swift. She moves to dive sideways, for all the good it will do.

A growl of exasperation reaches her ears, a kinetic flash accompanying the aggravated sound. Someone's silhouette whisks into her line of sight, a male whose body careens in front of her. One second before the arrow hits Wonder, the masculine frame blocks it, jerking into her and taking the brunt.

Both of them slam into the tree. A guttural noise pumps from the figure's throat, quelled behind his bunched mouth. He hunches into her for a moment, his hands braced above her head, his palms flat against the trunk. The projectile had slammed in between his shoulder blades, tensing them as if those bones just met the lash of a whip.

A leather sweater rubs against her bodice, the material carrying the scent of old books. His golden waves bow, processing the hit. Then his face raises, his inconvenienced irises pinning Wonder to the bark.

Rancor and bafflement wrinkle his features. Malice glares like she'd been the one to target him, like she'd forced him to shield her.

They stare at each other. The tenacious vibration of a bow breaks the spell.

A leer stretches across his face. He rotates, his bow loosing an arrow that fractures the one flying toward them.

The stranger charges. With a half-cackle, half-sneer, Malice leaps like a gazelle and meets the opponent halfway. Wonder breaks from her paralysis to join.

The elder is mightier, her years eclipsing theirs. Yet her disjointed motions suggest that she's stumped by this show of aggression within a peaceful land—and by Wonder's aptitude, as if she's intimately acquainted with the female's tactics.

She and Malice move fluidly, bending and whirling as if practiced for a thousand years. They're a sphere of motion, orbiting one another. When he blocks, she strikes, and vice versa.

Their harmony stupefies Wonder. They've never trained together, yet he shifts seamlessly around her while wielding his longbow like liquid, somersaulting and shooting another arrow, which the assailant evades. He's also on the verge of laughter, as though he's been invited to play in a sand box that he plans to demolish afterward.

So caught up in the moment, Wonder and Malice swerve in unison. They halt, their weapons inadvertently pointed toward one another. He blasts her with a furious smile, at which she rolls her eyes.

They swoop in opposite directions. Seizing an arrow between his fingers, he lashes it at the stranger's abdomen, narrowly missing but gaining an edge. Wonder takes the opportunity to cuff the figure from behind, sending her to the ground.

The elder folds into herself and goes still. But thankfully, she's alive, her lungs inflating with oxygen.

Wonder and Malice jog backward. Her joints shriek, her chest gallops, and each gasp feels like the serrated edge of a saw.

Malice hacks out blood and beams like he's just had an orgasm.

"Miss me, Wildflower?" he asks.

"You ridiculous son of a bitch. You think this is funny?" she snaps, struggling to keep her voice down. "The elder will suffer bruising and remember this attack."

"Then let's make things permanent."

"Are you serious?"

The demon god spreads his arms and seethes, "No, I'm fucking joking."

Her nostrils flare. "Stay away from her."

It's the wrong request. Sneering, Malice whips out a hickory arrow. In seconds, he has it pointed at the female's prone body.

"Stop!" Wonder dives in front of the projectile, catching it midflight, her fingers grasping the arrow's length, then tumbling across the ground and recovering on bended knee. Disgusted, she hurls the weapon to the ground, where it flashes back into Malice's quiver.

Another shot through the forest, which she thwarts with her quartz arrow, splinters Malice's strike in half. On his third attempt, she rolls across the ground once more, landing in front of the stranger and cutting off another blow with her archery.

Frustrated, Malice targets Wonder's womb. She returns the favor, zeroing in on his heart.

Panting, they glower at one another. Their arrows may not be capable of killing, but he's close enough to do lethal damage. With the right precision and severity, he can puncture the elder's skull or twist her neck.

He can slay her. He'd *tried* to slay her, and they've been here for less than an hour.

"Move," Malice fumes. "Or I'll help you."

"Disarm," Wonder commands. "Or I'll make you."

"Haven't you heard? You shouldn't tell a rage god what to do. It'll put him in a vengeful mood."

"I thought you were smarter than that."

Malice's arm tenses as her implication sinks in. An instinctive act of violence will prove his temper is stronger than his foresight. If there's anything he coddles more than his short fuse, it's his shrewdness.

But lacking any recourse, he maintains a steady aim.

Wonder does as well, thinking, wheezing, thinking, wheezing...inhaling. "Wait. I know what to do."

"So do I," he baits.

"You want to be sloppy or strategic?"

With a curse, he lowers his weapon while she disengages to hunt through grass, toadstools, and blossoms. Relief floods her at the sight of a purple lace flower that she plucks from the soil. Kneeling beside the deity, Wonder slips the petals into the female's mouth.

Tilting the goddess's head changes the angle of Wonder's view. And that changes everything.

She reels back. Oh, no. Blast, no, no, no.

Yes, she knows this goddess. Wonder has spent fifty years training with her.

Her Guide looks the same, with those dimples and that sage-colored hair.

Harmony

That's what the female had named herself after passing her role on to her charge. Harmony used to be the Goddess of Wonder, and now she's the Guide of Wonder.

A swell forms on the goddess's temple, but otherwise, there are no lacerations or abrasions marring her countenance. Nevertheless, Wonder's face drops into her palms. She permits herself a moment, then recuperates just as Harmony would have instructed her to.

Up close, Wonder squints and finally notes the ivory archery harnessed to the female. If only Wonder had recognized it earlier, or if only the goddess had perceived Wonder's quartz arrows. How had either of them neglected this?

But then what? Like Anger and Love, it's too risky to bring Harmony into this.

Resigned, Wonder finishes the job, nudging the flower between the female's lips. The petals will dissolve and seep into her mouth, an agent that will mend the wounds even faster than they normally heal. It shall fix the evidence, the damage they've done to her—as well as apply another symptom, not unlike the distortion caused by mortal mushrooms. With any luck, Harmony shall sleep through that part.

Wiping her hands, Wonder traces a thumb over the elder's chin, whispers that she's sorry, and gains her feet. In the silence, Malice stares with an inquisitive glint, to which she clarifies, "The goddess will think she was hallucinating."

"Ahh. I guess that'll work." He quirks a brow toward the budding woodland spread, regarding it like a human addict discovering an illegal pot farm.

Before he advances, Wonder orders, "Do not even think about it."

"Who?" He presses a hand to his chest. "Me?"

"We're not here to harvest celestial drugs."

"But it would make the sex much more invigorating. Just imagine how it would enhance the flavor of fucking like salt to a dish." His decadent eyes roam her curves. "A deep, round, hard dish."

She will not—she will *not*—let that crass comment melt any region lower than her navel. They haven't been trespassing for long, and already he's being difficult. To say the least, cracking frivolous, vulgar jokes while in enemy territory is wasted on her.

That...had been a joke, hadn't it?

"Where were you?" she gripes.

"Here, there, everywhere," he sings.

Never mind.

Their arrows have reappeared in their quivers. Malice hasn't bothered to change his attire, and the saddlebag is a burden while he's got hickory archery strapped to his spine. If she advises against the bag, he'll ignore her, which is what she'd do in his place.

The devil's humor collapses, taking note of something. Stalking up to her, his head bends to study her hand.

A slit of blood carves across her wrist, across her scars. It's dry, which means it must have happened earlier, when they'd transported here. It had been a bumpy ride, and they can tell from the demarcations that it hadn't been from her arrows, but from his.

He'd cut the pulp of starbursts.

Wonder swallows. Malice tosses her a sideways glance. "Hmm. Sorry," he says, sounding nothing of the sort.

She jabs a finger at him. "You got the date wrong. Look at the sky. Look at the sleeping body on the ground. The stars haven't shifted, and our people are milling about. It's not Stellar Worship yet."

"Ah, yeah. I may have botched the calendar. Hey, I'm not fucking perfect, but what's a single night early? There will be, what? One or two keepers roaming the Archives? We can handle that. Better yet, we can avoid them. It's a big building."

"You bastard."

"That would require having a father, which would require being a human. Do you know something I don't?"

"Just get moving."

In two strides, he backs her against a tree, enveloping her with chaos—his width and height, both nerve-wracking menaces. He looms, bracketing a pair of toned arms against the bark on either side of her head, his muscles straining to break free from the sleeves.

He's not robust like Envy or broad like Andrew. Rather, he's an approximation of Anger, tall and tapered yet capable of tearing everything in his path to shreds. Even so, Malice is in a category all his own; he has the most sculpted throat she's ever beheld and a torso built for rock climbing.

Not one word. He says not one word to her.

He just levels her with ashen eyes, a gaze on the verge of retaliation. Wonder lifts her chin, stunned to realize how close this puts her lips to his. His breath licks her mouth, his orbs swallowing her whole, his bulk blockading the forest.

She holds his gaze, refusing to back down. He would do well to remember the numerous times that she has wiped the floor with his backside, such as the night last year when he'd targeted Love and Merry, at which point Wonder had tackled him to the ground.

Not to mention recent events, when he escaped and stalked her through the library stacks. She has bested him before, and she can do it again.

For a ghastly length of time, he engages without blinking.

Fates. How does he do that?

At last, he steps away, letting fresh air swoop in. He puts his back to her, then changes his mind, raising a clawed finger. "Oh, by the way." Returning to where she peels herself from the trunk, he gets in her face, his mouth curling. "I hate you, too."

He slithers into the woods, letting the darkness consume him.

His ferocity is intolerable, but it's also explicable. For one, he's the God of Malice. For another, certainly he abhors her. Captivity will do that to a person.

But why does it sound like Malice wants to punish Wonder for something else entirely?

6

It sounds as though his grievances extend beyond the library vault.

Like he blames her for more than that. Like he has a history's worth of blame to offer.

Like he knows what she's done to him in the past.

And in order for him to know that much, he would have to be *that* boy.

Adolescent dragonflies swim between the trees. Bracken trembles, and petals splay for the miniature creatures to slide down.

Wonder catches up to Malice. They walk an arm's length apart, which isn't enough.

It's about time that she stops fooling herself. As a curator of legends and celestial loopholes, she's wiser than this. She knows the stars' enigmatic power and their infinite technicalities. She has the track record to prove it.

This cannot be a coincidence. His face, his tenor, his possessions, and his nightmares cannot be a coincidence.

Indeed, he is that boy. Or he was.

Accepting the truth spikes her veins with anxiety. He's alive yet not nearly the same. More importantly, he's depraved, submitting to horrid dreams, and living an outcast life. If he were enjoying a happy and malevolent life as a deity, his resurrection would bring her joy, and she would be glad for Malice. But this rekindled existence has done nothing but harm him, turning him into a monster who likes to endanger everyone else for his own gain.

This is her fault. If she hadn't destroyed his mortal life, he wouldn't have died, and none of this would have happened.

"How curious," Malice says, glancing at her. "Feeling wistful? Bittersweet? Nostalgic? Tell me, are you reminiscing?"

Wonder tightens her grip on the archery buckle across her chest. "What are you babbling about?"

"Your eyes have turned into spigots about to overflow."

She thrusts an arm across her stinging tear ducts. "Just because I favor open books, that doesn't mean I am one."

"Mmm, something we have in common. Have you been homesick? Is it finally hitting you that we're here? How's your soul coping? Go on, I like getting answers."

"You might get them if you'd shut up long enough for me to respond. Where are you going?" she demands when Malice veers into a copse densely populated with offshoots and a gurgling brook.

He points. "It's called left, otherwise known as west."

"I know that's west," she bristles. "I've taken this route a thousand times."

"So have I, and the best way to access the Archives is my way."

"We need to go east. The economy section—"

"What the fuck? You can't be serious," he whines, flipping his head toward her. "That passage is unreliable and too narrow for my testicles to fit through. And putting it mildly—"

"You consider this mild?"

"—it's also the most boring area of the repository. A fucking snooze-fest of ledgers."

"Are you an imbecile or an imbecile? That is precisely why it's the most frequently unmanned section. Furthermore, it's canopied by the most trees. Hence, it's easier to breach the structure from there without being spotted. I know what I'm talking about."

"Look at you. As ramrod as a cock."

"I am not getting defensive!"

"No, you're getting aroused. Don't worry, competition does it for me, too."

For Fate's sake, he sniggers as if this is hilarious. It's the most pretentious sound Wonder has ever heard, grating on her flesh as rivalry blasts up her veins. In the near future, she'll need a ladle with which to scoop the memory from her temporal lobe.

On the flip side, he's right. Blood courses through her scalp, prompting a heady rush.

Mmm, something we have in common.

Oh, he has no idea how much they have in common. Will she tell him? Malice has forfeited most of his rights, but not that one. He doesn't seem to have a clue about his past life as a mortal, but he deserves to know.

Yet she's dubious whether he *should* know. It might send him into a tailspin. By the same token, it will force Wonder to share the details of her role in his former life, which will make him despise her more than he already does, which will hardly induce him to be civil, much less cooperative.

The rivalry progresses during their quest, each of them quarreling over the subjects of research, clamoring for the last word. And when not sparring about that, they feud over an assortment of other logistics, like the best nooks to search within the Hollow Chamber's forbidden channel.

They fling their expertise at one other like darts, aiming to strike true and get higher points. It's a petty match to see who knows more, to win the game, to get the medal.

Huff. The only reward he's going to earn is an honorable mention.

Then again, what's become of her scholarly, investigative decorum?

Writing is universal. In retrospect, it's been a foundation in the relationships of her peers, playing a role in the evolution of their stories: books and journals between Love and Andrew, neon words and lyrics between Anger and Merry, libraries and letters between Wonder and Malice.

Not that they're a *Wonder and Malice*. The prospect greases her tongue with oil. She loved the boy he used to be, not the deviant he's become. Thusly, they've joined the ranks of Envy and Sorrow, another temporary couple without definition or a promising future.

Birds shake their bejeweled plumage while chirping a spectral melody. The woodland splits, the branches unlacing to reveal a resplendent edifice. The sight quickens Wonder and Malice's pace until they duck behind shrubbery.

Nestled within the beeches, the Archives rises from the earth, multiple levels of interconnected star-shaped towers shooting to the sky. Windows refract lights from the constellations. Exterior stairways soar along the stone fortification, and waterfalls course down the walls and grass-carpeted landings. The structure blends into the enshrouding boughs, coalescing with the trees like an extension of the celestial wild.

It's a great library of forests and starlight.

Wonder's mouth wreaths into a smile. From the corner of her eye, she notices Malice paying infuriating attention to her.

In the piebald light, his jaw ticks as though her pleasure is contaminating his mood.

"What?" she blusters.

"Nothing." He shifts expressions like he shifts moods, recklessly and with immediacy, his lips lifting. "Wandering Wonder. How do you like the western view?"

Damn him. She's neglected to notice the direction in which they'd been trekking.

Then again, she takes a second look. Examining the gate bookended by tumbling mists of water, a smug giddiness brightens her evening. "I wouldn't know. Would you?"

Frowning, Malice studies the *façade* and draws the same conclusion. She hadn't been the only one not paying attention to their destination during the hike.

This is the north wing, the building's very own northern star.

He curses, raking those talons through his hair. "I hate this entrance."

That perks her up. "Suddenly, it's growing on me. Why don't you demonstrate how much you hate it by trespassing first? I know you like coming first. There's something so—" she imitates him, flicking her fingers in rumination, "—so first about it."

His face cinches into a scowl. "Very funny, Wildflower."

"I like to think so, Demon."

"What happened to 'dearest'? Why does everyone else get 'dearest,' and I get its evil twin?"

"You wouldn't know what to do with the alternative."

"Wouldn't I?"

He just hates this entrance because it's not a challenge, even less so than the eastern gate. On this route, the only trial they'll face is navigating a dizzying maze of corridors that no equilibrium stands a chance against. Easy.

Not that it used to be easy. Wonder has gotten lost there precisely two hundred times prior to mastering its path.

Although the east wing is their best option, the rotation of the Archive keepers—whichever dutiful ones remain here until cessation officially begins tomorrow—should prevent an altercation in the north entrance at this hour. Nonetheless, Malice is correct. It can't be more than a few stragglers, and it's a large structure, so any guardians will be painless to dodge.

One can hope.

They race across the lawn and pause beneath the misty waters flanking the gate, where Malice withdraws the Asterra Flora from his saddlebag, slathering the contents over the winding calligraphy of bars. It's a clean rift, the bolt giving with a subtle tremor.

Slipping into the courtyard, they dash toward a pentagonal double door, where they apply another dose of the liquid. Just like that, they slip into the vestibule, where a procession of lanterns hangs overhead, each housing a single star. The encasements' cutouts emit strands of rosemary green light that dimple the bookcase walls, while narrow windows exhibit violet twilight, the glass panes embroidered with leaves from outside.

Wonder reads Malice's mind, and maybe he reads hers. Agreeing on a route is paramount, but before they do anything, they must tend to the basics. That includes reaching a safe zone until the building empties at dawn.

Demoted from a library maven to a library squatter. If she were alone, she would get cranky. Since Malice would feed on that emotion as if part of his diet, she pulls herself together.

"Whatever wardens are left, they're already in vacation mode," he murmurs. "I suggest we bunk in the southern dorms."

She was going to suggest the same thing. The librarian dormitories are closest to the most vital area of the Archives, the most important place for research. "Let's establish ground rules right now. This illustrious establishment has space for only one diva—and that diva is *me*."

"Ahh," he draws out. "If you're that certain, such a flagrant public service announcement wouldn't be necessary."

She fantasizes about digging a forest trench, dropping his opinions inside it, stuffing the remaining crevices with dynamite, and lighting a match.

For once, she regards him as just Malice. Just Malice, an insufferable yet indispensable knave. Just him.

Hustling into the belly of the Archives, neither of them utters a syllable about when or where to turn. Their footsteps brush the floor, and the deeper they go, the more this atmosphere glows. The inlaid bookshelves contain scrolls about the genealogies of constellations, with plaques mounted beneath each container. She takes advanced note of this section, should it be of use later.

Excitement lurches up her chest, eclipsing fear. She's never had access to this degree before, never had the opportunity to sleep and awaken in the depths of her happy place.

Wonder changes her mind about being reduced to a squatter. She has often joked about wanting to live here, and that's about to become a reality, however unlawful.

She cannot wait to get started. So long as they stay alive, everything will be fine. It's time for her to exercise the positivity that annoys Sorrow and exhausts Anger.

As the passages expand into aisled halls, branches and galleries multiply, as do study arbors, fireplaces crafted purely for ambience, communal tables and desks topped with candles, and velvet chairs large enough to rest in.

They segue into another corridor, toward another wing. Indeed, the leftover guardians must have been reduced to a handful. In any case, Wonder has trained herself, attuning herself to their schedule, in addition to their kinetics.

Which is why she cuffs Malice's arm at the same time he does hers—as the drum of boots pounds into the corridor from the acquisitions quarter.

They jerk their arms back, then spring into opposite niches, pressing themselves against the walls while glancing sideways at each other across the divide. Nearing footsteps match the beat of Wonder's pulse. Malice stares as though he's got X-ray vision, spotting the anarchy beneath her bodice.

An undulation of lantern light flickers across the ground, signaling an approaching shadow. The warden pauses, audibly ten feet from them. Such guardians are retired Guides, merciless to vandals and trespassers. They have the weapons to enforce punishment: longbows, crossbows, and other sharp options. The clank of steel suggests this warden carries a sword that's curved like a saber.

Wonder waits, and Malice waits, and the keeper waits.

Her companion leers and jerks forward, about to fling himself in front of the keeper for no probable reason other than enjoyment. Wonder makes a rapid, cutting motion, slicing her flat palm across her throat, ordering Malice to a standstill.

Miffed, he obeys but sticks his tongue out at her.

Those boots strike away, the pace reluctant but disappearing all the same, making for the encyclopedias and almanacs in the reference section. Wonder's ears perk, assessing whether the guardian is biding time, keen to trap them. She and Malice lock eyes for an eternity until he hops loudly from his hiding spot, his emergence ricocheting down the halls.

Wonder holds her breath. But no one returns.

Then she suppresses a growl. For someone who'd been determined to get here, he's not acting like he wants to succeed. But when has Malice ever behaved consistently?

They keep going, migrating from the north to south. Beneath the lanterns reside infinite levels, categories, and collections, a Magnum Opus of texts holding galaxies of pages. They should ascend to the dorms. Instead, they detour without voicing it, skittering down, down, down a stairwell. Perhaps it's a bookish siren call.

Wonder tiptoes while the fiend beside her slides along the banister. At the bottom, they reach another pentagonal threshold, beyond which an endless vista of stacks awaits, filled with magic and mysteries.

This is it. This is where she'll begin her search for answers.

The Hollow Chamber.

Malice flashes his teeth, anticipation and triumph brightening his face. And something else enhances his complexion: hope. It's an ephemeral transformation, a rare but infectious one as they swap a moment of worship.

One might call it a kinship.

It doesn't last, trepidation dripping into Wonder's mind. She has her own quest, but what is his? What does he need her for? What does he want from this place? Why is this so important to him?

How far is he willing to go in order to get it?

And will she have to stop him?

7

In the Peaks, some treasures have discernible aromas, whereas they wouldn't in the mortal realm. The instant Wonder crosses into the Hollow Chamber, the mythical scents of ink and sepia—which bring to mind the envelopes that Malice had insisted on packing—swaddle her like an old blanket. As if she's never left, she basks in their reassuring embrace.

Rather than reaching high, the subterranean hall digs deep, its levels corkscrewing into the earth like a drill, cramped with curving grids of aisles. The nooks and stacks contain all manner of texts and relics: documents, pamphlets, essays, scriptures, lexicons, portfolios, periodicals, manuals, folios, and tomes.

Overhead, at the crown of the funnel, is a sphere. It floats, a globe of miniature stars and rosemary rays, a source of illumination for patrons.

And for trespassers.

It's going to be all right. Everything will be all right.

Growing up, every archer is introduced to the Hollow Chamber and required to study it. Built and fashioned by history's original Fate Court, it's an underground repository of the arcane and ancient, housing volumes of trivial importance, information that has overstayed its welcome, outlived its value.

If one discounts a certain forbidden area.

A restricted section that she knows all too well.

Wonder and Malice stand at the railing that overlooks the sphere and floors beneath, all these enigmas with the potential to unfurl like petals. She's never been here with someone else. Absurd as it seems, she likens this feeling to mortals who join fandoms, eager to share in their geekery over a mutual love, all the while protective of it.

What's his favorite section? Where has he spent the most time?

What about her? What sorts of formats intrigue her the most? Which repel her the most?

Wonder tucks a marigold lock behind her ear and then glances sideways, just as Malice swerves away from her, his eyes searching for someplace to land. Scanning the Chamber, he leans over—far over—while squeezing the bar until his wrist veins inflate.

She returns to the scenery. Flecks of silver glaze the corners and slopes, hinting at precious book spines, artifacts of eras gone by.

"Since I was little, the Archives has been my playground," she whispers. "And my temple, and my school, and my home. Every safe and scandalous part of it."

"Which do you care about most?" Malice asks. "The safe or the scandalous?"

"I'm starting to think they're one and the same."

"I've always thought that."

"At first sight of the bookshelves, I became obsessed."

"Obsession is healthy." Based on his ghost of a smile, she's unsure whether he's being serious or sarcastic. "First time I ever came here, I made a beeline for the Chamber and tried to steal a book."

"Naturally, when you could have borrowed it."

"Where's the fun in that?"

"Why a text from this area? Was it from the restricted section?"

"Nah, I raided that place later. But the rest of the Chamber? These books aren't given a chance; they're dumped like piles of turds. I liked the idea of reading the outcasts that nobody else gave a shit about."

"That's what attracted me as well. The books that people underestimated."

"Yeah. But then a scribe caught me. Fucker grabbed me right before I got outside."

Wonder's head bounces toward Malice's profile. "You almost succeeded."

"I hate to break it to you, but almost doesn't count."

"Well, I don't condone thievery, but in other aspects of life, almost succeeding is better than never trying."

His mouth twitches. "How didactic of you."

Oh, why does she even bother?

Rest is the order of business. It's been a trying journey, so they exit the Chamber and take advantage of the vacant librarian dorms. They travel up the north tower, which houses a spiral of quarters along its column. At one landing, neighboring doors with diamond handles greet them.

Wonder and Malice gravitate apart, each of them grasping a knob. Inside the room, the ceiling gleams with renderings of constellations, and a plate of glass slopes before her, offering a vista of the forest. Frothy linens encase the bed, its frame as slender as a finger. The simplicity is aerial and elegant, with its wardrobe, writing desk, and bookcase.

Wonder sets down her archery, her muscles sighing at the

blissful loss of weight. There's so much to explore, so much to see and do. But presently, she's too tired to feel overwhelmed by anything, and that's a godsend considering who's bunking next door.

Speaking of that knave, Malice looms in the archway, free of his own baggage. He shoves one leather shoulder against the trim. "So this is where you'll get undressed, eh?"

"Absolutely," she answers with feigned sweetness. "Right after my arrow amputates your prick."

"Ouch. Christ, that's grotesque."

"Go to bed, Malice."

Instead of taking the hint, he watches her through cindered irises.

Does he sleep naked?

Wonder stiffens, trashing the visual before it becomes implanted in her mind and keeps her awake, with her heels pushing into the blankets. Besides, he just wants attention.

She holds out her upturned palm, wiggling her fingers. "We've arrived. Hand over my corsage."

He wiggles his talons in mock farewell. "I said I'd give it to you when we got here, but I never gave an exact date."

"What does that imply?"

"I don't know, but it sounds clever."

"I can break into your room and take collateral, too. Try me."

Because she isn't bluffing, those eyes narrow to slits. "I'll never stop trying you. Not until you break."

"You'll be trying for a very long time."

"It's lucky that we live forever, then. Sweet dreams, Wildflower."

When he's gone, Wonder thrusts the door closed and drops onto the bed. Yes, she wants her corsage back. And yes, she'll take it by force if she must. But that's a plan for tomorrow, among a million plans.

Malice might have his own agenda for coming here, his own answers to seek. That aside, this crusade to overthrow the Court is in his favor. He hasn't said so, but he's going to help her—in as much as he'll try to use her for his own purpose. Otherwise, this mutual abduction is void.

And he'll keep her corsage hostage until then.

What he hasn't grasped—or perhaps what he's counting on—is her rebellion. If he's plotting to bait and harass her, she'll bait and harass him right back.

Slipping between the gauzy sheets, Wonder inhales the fresh linens. Since slumber will come easier with a stream of meditation, she empties her mind until the world recedes into blackness. And for the first time, she's not plagued by his wails.

Somehow, she's certain: He won't have a nightmare tonight.

At dawn, Wonder knocks on his door. Then she knocks harder, pretending it's his skull.

Receiving no answer, she hisses. The remnant keepers have long since departed the Archives, because she'd witnessed them from her window as they'd glided into the forest, their robes blending into the mesh. Hence, she's allowed to make noise and haste.

She races to the Hollow Chamber, where she finds Malice reclining at a compact desk just inside the entrance, an open book spread across his lap. He props his feet on the tabletop, crossing them at the ankles while canting his head at her.

"Tardy on your first day?" he goads. "Overslept? Dog ate

your homework?"

"We were supposed to meet outside the dorms," she gripes.

How dare he leave without her. How dare he create an arbitrary schedule, act like some prized pupil, and then admonish her about tardiness.

How dare he beat her to it!

To cool her heels, Wonder weaves her hair into a tousled side braid. Meanwhile, Malice scrapes through his mussed waves. That's all it takes for them to peter out and trail off into silence.

Why does this feel awkward?

Malice has conjured new attire, having replaced the leather sweater with a Henley that strains across his torso, pulling taut over firm muscles. Alas, she misses the concealment of thicker clothing, her body buzzing at the sight of him. So this is how Hades looks at the break of dawn, when he's free to roam as he pleases.

Her own garb is as disheveled as his hair, and that feels too intimate for her liking. By contrast, he's not ashamed to scroll over her with aplomb.

Standing beside the chair, a tripod table balances a steaming pot of peony tea, plus a fruit bowl loaded with bloated cherries and blushing peaches. No pomegranates.

Heat coils from the pot and dashes into the air. Industrious, he's already procured breakfast.

She loves the selection. In fact, they're her favorites.

Hadn't she mentioned that to him recently? It must be a ploy.

Wonder pours a cup of tea. While balancing it in her hand, she avoids the cherries and snatches a peach with her free fingers. "Let's get to work," she says.

Malice vacates the chair. Gaining his feet, he leans in and

bites the orb propped in her hand, then straps his mouth around the rim of her tea, guzzling the contents.

Licking his lips, he sets the half-emptied peony tea in her palm. "I thought you'd never ask," he says.

Still holding the cup and fruit, Wonder watches him leave. Then she regards the refreshments, each one impinged upon by his mouth...his tongue...

She dumps both on the table.

They start in the restricted section, descending into the funnel's lowest level, a vanishing point at the base of the Chamber. There, a curved slab encircles them, giving the appearance of a foyer. In the center, a metallic telescope—a stargazer— points toward its own likeness, a painted mirror image set amidst constellations. Other than that, the wall bears no doors or grooves into which a partition might slide.

No, this segment of the Chamber doesn't open by conventional means. The stargazer is a key, and there are two ways to enter.

One, by rotating the lens just so, a maneuver that cannot be mastered by anyone but the Fate Court, the Archives keepers, and the librarians.

Two, by breaking celestial law.

It's how Wonder—and evidently Malice, during his own rebellious sojourns—used to sneak inside.

He rifles through his pocket to retrieve the capsule of Asterra Flora, then smears the liquid onto the lens, causing it to circuit and twist like a kaleidoscope. The mural shimmers, coming to animated life and thinning into a sheer screen of dew and twinkling stars. They step through the veil, a fine layer of dampness settling on their clothes.

Elated, Wonder inhales the atmosphere. Oh, how the fragrance of ancient ink permeates the channels, while starlit lanterns pour incandescent rosemary light onto the lanes. The beacons illuminate dust floating in the air, the motes lustrous and shining.

Mesmerized, she and Malice step tentatively, savoring this reunion. They wander in different directions, slipping around bends and strolling along the glistening stacks. These are the aisles of the forbidden, of the taboo, of the elusive. This is an illustrious cellar of secrets, many stored by the various Fate Courts over the ages, others tucked here by the stars, secured for those destined to find and enact them.

She gets reacquainted, running her digits over the books, privately instructing herself as she once had. Feel the pulse of each shelf. Bask in the gleam of every bookcase. Respect their darkness and seek their light. Listen to the pages crinkle. Follow them. Read them.

Wonder pulls away from a title, green granules clinging to the pads of her fingers. Beaming, she blows on the flakes, soot whisking up into a pixie dust cloud—beyond which Malice appears. As the nebula floats to the ground, he watches her, and she watches him.

He taps his chin. "Shall we get to it?"

She straightens. "We shall."

During this month of worship, they have free reign without the necessity of nocturnal escapades or vacating the premises in anticipation of the watch's rotation.

True, it's not foolproof. Wonder's Guide might resist the notion that she'd been hallucinating in the forest. Therefore,

Harmony might insist on an inspection of the woods and its vicinity. If she or any other unexpected presence breaks with tradition and comes sniffing here, Wonder and Malice will have to flee. She knows the rattle of every doorknob in this place, the creak of every hinge, the compression of carpet beneath a deity's stride, the echo of movement in the halls.

Does Malice know the same warning signs? Will it be enough?

Now that slumber is behind them, they'll have to tackle these questions first.

And so it begins. Drafting a contingency plan comes more seamlessly than she'd anticipated, compared to when they'd broken into the Archives. It strikes her how painless collaborating on solutions to unwanted company turns out.

By the time they have methods of offense and defensive in place, they move on to investigation. And that's where things go downhill, both of them facing each other on opposite ends of a long table, their palms flat on the surface.

"Tell me what you're searching for, and I'll tell you if I'm going to cooperate," Wonder states.

"I'll tell you when I'm ready, and you will cooperate," he replies.

"In other words, you wanted badly for me to come here with you, but you haven't a clue what exactly you need me for? I doubt that. You're Malice."

"And you're an Archive diva. If I can't figure shit out on my own, you're my research backup. Besides, isn't that same reason you need me? For your friends' little campaign against our rulers? You need my bookish ingenuity, in case you can't—gasp!—find the victorious answers all by yourself."

The prospect is a sucker punch to the ego, but fine. They'll draw from one another, if the need arises. She's not in a rush to assist him anyway.

Until then, they research separately, bickering over who gets priority over each section. The worst territorial cat fights circulate around the areas containing lunar folktales, the topography of the Peaks—in case there's a line, crater, or uncharted portal of entry connecting it to the mortal realm—the history of exiles, and inexplicable astral cases or testimonials, meaning incidents in which the stars have defied logic. She and Malice toss trivia at one another, to establish who's more deserving of each location. They fire bullet points as if these sectors are exclusive, up for auction to the highest bidder.

"Which ledgers list the most accurate data about weather patterns?" he grills.

"How can you spot a tall fable, from a plagiarized fable, from an authentic fable?" she retorts.

"Which millennium saw the most outcasts?" he volleys.

"Which type of format—illuminated manuscripts or scrolls—chronicles the most accessible spectral phenomena?" she quizzes.

When they finally come up for air, they decide to split the areas and then switch.

That's not all. He mocks her color-coded notations, a technique she relies heavily upon lest her mind stray. It's best to jot down the information before she loses it, eclipsed by a new concept or query.

In contrast, his method involves organized chaos. Rather than pen actual notes on actual parchment, he relies on the casket that is his brain, stocking his cache there.

They're defensive about their systems, endorsing them with condescension and superiority. Neither of them wins the round, though neither of them calls it quits.

The following nights pass in the same cutthroat manner. They charge through the Chamber, rushing down the lanes in a race to see who can do their research faster and come out with the most promising texts for their goals. One time, they power walk down parallel aisles, casting each other glances and then increase their speed while hunting for particular books. To their astonishment, they end up in the same spot, skidding in front of the same shelf.

Their hands reach for the same volume.

When their digits nearly collide, Malice flicks his fingers back to avoid her. Then he swings his arm and gestures to the title. "Wildflowers first."

As if he's doing her a favor, throwing her a bone, letting her win.

It turns out, they may have been looking for the same book, but not the same chapter. Not even the same page.

On another occasion, Malice uses an inkwell to blot her color-coded notes. Later that night, she swaps the analytical texts he'd scrupulously collected, exchanging them for economy ledgers, since he finds them oh, so boring.

Apparently, they're not above trying to sabotage one another.

It doesn't escape Wonder that such petulance negates the trouble and risk they've gone through to get here. Shame washes over her, that she's lowered herself to this level. Using this place as a tool to belittle her enemy is disrespectful to the Archives and demeaning to her purpose.

And now she knows what rivalry feels like.

And drat it all, she cannot find anything remotely helpful toward her classmates' campaign for free will. Presently, Wonder slams a book shut and flops backward in her chair, positioned at the head of a study table in between the restricted stacks. Although upholstered, the rigid seat croaks with her motions. She has set up camp in the philosophy sector, away from where Malice prowls the history stacks. The heap of books on the desk mocks her, inadequacy and frustration causing her fingers to curl.

The corsage of eucalyptus, stephanotis, and peony is hers. It's her good luck charm, and she needs it. And she's to blame for letting him have his way, which is unacceptable. And because it's unacceptable, the chair skids back as Wonder rises. He's far out of range, lost in his own task.

She'll be quick.

Hiking the tower to his room, she glances for the hundredth time over her shoulder and slips through the door. It smells of Malice—of old pages. But inconveniently, the space lacks the fragrance of a pomegranate. That's not encouraging, since the posy is presumably subsisting with one.

Also, he's a tidy soul. The bed is made, the space swept clear of clutter, except for his saddlebag and archery.

Wonder hunts the vicinity, rifling through the wardrobe and bookcase. The cabinets and drawers yield nothing of consequence, just extra leaflets and castoff books. Because he doesn't scribe notations, there's nothing to memorize, no hint of his private intentions.

There isn't a sign of the blooms, so she kneels before the saddlebag and pries it open.

And then she remembers the envelopes.

Wonder halts, her digits freezing. There they are, pressed together and yellowed with age, the parchment looking soft...and legible.

Here in the Peaks, she'll be able to read the contents. And it's wrong, so very wrong to intrude. But mustn't she? They share a tumultuous past, and that past had consisted of letters just like these.

Just one peek. Her fingers shake as she lifts one of the envelopes and tugs on the flap. She swallows, withdraws the paper from inside, and unfolds it.

Immediately, Wonder wishes that she hadn't.

At last, there's no denying, no rebuttal, no chance. Her heart seizes as a flurry of words materialize...careless and stupid words. It's penned in his handwriting, recognizable from the moments in which he'd vandalized her own notes just to spite her.

Yes, it's his handwriting. But it's not his prose.

It's hers.

These are her words, from another century, from another place. These are the words she'd once written to that mortal boy... words she had written to Malice.

Because he's that boy. That's no longer a surprise.

The surprise is this: He remembers her.

In some way, he remembers her.

This explains why these missives resemble the ones from their history. He must have conjured them to look this way, fashioning them into replicas and then transcribing the contents by channeling his nightmares. It's the only feasibility, seeing as the originals no longer exist, for Wonder knows what befell them.

The note in her hand is a clone of her dozenth letter. What about the first one she'd written? Might she find a facsimile in this pile?

Is this why he's here? To unearth answers about his past life, however much of it he recalls?

Wonder resists the temptation to dig in and learn more. She tucks the paper into her bodice, then fumbles to place the empty envelope back in its slot. The saddlebag is split wide open, with her guilty palm suspended over his collection.

Unfortunately, a shadow materializes. It looms over Wonder, swallowing her whole.

"Hmm," a voice creeps from behind. "Big mistake, Wildflower."

8

Daytime starlight slashes through the window. Blue streaks give the room a compass effect, the beams of light and dark pointing like hands. She can't tell whether her throat bobs from remorse, mortification, or a fragile emotion linked to the words in that letter.

If she turns, will she see him differently? Will she see *him*? That dearest boy?

His silhouette puddles across the floor while foliage outside the window shivers, the fringed leaves chanting, *Shhh*. A youthful dragonfly has flitted into the dorms, landing on the desk and then zipping away.

Wonder twists, pretending to follow its trajectory. The insect zooms past Malice's hip, and she focuses on the notch of his waist while bracing herself. Delaying any further will make her look weak and scarcely innocent.

Her eyes drag up his body, framed in the doorway. Malice idles on the threshold, his arms raised above his head, his fingers gripping the molding. This pushes him forward, angling him into a deep incline, a precarious and slippery slope.

This also places his attributes on display. The ridges of his biceps and the expanse of his torso, adding length and ripples to his form beneath the jeans and Henley. Destiny has converted him from a blushing mortal to a volatile troll outfitted in black, a dark specimen capped with the wrong color hair, those waves imbued as if he's an angel.

When she meets his eyes, both incarnations stare back, so that her heart cracks.

It's you. It's really you.

But what's happened to you? Why are you like this?

How I've missed you. How I loathe myself for what I did to you. How I despise you for what you're doing to me.

I hate you. I love you.

I don't forgive you. I'm sorry.

Wonder can look at him all day. And she cannot bear to look at him another second. It's too much. She needs to get out of here before she dissolves and splashes to the floor, every word gushing out of her.

Is this why he treats her with vitriol? But it's illogical. Malice may recall her letters to him, but he cannot know she's the author. She was invisible back then; they never met in the flesh, much less in any guise. They'd never once spoken.

He remembers her words. But he cannot know her face or voice.

Can he? If he has somehow discovered that she's the specter, it's undetectable. But that's Malice, seldom revealing what he wants, or feels, or knows. There are exceptions to this rule, but not many.

She gains her feet and matches his mask of indifference, blessed numbness settling over her. She has become accustomed to his unpredictable streak. She has gleaned the warning signs of when he'll attack, when he'll taunt, and when he'll withdraw.

That deceptive calm suggests the latter, but she's no fool: He's livid.

His lips twist as he crooks a finger, silently beckoning her. If he wants Wonder to draw near, he's got another thing coming.

Noting that, he boosts himself from the molding and prowls toward her, stopping close enough for her to see the charred flecks in his irises. And because she folds her hands in front of herself, he dips his head to examine the scars, which inspires him to swerve a fingernail, pretending to sketch the starburst marks. From the day they met in the Celestial City's library, he's been fixated on her wounds, while she has refused to give him a single tidbit of information. Denying Malice facts drives him to the precipice yet gives his adversaries power.

To this day, Wonder chooses power. Though her skin prickles from the illusion of his digit skimming her.

"Pain clashes with your skin tone," he observes in a ghastly tone of voice. "Was it worth it?"

The subtext of his inquiry isn't hard to miss. He'd seen her rifling through his envelopes, so it's best not to explain until Malice decides what he wants to say. Otherwise, she'll back herself into a corner and give him too much information to play with.

Was the pain worth it?

"I don't know," she replies, because she honestly doesn't know anymore.

To which Malice gnashes his teeth. "Either you're one hell of an overachiever, or you're a nosy-assed goddess."

Wonder finds her stamina, resilience sprouting from the depths of her stomach and sprinting off her tongue. "Does it have to be one or the other? Can't I be both?"

"Curious. You've got the Archives at your disposal…our home, away from home, away from home. What can my saddlebag give you that a million square feet of stacks can't?"

"Where is my corsage?"

"Christ. Is that all you want to know? Are you sure that's what you were looking for? Seems to me that you followed the scent of paper instead. Couldn't help yourself but to help yourself, is that it?"

"You arrived too soon. I had no chance to help myself."

In a nutshell, denial sounds guiltier. With Malice, it's better to subvert his expectations by owning up.

He calls the bluff, stalking past her. Wheeling slowly, she watches him squat and pick through the bag. He must have the letters organized in a way that only he can identify, just in case someone with curves decides to snoop.

Wonder steels herself. She'd made sure to place the envelope in its original spot, but pulling a fast one on Malice is a challenging feat.

If he grins, that means he's going to pounce. Unarmed, she flits her eyes over to the wooden longbow propped against his bed post.

At last, he rises. His shoulders relax, along with that wiry mouth.

Good. She won't have to use his archery on him.

"Are you satisfied?" she asks.

He runs the plank of his thumb across his lower lip, considering her. "Oh, I will be. Rest assured."

"Rest? I'm not the one who has trouble resting."

That's pushing it. She knows because his features spasm in surprise—right before he fishes a lone peony petal from his pocket. Wonder recognize this small token from her corsage, which he must have carried around, possibly for a moment such as this. Twirling the purple bud in his digits, he says, "And I'm not the one who has trouble doing this."

Making a fist, he crushes the petal.

"You odious, vile...!" Furious, Wonder bats at his fingers, wrestling with him until he exposes the bloom, still intact.

She stalls, then veers away, remembering herself. For a second, she'd forgotten how robust the Peaks' flora are. It would take more than his grip to wilt the nature of this land.

Malice had counted on her forgetting. "Your reaction was perfect," he says, stuffing the petal back into his pocket.

Wonder storms past him, only making it to the open doorway when his voice slithers up her spine. "Wildflower?" he croons, and when she makes no reply but merely glowers ahead, his words lick up her back. "Peek in here again, and I'll burn those flowers."

She twists halfway. "Burn them, and I'll shred the letters while you *rest*."

The rebuttal jostles a protective glare from him, one that warns her against it yet dares her to try. But would he really do as he says? Would she?

No. Yes.

She leaves the room. Nevertheless, their mutual threats echo for the rest of the day, well into the afternoon as she resumes her perch in the Hollow Chamber. Sagging into her chair, Wonder hunches, stamps both elbows onto the table, and drops her face into her palms, instructing herself to breathe.

She deserves a medal for that performance. To convince Malice that she hadn't taken anything from his bag, on the heels of admitting that she tried, is a victory.

Restraining herself from either cupping his jaw or slapping him has a place in the history books: the blooming librarian goddess with intractable willpower. It would make a grand tale.

Speaking of texts, she hazards a peek at her surroundings

and then plucks the delicate letter from her bodice. The paper flutters from her fingers like a plume. It lands atop the open book she'd been reading earlier, an anthology about the Peaks' natural resources, the chemistry and biology of its environment.

She just can't right now. She can't bother perusing pages that reveal next to nothing, amounting to gibberish.

Wonder moves to retrieve the letter and then close the book. Clasping the hardback rim, her eyes hook on to the layer of paper overlapping paper. The sepia sheet resting above the volume's text becomes…transparent.

She straightens, flattening the leaflet, pressing it firmly against the manuscript. What was a yellowing sheet one second ago has turned into a sheer surface. It blots out the anthology's original text, allowing alternative script to materialize, as if the sepia paper has become a magnet, pulling hidden cursive to the surface.

She scoots closer to the table, its rim pressing into her navel. It's not that Malice's paper has its own sort of magic, because his handwriting remains, interfering with this new secret message. She tilts the letter so only its blank areas cover the manuscript, so that it doesn't obscure the mystery beneath.

Her gaze jumps across the words. As it does, her scalp tingles—a familiar and enticing sensation, fraught with risk and reward. She has lived such a moment twice before, walking a fine line between ignorance and discovery. In this maze of shelves, she experiences it for a third time.

It's a legend.

She reads fast, then rereads the script, then translates its celestial vocabulary. In Love and Andrew's story, the secret quest had involved uniting hearts. In Anger and Merry's story, it had involved winning and breaking hearts.

And what does this new legend share?

Her finger rides across the paper for yet another round.

If a deity releases their own heart, that deity will heal from their greatest mistake.

Wonder's head snaps up. Only one regret festers within her. Only one person.

So if she releases her heart from the past, she'll recover from it. She'll free herself of the guilt and pain. In turn, that will make her stronger, won't it? It will empower her for whatever battles against the Fates may lie ahead.

And the ache for Malice's ghost will vanish. She'll stop hurting, stop loving who he used to be. She'll stop wanting.

He will mean nothing to her.

Won't that be a relief? Won't that be nice?

All she has to do is release her heart. The question is, how?

9

There's more.

There's more because she uncovers more.

Sometimes a crack in research becomes a crater. Sometimes the secret has more to say, more clauses to impart. Any respectable Archive diva wouldn't merely take a legend at face value without making sure this is the extent of it. There might be branches, a family tree of mysteries.

She tries different techniques: twisting the overlapping paper like a knob opening a door, turning it clockwise above the manuscript, then counterclockwise. When that fails to clear a path of new information, she presses down harder and steers the leaflet across the surface, highlighting and obscuring certain parts. She treats the page like a map, sweeping the sepia sheet across its typography, bearing northward and then southward.

Still nothing.

But there *is* something.

A tremulous sensation passes through her, similar to past visits when she'd uncovered other forbidden scripts. This is her, in her element at last. This is her, remembering what it's like to ally with these books, privy to their secrets. How she loves this feeling!

There is more, there is more, there is more.

She will figure this out. Perhaps it's not on this page, but on another one. So begins an investigation of the manuscript as she flips from chapter to chapter, repeating the process and layering paper over paper, gliding the sepia sheet across ravines of calligraphy, scaling elevations of ink. This, with the aid of a yellowed and weathered letter belonging to her rival.

But enough about him. This is about two pieces of paper reacting to one another.

Wonder almost reaches the end of the book when there *is* more.

Trying one last method, she lifts the sepia paper and then releases it, letting it flutter atop the manuscript like a quill's plume. That's what she had done upon her first discovery hours earlier.

Has it truly been hours?

Yes, it has. This tome is large and heavy, a breeding ground of text. Although she's immortal, the book's density would nevertheless fracture her toe if she dropped it. Therefore, it has taken a while to pore through its girth.

Wonder watches as the stolen paper drapes itself over the anthology, as delicately as a feather. The moment that happens, text surfaces like seaweed from the bottom of an ocean. Except the sentences have the shine of tinsel, drafted in the same nimble penmanship as the first part of this legend. It's the handwriting of the stars, emancipated after who knows how long.

Her kind has many assumptions, including that gods and goddesses are incapable of feeling love. But oh, what a falsehood. For deities indeed possess hearts, and those hearts beat, and writhe, and shrivel, and grow.

In fact, that's how immortal kinships and friendships begin. This begets brotherhoods and sisterhoods, if not families.

Therefore, the legend says that while a deity might release

their own heart, they might also recover that heart. Wonder mouths the words, tossing them about in her mind. To recover one's own heart can mean a thousand things.

She pushes away from the table, her chair scraping the floor. Perhaps this legend is only able to reveal itself when human paper makes contact with immortal paper? And is it a coincidence that a letter belonging to her antagonist is the key to this secret?

She tests that theory, tearing a blank paper from the notebook she'd procured in the Archive's storage facilities. The random page yields the same message, which causes simultaneous reactions, her breath whooshing while her shoulders slump. So it is coincidence, yet not. Although she could have used any paper, kismet has seen fit to deliver this information via a particular sheet, one so near and dear to Malice.

If a deity releases her heart...

If a deity recovers his heart...

This has no bearing on her mission. Does it? Or what's the correlation?

Though somehow it's important, if not to the battle ahead, then to those involved in that battle. And in some roundabout way, it's relevant.

The first part, certainly to her. To release her heart, must she endure a specific test? Resist a specific temptation? Reject a specific moment?

Must she utter certain words? Perform certain acts?

In any event, she'll be ready. She has endured a lifetime of heartbreak and torture. Yet here she is, still a library diva, still an archeress, and still damned intelligent.

She can do this. She must do this.

The second part may very well pertain to Malice. To recover that black, pounding organ in his chest, what task must he face?

The legend spills across the pages, a declaration bleeding to the edge of the manuscript.

If a deity recovers their own heart, all that came before shall be rekindled.

All that came before…before he lost his heart…the time before that. It shall be rekindled.

What facet of *before*? What shall be rekindled?

"His memory," she whispers, her mouth going dry as a prairie.

If he succeeds, he'll get his memory back. He shall relive all his blessings—and his torments. He will reconnect with every memory, every single one, and not just the happiness but the source of his nightmares.

The bleakness and hope of this promise scrambles like an egg in Wonder's psyche. She didn't uncover any of this by accident. And if so, Malice deserves to know. If he doesn't remember who he is, he'll want this opportunity.

But will the outcome strengthen or destroy him?

And what about her? By releasing her heart, will she gain something vital or lose something valuable?

10

She awakens with her cheek swimming in a puddle of drool. Her head lifts from the desk where her arms cross like a makeshift pillow. Dawn siphons through the windows, a gradient of hydrangea blue that bleeds with the interior's rosemary tints from the star lanterns, while green granules akin to literary pixie dust swim through the aisles. The last thing she remembers is the legend leaching clarity from her eyes, straining and distorting her vision.

Here are the side effects of pulling an all-nighter: drool and soiled clothes that cling to her ribcage and hips. Wonder's groggy and grimy, and she couldn't be more pleased by this wave of nostalgia. She would willingly fall asleep amidst books any day.

An additional perk is that Malice is nowhere to be seen. She imagines if he'd been here, eager to berate her sleeping habits and scorn her appearance. He would gloat that he doesn't need to stay up in order to conquer the Archives.

Bully for him. She's more dedicated than that, which is why she's found what she's found.

After tidying up and placing the books where they belong, Wonder carts the anthology and the letter to her room. It's time for rejuvenation. Upon her arrival from the mortal realm, she had outfitted the wardrobe closet; rifling through her options now, she dons a silk robe and then pads barefoot into the corridor.

Malice's lair is deathly silent. He must be lurking in one of the wings.

She would bet her corsage that his door is locked. She confirms as much when testing the knob.

Descending the tower, Wonder steps from the building and into a courtyard, fashioned into a bathing area for residents. She sighs at the beautiful sight of a sunken pool built into the ground and shrouded in greenery, the branches of a willow draped around the rim to form a curtain.

The tresses of steam plaiting from the water is purely aesthetic, temperature being a moot subject. But the effect is pretty, especially beneath the firmament littered with morning constellations. The fragrance of elderflowers wafts through the air, and lotus buds float in the water.

Checking the perimeter, Wonder twists her locks into a messy bun, then hooks the robe over a bough. A breeze dances around her limbs. She wades deeply, the splashing sounds reinvigorating. Partially submerged and reclining against the ledge, she brackets her arms and tips her head back, her breasts dripping and puckering at the surface, her legs floating in front of her. Every dilemma and discovery vanishes from her mind as she drifts into therapeutic randomness.

She whispers to whichever dawn stars are listening. "Do constellations get sleepy? How intoxicated can you get off the scent of wildflowers? If a book contained an entire life, how many pages would it be?"

Eventually, she runs out of questions. Lotus flowers swim around her, tickling her knees and settling atop her feet. She rubs one of the blooms until a foaming cream seeps from the bud, then she lathers herself, bathing her skin with its generous essence.

A breeze thrusts itself into the alcove, and her skin pebbles from the onslaught.

Wonder whisks around while ducking. A thorough scan confirms there's no one here, because everyone is in spiritual retreat, and she's secluded in this giant structure, marooned with only one other soul. And if Malice were spying, she would know it, because he would let himself be known. He'd rather be a loud antagonist than a silent creeper.

The very thought of his eyes on her wet body produces a tiny bolt of desire. Unbidden and intrusive, it shoots through Wonder until she shakes off the disturbance.

No, he wouldn't gawk. Rather, he would probably steal her robe and force her to traipse naked through the Archives.

She finishes washing, then rinses herself off and exits the pool. Her soles make flipper sounds against the rim's tiles, sprinkling the plants with dew. Reaching toward the branch where she'd draped her robe, she feels nothing but air.

Wonder halts. A scream solidifies in her throat and cannons off her tongue. "Malice!"

Nude, she marches into the Archives, soaking the floors and carpets. The lanterns glaze Wonder in rosemary, turning her into a garden, emphasizing the rocks of her nipples and the sprigs of hair between her legs. If deities were modest, this graphic trip would be unforgivable. But since neither applies, it's merely a gross annoyance.

That doesn't dissuade Wonder from tearing a linen curtain off a window rod and wrapping it around herself. By the time, she reaches the dorm stairwell, she's ready to maul him. Rounding the narrow corner kindled by morning starlight, she halts.

Lounging against the passage wall, Malice wears a leather V-neck shirt as glossy as black licorice and ornamented with fine whiplashes of chain. His jeans have been replaced with onyx hose, a customary choice in Peaks, while the black boots studded with hardware reflect his tastes from the mortal realm.

Grinning, he flaunts her silken robe and fondles the sleeves. "You've got feminine taste."

She grouses, "And you're a toddler."

"How many times do I need to remind you? I'm the devil. I like being the devil. It's so devilish of me. By the way, I think we're even now. And to clarify, I wasn't spying. I grabbed this dainty little thing while barely seeing your head above water."

"I didn't take anything from your saddlebag."

It's a lie, but he doesn't know that. Right?

Malice trails off, going oddly silent while she stomps up to him, exposing herself in the beams of green light. Her fingers swipe the garment from his hands. To her surprise, it's easy to do. He hadn't even bothered to get vexed and hold it out of reach.

Why? Oh, she sees why.

Malice's eyes dip down her body, the curves trussed up in sheer cloth and speckled with wet spots. She becomes hyper-aware of the beads licking down her neck, her breasts pumping against the textile, and the flush of her complexion. This compact area reduces her oxygen supply, and his breathing has a new weight to it, which increases in frequency.

He's astonished. But what had he expected? For her to be dry and fully clothed?

Yes, he had. She's a fool, irritation having overwhelmed logic. It had been a harmless jest, since she could have conjured a replacement for the robe. She hadn't needed to traverse the Archives naked. If she hadn't taken leave of her senses, she'd have drawn that rudimentary conclusion.

His smug features lose their mirth. The more his eyes trace her, the more acute the sensation. The more droplets seep into the cloth, the more gluttonous his expression becomes.

She feels every sweep of his gaze. The tick in his jaw matches the one in her pulse. Her thighs tighten, a rawness building at their juncture, as if her very survival hinges upon this moment.

The boy from history nudges to the forefront of her mind. How long has she dreamed of him looking at her this way, with the sort of disorderly hunger that makes her want to bite something?

Step closer. Unwind the garment and see if he's capable of blushing, like he used to be.

Malice rakes a hand through his hair, and those gilded waves spring back into place. Unfortunately, a second later, vulgarity rinses the awe from his face. Even if she could tap into his emotions, she doesn't need to—not as the dark, self-indulgent taste of wine floods her palate. It's a sensual slide down her throat, tainted with lust and lechery.

Any moment, he's going to say something perverse just to aggravate her.

Malice ridicules, "I take it my gibe derailed you. What a productive morning."

Wonder huffs, "I'm not going to shower you with attention."

"And I'm not going to shower you with discretion," he spews. "It's not my problem if your tits are soaked and jiggling in my face. If you don't want it to happen again, then get your shit together and remember your magic. Don't make yourself an easy target."

"Enough, or I'll declaw you!"

"In my sleep, no doubt."

"Think again. We've established more than once that I can

trounce you while you're awake, with your eyes wide open. So take my advice and put away your arsenal."

Gliding his tongue across his incisors, Malice backs Wonder against the wall. The proximity causes his shirt to brush the damp cloth scarcely concealing her nudity.

How can a moment be infuriating and stimulating at the same time?

How can someone be dear yet damning?

Malice's pupils dilate. His palms make a loud and theatrical smack against the stone on either side of her head. "But I haven't even whipped my arsenal out yet," he intones with a sneer, his breath a drizzle across her lips.

In a flash, Wonder drops the robe and flips them around. His back hits the slab, a sound of surprise lurching from him, which turns into a hiss when she clamps onto his pinky nail and exerts pressure, threatening to yank the talon from its root.

There'd been a time when seeing him hurt would have been unthinkable. Most times, it still is. Just not now.

"Go ahead," she speaks through her teeth. "Try it."

He spurts out a pained cackle. "So the wildflower doesn't like to be trapped—"

"—any more than the demon," she finishes.

Those pupils shrink. Releasing him, she snatches the robe off the steps.

He has taken her corsage, while she has looted his own possessions and then blatantly denied it, so perhaps they're even. And as he'd said, he hadn't peeked while she bathed. His mouth twitches whenever he's not telling the truth, but those lips are doing nothing of the sort. Instead, they're clenching.

Wonder shoulders past him, slamming up the steps while he stalks past her, striding down the stairs. On his way, he swings a hoop around his finger, an ornate moon-dusted key hooked to the ring. Just as she'd thought, a key to his room. Locks in the Peaks are resistant to immortal strength, meaning they're not penetrable with the assistance of mere muscle or elbow grease.

For good measure, Wonder swipes the key ring from Malice while hiking up the steps. Without stopping, she flicks it out the nearest stairwell window, ignoring Malice's curse. Smiling to herself, she trots toward the dormitories.

Thirty minutes later, she's dry and armored in a gown dyed leaf green. The bodice drapes into a V along the spine, a sash wraps around the dropped waist, and the skirt cascades down her limbs. She threads her hair into loose twists at her nape.

The pièce de résistance? Freesia buds spring from the outer corners of her eyes.

Deities aren't always the most mature beings in the universe. Epicurean, sensuous, excessive, petty, sometimes belligerent, and oftentimes spoiled, yes.

But not all of them. Others are regal, dignified, and patient.

For shame. Just because Malice behaves atrociously, that doesn't give Wonder leave to act the same. Or else, what has she learned?

From her friends? From her expulsion? From her life?

She's ready to be civil. Their earlier spat had been a mishap, because if she wants to succeed in this mission, she needs to wave a white flag, cease acting like a child with a competition complex, and encourage him to do the same.

Her unshod feet make for a quiet approach into the Hollow Chamber. It takes a while to locate him, but immortal ear canals pick up the shuffling of books.

The disturbance comes from three levels down. The grand stairway winds alongside the funnel, tapering toward the bottom floor while plankways and bridges intersect beneath the hovering astral sphere. On her way, Wonder detours along a fork in the maze of stacks. Stopping by the storage facilities, she collects sheets of parchment, needing the additional supplies anyway.

In the social science quarter, the honeycomb shelves force texts—customs, laws, and community—to slant rather than stand upright. Other volumes levitate overhead, their bindings spread like wings, soaring so high that one requires a rolling ladder to pluck them from the air.

Wonder plants the writing materials on an alcove's table but keeps a single paper between her fingers. Just as she rounds the appropriate corner, there's a distinct "Fuck" from the end of the bookcases. It's punctuated by Malice slapping a title shut, hard enough to give it a concussion.

He's made a column of books on the floor. Those must be the duds that he has gone through so far.

Wonder twists the paper into the shape of a telescope, peeks through, and pretends to adjust the focus. "What's this? There's a star that curses."

Malice swings toward her without preamble. Brows crinkling, he forms his hands into his own telescope, his wrists jerking as he zooms in on her. "And there's a star that drifts."

The analysis jolts through her with uncanny accuracy. Something tells her that she's hit the bull's-eye with him as well.

"And there's a star painted black," she adds.

"And there's a star covered in petals," he rasps.

"A deceptive star."

"A meddling star."

His lips quirk, and the corner of her mouth lifts, and reluctant chuckles stumble from their tongues.

Their fake telescopes unfurl as they lower their arms. He appraises her gown, then the freesias ornamenting her eyes. A slow drip of awkwardness leaks into the aisle, though it's something of a cease-fire, at least for the afternoon. But she can do better, because if there's one way to get Malice to talk, it's to push his book button—the egotistical little device that sets off a chain reaction of gloating.

Wonder knows, because she possesses the same button. She doesn't need to rely on subtext or nuance with him. Not when it comes to this.

In the past, Malice has uncovered his own legends here. One of them had played a pivotal role in Anger and Merry's story. By chance or divine intervention, that legend had clashed with the one Wonder had found, which also affected her friends' romance.

"Before Anger and Merry became lovers," she begins. "Where did you find the legend? The one you presented to Anger?"

Malice places a hand against his heart as if flattered. "Well, hell. You're interested in my underhanded tactics?"

"You know, it's amazing those curls actually fit around a head as big as yours."

"Are we comparing notes?"

"Show me yours, and I'll show you mine."

"Ahh, research porn," he coos in approval. "I might have a hard-on. Can you check?"

"You're shameless, unsavory, and obnoxious. And the answer is a resounding no."

"I was being rhetorical, though a scholarly game is pretty kinky."

Wonder pledges, "I'll be sure to keep score."

"No need to. I'm going to win. Only problem is, I don't have the evidence here. I stole it right before I was banished, and when Anger's story was over, he confiscated it from me. I like to think he wanted a souvenir of our illicit affair. Good times."

"Oh." Wonder hadn't known Anger did that. But then, she can't know everything that everyone does. Her face falls, intrigue slumping with it.

Malice considers her. "Buuuut…" He crooks a finger. "Follow me."

He saunters in her direction and claims her hand on his way from the passage. His palm is softer than she'd imagined but no less stifling, nor less stunning. Touching him, and being touched by him, forces her eyelids to pinch shut.

For a moment. Just for a moment.

At last, Malice is actually clueless about something. In this respect, this glaringly singular event, he has no idea what the contact means to her.

A million days and nights of wanting this connection—with his former self, not with his present self—seizes her by the jugular. Poignancy drains her mind of pragmatism. She allows herself this while his back is turned, while he's unable to see the damage it does.

Nonetheless, is she imagining it, or does his grip stutter with its own electric current?

He leads her across the gangway and down the funnel's stairs, once more into forbidden terrain, to a branch where towers of books rise from the floor, each offering a challenge. At one column for example, pick the wrong title, and the tower will rearrange itself, confusing the visitor. The galaxy's skeletons and loopholes remain secret for a reason, with the assistance of intricate storage.

The deeper Wonder and Malice wend into the labyrinthine area, the more suspect she becomes, her consciousness tingling with memories. She has explored this particular stretch before.

At another column, Malice releases Wonder. She inhales through her nostrils and pulls herself together right before he jerks his head at the pillar. "Far be it from me to disappoint." He rubs his palms in preparation. "Hmm. I do believe…"

The least impressive title in the bunch, with a weathered spine and faded gold-leaf, fits in his hand as he slips it from the collection. Deftly, he flips through the pages and then stops.

Malice rotates the open book toward her, to show that one of the pages has been sliced from the inner crease. Wonder grabs the book and peers closer, then peeks at his gleeful expression. Pride stains his cheekbones peach, a youthful reaction synonymous with discovering buried treasure. She has seen that flush in a prior life.

"You cut out the page," she observes.

He makes a shearing motion with the sabers of his index and middle fingers. "Manicures like this are practical for lots of things. But my finding wasn't merely a page."

No, it hadn't been. Again, Wonder has an inkling.

He demonstrates, tugging on a random page. At which point, the paper unfurls. Extending from the book, it turns into a scroll, rolling like a bolt of cloth to the floor. However, nothing about the text itself alters.

Malice gives the scroll another tug, and the volume's crease sucks the page back into place, reminding Wonder of a yo-yo. "The tactic was right," he says. "I just had to find the right page. When I did, it yielded—"

"—a secret," she finishes. "With an insignia at the bottom."

He tilts his head. "Do tell."

She taps the cover. "Page two hundred and six."

Using the same process, the sheet unravels into a scroll, except this one reveals a hidden message that cavorts across the surface, replacing the original content. It's the second half of the legend that brought Merry and Anger together. It's the part that Wonder had uncovered.

Malice scans the text. "My, my. Looks like I missed a spot." He shrugs. "Then again, I was in a hurry. The keepers had just caught me red-handed, so I couldn't check the whole book."

"That's when you got exiled?"

"Another five minutes, and I would have found this."

"It took me only three minutes."

His eyes crinkle. "Is that so?"

The afternoon turns into a book-a-thon as they gallivant from corner to corner, leading one another to the points where they've stripped mysteries bare. The majority have been taboo accounts, a rare few life changing. Wonder presents a diminutive book camouflaged and tucked within a book, within a book, within a book. It contains a list of forgotten supernovas.

In a rotating case, much like a rotating door, Malice fishes out a chronicle that only relinquishes its secret when treated like a flip book at the right speed. From there, a code can be deciphered about how to cheat at antiquated games.

There's a list of the stars' oldest criminals; these extra pages sprout when one plants a seed in the hardback's crease.

There's an account of the stars' lost criminals that can only be read beneath a glass shard, like a makeshift microscope.

There's manuscript that manifests riddles when doused by rain, another that shares ancient recipes when smeared in ink. "In order to read it, you have to ruin it," Malice explains.

The contest isn't hostile today. It's animated as they find a common ground, exploring the stacks while bonding over locations, stories, and research.

Biographies of infamous deities, psychological analyses

about dreams, and riddles are Malice's guilty pleasure. Travel accounts are Wonder's default for procrastination.

It becomes a game, and it becomes a fun one. They go so far as to offer each other tips and cautions: what niches to peruse and which ones to disregard.

During a debate about the assets of human libraries, Wonder pauses near a recess and gestures toward an area housing ancient journals, where intricate straps and thongs encase the texts. The closures are so expertly tangled that it would take patience to unbind them. "I've always wanted to tackle this section, but I haven't graduated to it yet," she jokes. "For the life of me, those straps are so…Malice?"

He gawks at the books, an unhealthy white paste coating his skin. His foot is arrested midstep, and his fist chokes the banister.

Wonder's gaze jumps between his stricken face and the books wrapped like mummies. "Malice."

The second her hand meets his elbow, he flinches violently, the floor vibrating beneath them. His chin jerks toward her, his eyes slitting. But to her surprise, something in her expression must tame him, because he shakes himself. "It's nothing. Drop it."

He vacates the quarter, compelling her to jog after him. The hours have cycled swiftly, nightfall greeting them when they exit the Chamber. Malice is twitchy, and she wants to probe, but she doesn't. He'll only shout or say something foul.

Pewter moon rays soak the dorm foyer. They halt at the landing, two blots in the center of glowing light. She wants to ask, but he's not ready for that.

Perhaps, neither is she.

"I have a confession," she whispers, and that gets his attention. "I forgot to keep score."

His mouth lifts with humor. "Slacker."

"But we don't make a bad team."

"Not too shabby."

"We could be a force to be reckoned with. But we won't get anywhere unless…"

Unless they work together, they won't prevail in either of their goals, neither her peers' campaign, nor whatever he's hunting for.

Malice translates her thoughts. "Fuck it. Count me in, but I'm still a better researcher. Get used to it."

"I think not," she declares as he walks away. "Malice?"

He stops and swerves his head over his shoulder. "That's me."

"In the forest, with that elder. Why did you…?"

Why did he jump in front of Wonder when Harmony took that shot? Why did Malice throw himself into that arrow's path, and for someone he despises?

Processing the question, he gets cocky. "I just wanted to annoy our visitor."

She hadn't told him it was her Guide, which is illogical. But at the time, she'd needed to come to grips with the discovery first. Soon enough, she'll let him know.

"Thank you…for annoying her," Wonder concedes.

"I don't usually hear that," Malice remarks.

"Your name said without rancor?"

"No," he responds, "I don't usually hear, *Thank you.*"

"Forgive my pretention, but gratitude is earned. It requires doing selfless things for other people. You could try filling that quota more often."

"Where's the fun in that?"

Wonder shakes her head as he disappears into his room. In her own sanctuary, she changes into a camisole and pants that cinch at the ankles, the satin caressing her flesh.

She sinks into the down, replaying the day's pleasantries. The vision of them exploring the Hollow Chamber flits through her mind, his wisecracks making her chuckle aloud until the evening blurs into nothingness.

And then the world explodes back to life. A piercing cry severs Wonder's dreamscape, and she lurches from the linen pillows, gasping out of slumber. She knows that mutiny coming from Malice's room.

It's the sound of a nightmare.

11

She catapults from the bed, bursts out of her dorm, and sprints toward his lair. Her bare feet slap the floor, cutting through slashes of midnight.

Dammit, he's barred himself inside. This wouldn't be a problem if she were dealing with a human latch.

Wrenching on the knob is fruitless, the door's framework refusing to budge. Wonder tries twice, using enough vigor to rip a mortal barrier from its hinges, but still, the bolt resists her. Other than his moon-dusted key or the Asterra Flora, there's no way to invade the dorm.

The howls escalate, scraping from his throat. Wonder slams her palms on the *façade*. "Malice!" she screeches. "Malice, wake up! Wake up!"

Whatever horror he faces, it's evidently causing his bed frame to rattle. His wails shrivel into whimpers and then grate back into hollers. Wonder's throat swells as she rams her shoulder against the door, but the craftsmanship is too solid, impervious to the pounding of her weight. She can't just leave him like this.

Wonder reels back, then dashes to her room to retrieve the quartz archery. Skidding in front of his cursed door, she nocks an arrow. At the right angle, with the right force, hitting the keyhole dead-center, it could work. If her wits have gotten her into this building, they can get her into this forsaken room.

She lets it fly. In a spectrum of light, the knob convulses.

She strikes again, and then again, and then again. The lock collapses in its frame, and the door jolts from the molding.

Dropping her weapons, Wonder blows through the partition, which dents the opposite wall as it swings inward. She freezes, plugging her mouth with her fist to contain a gasp.

At the dorm's heart, Malice thrashes under the sheets, the chaos bringing ghosts and exorcisms to mind. He spasms, his arms pinned to his chest, crossed like they're stapled that way. His bare torso writhes atop the mattress, a serpent desperate to break free of its cage.

This is worse than the previous ordeals in the Celestial City. But that's nothing compared to what he blares.

"It's true!" he screams at the ceiling. "It's true! She's real, she's real, she's real! Keep away, let me go! She's real!"

The serration of his voice dislodges Wonder from her stupor. Slamming across the room, she drops onto the mattress's edge and grapples with his shoulders, yanking him upright. His waves press flat around his face, his cheekbones strung tight. He seethes, his claws batting at her, wrestling with apparitions.

He whips her sideways onto the bed. Wonder yelps, then lurches at him, using adrenaline to dominate his movements. Seizing his elbows, she shakes him, and when that doesn't work, she resorts to the same tactic from the vault.

She slaps Malice. It doesn't work. He bucks against her hold, growling in outrage as though restrained by something other than the blankets.

Instead of another blow, perhaps he needs something else from her.

Wonder gentles her tone. "Shh. Malice, shh."

Cupping his warped face, she holds him steady. "It's a dream, just a dream. You're free."

His body gives, the muscles cramped and quivering, and his wheezing begins to tremble at the edges. The careful moment reminds her of legends floating to the surface of a page, requiring delicacy.

He holds on to himself, those arms crossing once more, either for protection or to ward off something. The haunting vision of him as a mortal imprisoned within a cell stings her eyes. That's what he's dreaming of. Now that she has confirmed who he used to be, it's obvious.

All her fault. All her fault. All her fault.

Wonder drags her fingers from his jaw, and it takes a steel grip to pry his arms from his naked chest, but he lets her.

"It's all right," she soothes. "Wake up, Malice."

"Untie me," he slurs. "Let me go."

"No one's tying you down. Not anymore. Wake up, now."

"I'm…I'm wayward…I'm a wayward star."

Wonder sucks in a breath. Did he just recite…did he just say…?

His face cranks to hers, his eyes splitting open and leaping all over her. Wild irises flash like cymbals, then dull. The atmosphere calms, the noise dissolving into the walls, leaving only tired gusts of air. He just stares at her. It's a blank slate, sedated but lost, and she cannot tell if he recognizes who she is. He's unconscious of his ramblings, only partially aware of anything.

Malice focuses on her eyes, his gaze dashing all over them. "Wildflowers," he says in a hoarse tone. "I see wildflowers."

The freesias springing from the corners of her lids. She'd neglected to remove them before sleep.

Wonder nods. "Yes. You're home."

Is he? Where is home for him? Where is home for her?

The answer feels irrelevant outside of this room. Starlight drenches them, tinting the world in violet. She scans him for remnants of the nightmare and finds none. His naked abdomen flexes with his inhalations, and the sight of a thatch of blond hair disappearing into the low waistband of his pants stumps her.

Wonder gulps. She's never seen him divested of a shirt, the sculpted muscles stacked and thumping with oxygen, so very alive and close. Her fingers tingle with a hundred and fifty years of longing, itching to mold his skin, to make him sigh, and then to turn that sigh into something pliable—and savage.

It's either suicide or survival, but she broaches the distance. With Malice's gaze pinned to Wonder's, her digits steal out to tuck a curl behind his ear. He doesn't recoil, so her index finger grows bolder, sliding into the slot behind his lobe.

Malice's square chin tilts, his eyes darting toward the contact. Tension radiates from his shoulders, caught between a protest and permission.

Then he resumes studying her. "You're tired," he says, the drowsy words injected with a tranquilizer.

Wonder bobs her head. She whispers, "And you're awake."

His hand snatches her wrist, bringing her with him as he pours himself beneath the blankets. She allows it, too stunned to withdraw. It's natural, the way he curls into a fetal position and faces her, watching as she draws on the linen, cocooning them inside its weave. It's as if he's never seen anyone do that, and it fascinates him.

He's not wholly present. If he were, she cannot fathom that he would appreciate being seen in this state, nor being coddled.

A terrible, gut-wrenching relief flows through her. It's the fuzzy texture of safety and the coarseness of loss. She has dreamed of sleeping with him like this, of feeling his weight drag down the mattress, his shadow hugging hers after hours of...not sleeping. In each of her fantasies, they make love to the point of sweet agony, then fall into exhaustion.

In those imaginations, she isn't scarred, and he isn't crazed. Nightmares cannot infest him, and remorse cannot plague her. In that other life, they're just like this—peaceful, with the free will to love each other, not the fate to abhor one another.

It's true! She's real, she's real, she's real!

This must stem from his past, which is also her past. He must have been ranting about her. Who else can it be?

I'm a wayward star.

That had been the most excruciating part. She knows that recitation, had penned it ages ago, and had reread it recently—in the letter that she'd stolen.

The truth floods Wonder's senses, tugging her into oblivion. She's remorseful as her vision wanes. Life blurs until all that's left is a set of rogue eyes, wide open and riveted on her.

12

Dreams beckon Wonder, submerging her into a watercolor sea, where she pirouettes from one color scheme to the next, swimming in seeds and petals.

Then dawn calls for her to return, its resonance as dainty as a melody pouring from a flute. It's been so long since she's had such delicate visions that Wonder rouses effortlessly. She feels like butter, her figure swaddled in linens and the leisurely blue haze of morning.

A weight burrows beside her, rising and falling under the blanket, a bundle of masculine hums. His face is the first thing she sees. The fans of his golden lashes twitch, the hatches of his deep-set lids indicating blessed sleep.

It's the visage of an angel and a demon, benign and malignant. Like this, Malice is a star, pure but blinding.

And he's right here, his breath stirring Wonder's hair. At her age, it's hard to believe there are any new emotions left to feel, much less new experiences to have. But this moment proves her wrong. She has neither seen nor experienced anything remotely comparable to this.

And now she knows what gratitude feels like.

Yet it dwindles quickly, overshadowed by reality. His nightmares comprise the tattered remains of his past, a past that's pulling him into fragments. Does he know the vision was once reality? Does he know that it really happened to him? She still hasn't gleaned exactly how much he recalls.

Regardless, after last night and everything she's heard, Wonder has to tell him about the legend. If recovering his heart will revive the memories and the part of himself that died, then he might find peace. With any hope, he'll never scream again, not as he had last night.

Then again, there's no guarantee. She can only beseech the stars that remembering won't otherwise lead to additional nightmares.

And friends or not, rivals or not, enemies or not, this will end only one way. Either Malice won't get his memory back and continue to suffer this trauma, in addition to despising her. Or he will get his memory back, a platform on which to begin healing, in addition to remembering what she did to him. At which point, any speck of companionship will vanish, and he will rue the day she was born.

It will always cycle back to hate.

But if Wonder succeeds in releasing her own heart, how he feels about her won't matter, because she won't care. She'll have emancipated herself from this emotional clutter, her mission in life narrowing to that of an immortal librarian and archeress, not a pining one obsessed with a dead boy, nor a grieving female who knits other couples together in order to compensate for loneliness. She'll be strong once more, pumped with vigor for this struggle over equality between realms.

There's one fatal flaw to this hour: Their hands are still clasped between them. As Wonder tries to wriggle free, his fingers tighten. Her gaze springs to his eyes only to discover those chasms awake and piercing.

"Slumber is a fickle pastime," Malice intones. "It renders you helpless yet sets you free."

"I want my fingers back," Wonder says. "Let go of them."

"I'm sure you do. It's nice to have fingers. They're practical for touching and fondling things that don't belong to you. Things like secrets."

"You're referring to more than just secrets."

"You're right. I'm referring to fornication."

She jerks her digits from his grip. "I see that side of your cerebrum is intact."

"I see the topography of your own cranium has reached maximum capacity and needs to unload."

Malice does this whenever he's uncomfortable, whenever he gets desperate. He tosses out suggestive comments, making others squirm so that *he* doesn't have to. Based on his belligerent expression, he knows that she knows.

His features ricochet between sober and silken and scathing, between harsh and harsher and harshest. It's ill-advised to show him compassion or pity. Even while holding her fingers prisoner, his eyes shout the obvious protests: how she shouldn't have barged into his room, how he wants her out of here so he can fester and break something.

But he's right. Her mind is filled to the brim, crammed with too much of him and not enough of her. And that, she will not stand for.

Wonder meets his stare. "I found something."

She tells him. She tells him when, and how, and what. She tells him about the legend.

Wonder omits two things. One, the portion about releasing her own heart. Two, how she'd used the letter from his saddlebag to uncover the legend's text. Instead, she replaces that detail with a random sheet of paper.

When she finishes, Malice's silence permeates the room, amplifying every shuffle of the blanket. If she gives him enough time, he'll fish through her thoughts and hook on to the missing pieces. Already he's picking through her words, scavenging for ulterior motives or errors of logic. That's what he does—overthinks and overcomplicates.

Whipping back the linen, Wonder swings her legs over the side. As she stands, Malice's pupils latch on to the strap of her camisole, which has slid down her shoulder, exposing the summit of a breast. A scant two inches more, and the bud of a nipple will make a grand entrance.

She yanks the strap back in place. But it only encourages his gaze to detour, an excursion down her unkempt locks, then continuing across the satin plains of her sleepwear before making a return trip, ascending to the freesias at the crooks of her eyes.

She cannot remember a time when Malice has ever been this quiet. No snarls or sarcasm.

"I'm telling you this because of the nightmares," she says. "Because nightmares are usually about fears or guilt or injuries. Whatever's plaguing you, it's feeding on your soul, and don't get me started on what it's doing to your sanity. I cannot embark fully on this mission if your capriciousness keeps getting in the way—not when you consider this quest a mutual abduction, and not with you ruining my sleep. If you recover your heart, perhaps success shall reward you with a piece of…of whomever you used to be before those nightmares.

"This isn't a merciful or kindly gesture. It's a pragmatic one, so don't get fussy about it. There, I've done my duty and told you," she finishes. "It's your choice whether to believe it or not, but I don't have time to sit around and wait. I have my own priorities to hack through."

Wonder exits the room and rushes to her dorm. She needs to peel these garments from her skin before she does something stupid like trace the satin contours. Fates, it's like he's cosmically bound himself to the material so that she can feel his stare all over her.

She rips off the camisole and pants, then gets dressed in a hurry, choosing fresh harem pants and a customary off-the-shoulder blouse. To complete the look, she affixes her ponytail with a chrysanthemum.

At last, she harnesses her archery. Dangers abound outdoors, as they do indoors. Nevertheless, she selects one peril over another, because research can wait.

In other words, she needs air.

Inside the palm of the valley's woodland, the repository bridges the distance between the heavens and the underworld. Beeches climb into the hemisphere while their roots thread into the grass, the environment half celestial landmark, half sylvan shrine. It's of the sky, earth, and soil.

Pausing beneath the arcade of gnarled branches and leaves etched in amethyst, Wonder indulges in a deep, spectral breath. And the instant she steps into the woodland, her mood improves. Even a goddess needs a hiatus, or a holiday, or at least a siesta.

Caution first. A month of spiritual withdrawal though it may be, breaking curfew for a brief session of merrymaking is a minor infraction. Someone might partake in a stroll, a gallivant, or a tumble. She stands vigil, scanning the vicinity for signs of frolics or escapades: the tinkle of a deity's voice, chimerical laughter or moans, the crackle of bracken, or the twang of a bowstring.

There's nothing but the serene drone of adolescent dragonflies, glowing creatures that flit through the boughs, their organza wings vibrating. Soon enough, they will grow larger than she. For now, they're content to hunt pollen and chase dawn's starlight.

Wonder hikes along one of her favorite trails, which winds into the mystic netting of brambles and lithesome blooms. Her stomach grumbles, because it's been a while since her last proper nourishment. On the way, she collects a sprig of edible crocuses, nibbling on the tart stems, the purple petals releasing sugar on her tongue.

A glade of lilac florals and lavender toadstools spreads before her, the area encased in willow drapes and canopied by climbable offshoots. A brook carves through the soil, water bubbling over stones and feeding blackberry shrubs.

Whenever not perched on the hyacinth hill, she'd made bookish camps here, as an archeress-in-training. Life was simple then, though not nearly as rich.

Wonder sets her eyes on a knot in one of the tree trunks. It's hardly a challenge, especially from so few paces away, but she's not in the mood to be picky. Nocking her bow, she cranks her arm and lets a quartz arrow fly. The tip slams into the bark and vanishes in a splash of light, the weapon reappearing in her quiver.

After a few rounds, she feels secure and isolated enough to challenge herself. She spins and shoots, targeting the same spot while in motion. The dragonflies play along, offering themselves as kinetic hindrances, cavorting around her in an attempt to thwart her aim. Laughing, she whirls among them while striking her mark.

She looses a final arrow. It whistles, slicing the air.

The sound doubles just as another projectile shears past her, torqueing from behind. It punctures the willow, landing beside her arrow to the very second.

Wonder has enough time to register the turkey fletching as it vanishes. Whipping around, she aims her bow at the dark figure slouched against a willow's column. A nebula of golden hair caps his murky silhouette as he taps the swan's neck of a longbow against his hip.

Fates. If his relaxed posture after taking that shot is any indication, he moves with stealth.

She has often admired that choice of hickory for his weapons. The rustic appearance is modest, a deceptive contrast to its power.

The demon god watches her. There's something compelling about the obscurity of his features, screened off despite the break of morning. Against her better judgment, this encounter reminds her of fairytale scenes between a heroine and a villain, that first inciting incident when they meet. The prospect sends a tingle through her navel.

"What are you doing here?" she asks.

"Staring at you," he murmurs. "Call me a voyeur, but it's becoming a hobby. I watched you party with the dragonflies on the night we got here."

"You were following me?" She plants her fists on her hips. "You rascal. Why didn't you announce yourself? What were you waiting for? A smoke signal? For all I knew, you'd landed in enemy hands, on the other side of the dale."

"Having dropped into Joy's bed, maybe?"

Wonder goes rigid. She'd had that exact thought upon their arrival. "Are you clairvoyant?"

"If I were, you'd know it. I'd give you so much shit for everything flitting through your perky skull."

"You could have misdirected yourself."

"Christ. We'd been in the Peaks for only a hot minute, and that's all the credit you gave me? I enjoyed spying on your dragonfly disco, like I enjoyed you bathing in the courtyard, like I enjoyed you shooting a moment ago."

"I thought you didn't watch me in the pool."

"I didn't. And I did. Take your pick."

"Hunting for my weaknesses?"

"Confirming your strengths—and the span of your hips." He traces her curves with the tip of his bow, moving it like a drawing pencil. "I like your hips."

She nocks her weapon. "Do you like your scalp right where it is?"

A smirk leaks from his voice. "Aim south. I dare you."

"I'd rather aim for that husk you call a brain. It matters more to you."

"More than my cock? Maybe true. Possibly true. Likewise, I'd say you value your own brain more than your target skills. On the other hand, both are equally impressive."

"Was that a compliment?" Truly, the statement surprises Wonder, especially when it curls like a tease, on the precipice of a chuckle. She rectifies the situation by clearing her throat and gesturing to his weapon. "Why wood archery?"

Malice sets his longbow against the tree and stalks toward her, the hydrangea of dawn slashing across his countenance. "Because it burns," he says. "Why quartz?"

"Because it doesn't," she replies.

"Ah, ah, ah," he sings, halting an inch from her. "Heat resistant, it might be, but everything has its limits."

"Because it heals."

Her amendment crinkles his brow. He glances past her, reflectively. "That must be nice."

Wonder dodges him, slipping around his body. Divesting herself of weaponry, she sets it beside his own and scales the nearest tree. Elevated a few yards above him, she hooks her limbs over a branch and hangs upside down, her hair unraveling like a banner.

She cannot say why she has always fancied this position. Perhaps viewing the world from an inverted angle makes addressing serious topics bearable.

Amusement springs across Malice's face. It turns out, he's a good climber, settling on the branch below her, where he reclines against the trunk. He sprawls one leg along the bark and bends the other.

They study one another, until Wonder says, "I can see up your nostrils, dearest."

"So immature," he observes. "You should be more worried that I can see up your shirt."

Her thighs stiffen over the offshoot, then go limp as she reminds herself the blouse is tucked into the pants. "You shall never get that lucky."

"Let's say your honesty this morning won me over. Ask me what you're dying to know. You only get one question, so make it a good one. Choose your 'What the fuck' carefully."

"Also, I have never had the misfortune to know someone this condescending."

"Why, thank you."

What are your nightmares about? Who do they feature? How much does this legend mean to you?

"Does it hurt?" Wonder asks. "Does it hurt when you scream?"

Malice startles. "Not what I expected."

Neither had she. The tint of morning trickles through the foliage, freckling the grass.

His jaw flexes. "You shouldn't have barged in."

"Let me guess. Your malevolent ego doesn't want anyone seeing you like that."

"I don't want a certain floral goddess seeing me like that."

"Because you have a menacing reputation to uphold? Because witnessing your vulnerable side gives me the upper hand? I'm not interested in either, Demon."

"Yep, it's inconvenient for my reputation, but that's not why I'm peeved. I have claws, and you have enough scars. Get my drift, Wildflower?"

Shock lances through her. Deities detect emotions in humans through sensory signals—taste, touch, sight, smell, and sound—but not in each other. Be that as it may, she feels the muslin texture of vulnerability, hears the brass clang of bafflement, and tastes the honeysuckle extract of caring. During his unconscious ravings the previous night, he could have inadvertently flayed her skin or crushed a bone. He could have taken her by surprise and made her bleed.

"My turn," he says, inclining his chin toward her scarred wrists. "If we're getting real, then let's get real: Did those hurt?"

Wonder swallows. If she wants him to open up, she must as well. "Growing up in the Peaks, did you hear rumors about me?"

"If I wasn't in solitary, I was in the Archives. If I wasn't in the Archives, I was in solitary. The commute between both kept me busy. Even if it hadn't, I wasn't a social butterfly, plus my classmates consisted of rage gods and goddesses—not the cliquey sort who got off on gossip."

That confirms what she had already concluded. He's too perceptive for details to elude him, and he's been badgering her about the scars since they first locked horns in the Celestial City. With a few scraps of hearsay, he could have drawn the right conclusion. Stars be praised, those facts have never reached his ears.

Wonder swings upward, sits upright on her own branch, and matches his position. A breeze cuts through the woodland and perfumes the land with the ghosts of absent lupines, sucking her into the memory of a western prairie.

"Growing up, I disobeyed the Fate Court and paid the penalty," she says.

Malice peers at her. "Who was he?"

"Who was who?"

"The dipshit you sacrificed your hands for? The one who inspired this disobedience?"

"He was sweet." After a moment's hesitation, Wonder drifts, conjuring that ruddy, mud-streaked face. "He was as bright as the sun over a countryside, and he blushed like a rose, and he loved animals."

"Can't say I ever met a god like that." Her companion sniffs, dragging her from the vision. "So that's your type? A vestal pile of sainthood?"

"Better than a diabolical pain in the ass."

"Pain is underrated, especially in the pelvic region."

"Come any closer, and my boot will prove your testicles wrong."

"What sort of *coming* are you referring to? The technical or the carnal?"

Wonder bursts into a scandalized guffaw, and Malice cants his chin, looking suddenly grim as he listens to the sound. "You cannot help yourself, can you?" she chortles.

"Speaking of which…" He indicates the scars. "Was he worth it?"

Her laughter dies, and her mouth stays unhinged, bereft of an answer. *Yes* is too weak, and *No* is too aloof.

Malice waves off her silence. "Don't answer. Replying to questions is boring."

"I guess that makes us even," she remarks, considering he hasn't said whether his screams hurt. "You're going to pursue the legend, aren't you? Is that why you're here? To cure the nightmares?"

"Ahh, well. Nightmares are so ghastly, so tenacious, so nightly."

"Answer me, Malice."

"But you know the answer."

She does. The density in his voice says it all.

In the dappled illumination, Malice leans forward. "We should do this more often." An eager gleam brightens his face. "Maybe during our next talk, you'll tell me the other half of this legend. You know, the part that has to do with you."

Wonder blinks, about to deny it. But really, she should have anticipated this, so what's the point? Of course, Malice would figure it out.

She raises her chin and mimics him. "But where's the fun in that?"

Malice grins. Ever since their stroll through the restricted section yesterday, they've reached a truce and agreed to join forces. Yet she cannot celebrate because if they accomplish their goals, the spell will break. He'll get his heart back, and she'll put a leash on hers.

The only mystery is, who will succeed first?

13

But no, there are multiple mysteries, a million mysteries. One of them occurs right now, as they make themselves comfortable on the branches, squandering valuable time by talking.

Just talking.

She doesn't know who starts it. Perhaps they simply need a break. But what begins as a flimsy chat continues as a discussion, growing roots and vines. What's tentative in the morning becomes introspective as the sky changes color with the hours, arcing toward noon. It's the seed of a moment pushing through the soil, unfurling and spreading its arms.

They abandon legends, speaking instead of books and research, and of the Archives.

"What do you love about it?" Malice asks from his perch.

Wonder scrubs her heel against the bark. "I love the possibility, the gateway between the known and unknown. I love that I can be one thing or many things. I love that there are choices. I love the safety of making my own decisions."

"Christ, I just love the rush of a good page-turner."

She chuckles. "Be serious, for once in your misbegotten life."

"It's not about safety for me. It's about risk. Finding out the truth can be a blessing or a shit storm. You won't know until you find out, but then, you'll finally get a grip on what you're dealing with instead of life keeping information from you. You'll be able to hold the facts in your hand."

"And decide what to do about them."

"Exactly. I like the sound of your laugh, by the way. I could lap it up by the spoonful."

Wonder bites the inside of her cheek, stifling a retort. As for safety versus risk, she suspects that he understands her as well. Finding a haven in books takes trust; facing the risk in books takes courage. She has never considered this before, but each has merit.

She asks, "So you believe in free will over fate, then?"

"Why choose between one or the other when I can have both? I can be a mishmash of action and reaction, which is much more interesting anyway." Malice counts off his fingers. "The Archives prove it. Humanity proves it. We misfits prove it. We have cognitive thinking, and we have nature, and they coexist. It's not rocket science, just chemistry."

"If that were true, finding a common ground between choice and destiny wouldn't be this difficult."

Malice juggles that in his mind. "I guess not. But it doesn't mean we'll never solve the puzzle, right? Be gone, little tyke." He swipes a hand, batting a young dragonfly from his ear. "So what do you hate about the Archives?"

That's a new one, and Wonder feels guilty when she dwells on it. "The same things."

Malice nods. "I'm with you."

They love and hate the Archives for the same reasons: possibility and risk. And it turns out, they adore and loathe their upbringings, their intended roles as archers. The servitude and the entitlement of it turns them into equal parts servants and superiors of mortals.

Being classified as neither is better. It feels right.

Inquiries pour out of Wonder and Malice, a staggering amount piling atop the boughs. Each quandary is the criterion of another, one thought bouncing to the next.

He dares her to question: Would she value answers, truths, possibilities, if they were dark, or flawed, or disturbing? What good are legends, if they teach nothing? What help are they, if they're only meant to please or coddle? What's the point of knowledge, if it's only there to validate assumptions?

She dares him to question: Would he value research if it didn't grant him absolutes? Would he keep faith in the unanswerable? Would he ever be content to merely speculate? Would he appreciate a legend, if it had nothing to do with him but benefitted other people?

"What answer are you really searching for in the Chamber?" Wonder broaches. "Why is it so important?"

"How about you? Are you binging on this sacred ground for the answers you just want to hear?" Malice volleys. "Are you looking for the ideal instead of the truth?"

They fall silent, tripping over those questions. Perhaps they're aware that visceral responses will result in shouting matches, which will desecrate the companionable mood.

Bickering is not worth ruining that, but Wonder packs Malice's queries into her mind, to carry with her. She senses him doing the same as the atmosphere turns into a picnic. While their questions marinate, they leap from the tree. Rather than conjure refreshments, Wonder prefers to harvest blackberries and edible blooms, while Malice scoops mineral water from the brook after emptying and washing his quiver. In the interim, she catches him glancing at her across the glade, and he catches her as well.

Lilac perfume wafts in the air, toadstools contain poison, and willows swish like horse tails. Wonder and Malice resume their seats, this time relaxing across from one another on the same branch, their legs spanning the divide, their boot soles bumping. Employing his quiver as a makeshift drinking vessel causes them to snigger.

To compensate for the harder questions, they gush about their favorite titles and sections of the Hollow Chamber. It prompts a series of, "That's the best chapter" and "I know, right?" and "You've got to read that one."

Malice tosses berries into his mouth and talks with his cheeks full. Wonder sucks juice from her pinky, aware as his eyes follow the slide of her tongue. The neckline of his shirt slumps, revealing his collarbones and the sexiest throat she's ever beheld. His Adam's apple dangles before her like a plump grape, provoking a thirst that water fails to satiate.

As the day wanes, she familiarizes herself with details previously neglected. The fine hairs on his knuckles, the pump of that neck when he drinks, the glimpse of him tickling a dragonfly when he thinks she's not watching. Their shared devotion to reading and learning, the recollection of hardbacks spread open in his hands, and how he licks his thumb before turning a page.

By eventide, they're talk-drunk, lulled by the bubbling of brook water. Constellations convene, dusk soaking the forest in violet ink. Where have the hours gone? It's irresponsible and unforgivable to squander time. Wonder should be sorry.

She should be.

Malice tosses his gaze around the forest. "Hmm. I think I'm a night person. Nighttime is so very dark, so moonlit. Have I mentioned how much more beguiling the moon is than the sun? This is the witching hour, when the stars are more active, doing all kinds of shiny things."

Wonder teases, "Such as *shining*?"

"Like they're fucking with you." He swings his head toward her. "You look like a cherub, sitting over there all pretty and plush."

"Enough with your trifling. But if you ask me, you look like a satyr, sans the horns."

"I can live with that. Have you ever been toyed with?"

"Not in your context."

Malice rises on all fours and crawls toward her like a panther, those black pants straining across his thighs and rump. Locking eyes with her, he swipes their provisions from the branch, discarding them with a backward swat of his wrist. Blackberries and petals spill to the grass, inviting the dragonflies to scramble after the pickings.

He stops when his nose brushes hers, forcing Wonder to uncurl from her sprawl, her stomach swooping. "What context is that?" he murmurs.

"I'm not playing that game with you, Malice," she whispers.

"Of course, you won't. It would require more expletives and less clothing. What would you know about those things?"

It sounds like he's fishing—or doubting, or daring—but too bad.

Wonder crosses her arms, concealing the trembles.

Malice relents. He rights himself, straddling the bough, those solid thighs parting and clenching the bark. His feet dangle off the sides, the pose simultaneously impish, vicious, and luscious.

He demands to know if she's a day or night person. For her, it's the former because that's when flowers flourish, and because that's when a whole day of discovery stretches before her.

They indulge in more commentary. Malice is especially chatty, and when he's not being crass or conniving, his eclectic train of thought diverts her. It's a trait that his alter ego hadn't possessed, as far as she knows, but it's a charming place to reside.

Their knees tap as he lobs a question her way. "So what's the other half of the legend? And what's it to you?"

Wonder notes her reflection in his pupils. "I'll tell you in the next life, when you're reincarnated into something with whiskers and a tail."

"And fangs? Please tell me I'll have long, hard fangs in this next life."

"To compensate for your missing tongue?"

Rather than his closeness, it's his laughter that disturbs her, sounding so very like…so much like…

Watching her reaction, the mirth dies on his face. With one flick of a switch, he buries the humor in a coffin, stuffing it beneath a tantalizing inclination. "Don't do that, Wildflower," he warns. "Don't give me that look, like you enjoy my voice."

"Why?" she sighs—then yelps when he straps an arm around her middle and hauls her atop his lap. Her thighs split around his waist, her pelvis rocking into his.

The yelp flutters into a gasp when his hips give a subtle but intentional jerk, emphasizing the ridge pressed against her groin. "That's why," he rasps, the noise scraping her flesh.

Her body seizes, her blood running a swift course for that intimate spot, so close to him. But his words are a bluff. The reality is, his length isn't fully amorous, not wholly aroused. However, its size gives the illusion of being erect.

If his actions were genuine, Wonder would shatter, perhaps grind atop Malice and bask in his hiss. But that's not an option. He's just using another crude tactic to prevent her from doing or saying something that he doesn't like.

What is it about her reaction to his voice that offends him?

Thankfully, her tone remains steady. "You're trying to scare me off."

He steals a chrysanthemum petal from her ponytail. His tongue swabs the bloom into his mouth, where she imagines it dissolving inside him. "Is it working?"

She beams, a bright and badass expression that provides the answer.

Not on your life.

Malice's lashes flap with uncertainty—and then wrath as she bounds from his embrace and shoves him off the branch. "Hey!" he snarls, tumbling sideways onto a lower bough, his body hooking over it and sparing him from a crash landing.

While he curses and glowers at her, Wonder blithely hops to the grass and struts off, concealing a grin. Another round in her favor.

⸺

At midnight, the sky darkens to violet. She wrestles with the linens, her calves tangled in the sheets as they abrade her skin. Something this soft shouldn't be this rough.

Her nightgown straps cut into her shoulders, and her breasts crush against the satin, and it all feels wrong—no better than a restraint.

It begins to rain, droplets pattering against the window, the rhythm jabbing at her consciousness. Usually, this weather lulls her into slumber.

To the contrary, the room's airflow thickens. For the millionth time, is this what heat feels like? Is this a hint? The dynamics of temperature had been a mystery until Andrew joined their band of rebels. At which point, Wonder had picked the former mortal's brain about the intensities of heat and cold.

Sometimes, she's on the brink of understanding. From what she's been told, heat is the congestion of oxygen, a buildup of one's blood and pulse—such as that which exists between her legs.

And in between Malice's legs. She knows this now, too.

In the forest, that brazen airflow had swirled from his center to hers. Damn that incident for depriving her of dreams.

It's not merely that. Two unnerving thoughts stomp through her mind.

First, it's one thing to know the boy he used to be, but it's another to talk with the boy he's become. Which person does she identify with better? Which one is more real to her?

Which one knows her?

That last puzzle piece isn't really a question. Not if she cares to admit it.

Second, and most profound, is this: She'd had fun today.

She'd had too much brawling, bantering fun. It's baffling, but whereas her classmates know the grander parts of her life, she had told Malice about the smaller facets, which are somehow as pivotal. Perhaps more so.

Her favorites. Her bookish escapades. Her resentment and gratitude toward magic and archery. Even some of her childhood had trickled out, along with memories of Harmony, her Guide.

Oddly, Wonder could have kept going. And oddly, he'd absorbed everything with an interest void of artifice or agenda.

Wonder shoots upright. Ugh, her archery!

She'd forgotten the longbow and quiver in the woods. If Malice were a gentleman or considerate god, he'd have brought the weapons to her upon his return indoors. But after pushing him out of their nest a few hours ago...well, she hasn't seen him since then.

The weapons might still be out there like so much evidence. If another deity breaks worship curfew and decides to take a midnight stroll...

It's unlikely at this juncture and in the midst of a tempest, but she cannot afford to be lazy.

Wonder flings back the covers. An inconvenient jaunt later, she's drenched.

Clouds convene over the forest, causing rivulets to cut through and rustle the mesh of leaves. The onslaught reduces her nightgown to film, plastering the material against her as she picks through wildflowers on bare feet.

She casts about for company. Oh, honestly. Does she truly expect someone to venture here during a storm? Who would expose themselves to the elements at this hour? Who would defy curfew or the law of nature on a night like this? Who would be that foolish?

Who would be that insane?

Wonder's heels skid on the grass. She flounders, her soles slipping across the glade. Her hand shoots out, grasping a willow trunk to balance herself.

Malice stands in the clearing's epicenter, making himself into a visible target. But that's not the problem.

The problem is, he's naked.

All thought, sense, reason, logic, musing, contemplation, worry, caution, questions, and answers drain from Wonder's mind. Along with the deluge, consciousness washes down her body.

This would be an optimal time to spring into action and dash behind the tree. But stars help her, she cannot move. Where have her reflexes gone?

To any common deity, nudity is hardly scandalous or private. However, it's impossible to apply this rule right now.

Not to him. Not to this.

Almighty Fates. He has shed his clothing, the black garments a puddle beside him. With his back to her, Wonder gawks at the expanse of creamy skin, the muscle and sinew rippling across a lean but toned figure—a doused figure, beads cascading down the pillar of his neck, the wings of his shoulder blades, and the taper of his waist. They roll over the swells of his backside, rounded and tight and smooth. A pair of indentations sculpt into his rear, hinting how they might contort while thrusting into a waiting body.

Malice's hands reach behind and carves through his wet curls, darkened by the rain. The movement readjusts the structure of his form, the lines and bones shifting.

Wonder's lungs cease to work. That same compression of air from the branch, and from her bed, and from countless other moments, incapacitates her. Also, there's an influx of blood, a suffusion that might be akin to heat, that flows at the nexus of her hips.

He's bathing. That's what he's doing.

Has he been here since she left?

And what's marking his bicep?

Malice's upper body twists sideways as he rubs water from his forearm. In her stupor, Wonder gets a view of slender, black threads feathering across his flesh. It's ink. The image of a fletching appears on one end, which morphs into a quill at the other.

When they'd slept in the same bed, she hadn't seen this.

Perhaps she'd been too preoccupied by his ranting and raving. It's an intricate design, crafted by an immortal artisan of the Peaks or a fellow outcast in the Celestial City.

It's a haunting sight. A tattoo hadn't adorned his mortal self. This novelty is all Malice.

She envisions how that rendering would rise and collapse, contorting while he takes another deity up against the nearest tree, the tattoo spreading its plumage as his body undulates, the quill rhythmically scribbling nonsense while he gyrates.

Wonder pries herself from the fantasy. He shouldn't be out here, but he'd never listen to such a flimsy lecture.

Her archery slants against another tree, poised right where she'd left it. If she moves to snatch the weapons and withdraw, he will catch her.

She backs away, tiptoeing from the scene until she's out of his periphery. Malice will finish washing, and when he does, she'll return for the bow and quiver.

Wonder beats a retreat to the only place that gives her strength. She drips her way through the Archives and into the Hollow Chamber, rushing down the subterranean stairs and across the walkways, wending into the lower-most level, then tucking herself into the restricted section. Disappearing around a bookcase, she slumps against the shelves to catch her breath. Her body dampens the carpet, while other parts of her dampen in a more succinct way.

Her head cranks backward as she gulps, staring at the nebulous prisms of green light floating overhead. "Cursed Fates."

"You forgot something."

Wonder whips toward the aisle's entrance, a squeal lodging in her throat.

Malice stands there, watching her while bracing his palms

on opposite bookcases. He isn't huge, but neither is he small. And his personality alone is massive enough to fill in the gap between the stacks.

A set of hickory weapons rests on the floor, tipped against the shelving. As for her archery? He's got it harnessed to his back, the buckle tensing across his chest.

His bare chest.

Because he's still naked.

14

Wonder refuses to glance away, because that's what he'd want. She keeps her attention level with his, narrowing her eyes while all hell breaks loose inside her. She inhales fresh rain and millennia of pages. The Chamber illuminates the forbidden shape of him—the carnal grid of his torso and the pillars of his limbs.

His wiry mouth morphs into a sneer, but that jeering smile melts once his eyes blaze a trail across Wonder. Her wet attire is plastered to her body, one of the nightgown straps slashes down her shoulder, and her nipples jut through the garment's satin material. And she doesn't have to follow his gaze to know that a very discreet patch of hair is visible below.

To say that his expression turns feral is an understatement. Never could Wonder have foreseen the smoldering effect she's having on him. It might exceed the havoc he's wreaking on her.

Despite every naughty thing he's ever said, not once has she surmised his interest to be genuine. Routinely, she has branded his remarks as tricks, a means to undo her, no different from anyone else he's gotten his claws into.

But this…can it be? Can that look be real?

Is her heart pounding for Malice? Or for the past?

What's happening to her? What's happening to them?

"If I forgot my weapons, you've forgotten your clothes," she comments.

"Stuffed the latter in my quiver," he says. "As to the former? It's not archery that you forgot."

"What, then?"

"The eyeful of my cock that you'd been hoping for."

So he knows. Of course, he does.

"You're an idiot for being out there. I'm aware this is redundant, particularly in your case, but what's gotten into you?" she accuses.

"I'm more interested in how to get into *you*. Tell me what *you* were thinking."

"I repeat: I was thinking you're an idiot."

Malice breaks from his stance while unbuckling her archery. He lowers the bow and quiver, his chest contracting and his tattoo jerking as he lets the weapons fall. She's about to reprimand him for handling her possessions that way, but then he swaggers across the aisle, those hipbones rotating into her line of vision. It's fortunate that she's a multitasker, which enables her to resist peeking below his waist, to retreat from his advance, and to raise her chin.

Her spine hits a dead end. What's boggling is that he doesn't make contact, nor cage her in with his arms. He just looms there, within touching distance.

Somehow, this portrays him as unreachable. And somehow, his nudity pits her as the vulnerable one, like it's silly she's dressed at all, like she's a coward. Add this to the list of reasons that she despises him.

"Go ahead," he says. "Look at me. See what's behind curtain number one."

"There's no curtain in sight," she scoffs. "Even so, the view doesn't make you special."

"Tsk, tsk. Neither does being a prude. But then, I'd say you're not as puritan as you let on. Otherwise, you'd be wimpy for a goddess. Or prove me wrong. Occasionally, I like being proven wrong."

That will either deprive Wonder of her remaining power or resurrect some of it. In any case, what's the use? She wants that eyeful.

Wonder permits herself a glimpse, skimming over his sopping curls and taut mouth. The whole time, he watches her as she travels to his pectorals, the hardened buds, and the grille of his abdomen. Her pulse quickens once her gaze topples down the lane of hair below his navel, between the slopes of his hips—down to the firmness between his pelvic bones.

Dear Fates. Her lips part of their own accord.

It's sensual, the way it rises, twitching when her attention lands there. Its length solidifies, on the verge of extending more. There's a straight column and a swelling peak, and it's all his.

How profound, the pleasure that one anatomical part can elicit.

What does he taste like?

Malice hums. "Did you like what you saw in the rain? Did you want to fuck me?"

Wonder's head snaps up. She gapes at him, feeling pink imprint on her cheeks, the same tint painted on his lips.

Before she can stammer a reply, he intones, "I bet we'd fit. I bet you'd be tight as a tube around me. I bet you're wetter right now than I was outside."

"How dare you!" she grits.

"I'm not the one who was peeping. You sound like a virgin, but you're not one."

"I'm two hundred and six."

"And I'm one hundred and fifty-six." He shakes his head in mock horror. "You wanton cougar."

"My dalliances are none of your concern."

"Meaning, it's somebody I know." Like a master of secrets, he checks her expression, examining it until his visage brightens. "Anger."

Wonder's nostrils flare, but not as wide as his do. He takes her silence as confirmation, his features hardening as though he's about to go on a killing spree.

She feels compelled to voice a caveat. "He hadn't met Merry yet."

It was only one night, ages before they'd been assigned to the mortal realm. They'd been lonely and heartbroken over other people. Back then, Anger had carried a secret torch for Love, and Wonder had been dealing with her own unrequited feelings for a mortal boy. And so, she and her classmate had taken refuge in each other.

"Did you enjoy it?" Malice interrogates.

That's a horrible thing to ask. "Let me pass."

"You did, didn't you?"

"Let. Me. Pass."

"You enjoyed it a lot."

"Yes!" she spits. "I slept with Anger eons ago, another lifetime ago, and I enjoyed it. And then I woke up the next morning and wished it had never happened. Because he wasn't…"

He wasn't you.

But for that night, she'd pretended it was. It's the reason she'd climaxed at all.

Malice picks up on her thoughts like a scent. "Because he wasn't that mortal mate you obsessed over." He steps closer, whispering, "And me? Am I another filler?"

She cannot answer that. And he doesn't let her.

"I'm guilty, too," he says. "I've seen humans go at it before in parks, and in clubs, and in cars, and in the Carnival of Stars. Before that, I watched archers hump, some of them having invited me to stare. It fills the void until it doesn't, because it tells you only so much about what you like."

His tenor deepens. "What do you like, Wildflower? I think you pine for a sweet romp. I'm guessing you got the opposite with Anger. It's a perfect visual, how that stallion must have plowed you into the mattress, his cock shaped like a pommel and welded like iron. Did you writhe and beg for more? Or did the orgasm pop out like a sob?"

"I pity that you have to try this hard to be in control," she says.

Malice's jaw clicks. "I think we'd do much better together." One of his saber nails claws down the wall behind her. "I think you wanted to bounce on my prick in that tree—that would have been fun, watching you shout to the stars, that mouth wide open and emptying itself of noise. I think you've wanted to mount me from the beginning, the same way I've wanted you, even while we loathed the idea. I think if I kissed you, you'd kiss me back, letting my teeth mark you, letting my tongue fuck yours. I think if I pinned you to the bookcases, you'd ride the shelves until books shook from the slots—"

Wonder plows into him, barreling them around until Malice's back rams into the wall. A shocked grunt rips from his throat as he registers their switched positions, that he's the one imprisoned now. She'd done this in the dorm stairwell, and the maneuver shuts him up like it had before. In fact, his pupils blow up because this is closer than they were a second ago. This is her, wrenched against his bareness from head to toe.

Suddenly, his chest beats against hers, rapid and shallow. He looks young. And nervous.

She doesn't care. She's had enough.

It's about time he gets as harsh as he gives. This attitude adjustment is overdue, to see whether he likes being baited, to see whether he can take it. If he wants a match, he'll get a match.

Wonder curls into him, pliable curves molding into chiseled angles, testing what the contact does to his cocksure demeanor, which isn't cocksure any longer. His mouth slackens, his inhalations reduced to spurts.

His eyes leap with trepidation. How unusual.

"You talk too much," Wonder seethes. "You like listening to yourself far, far too much. But now you're going to listen to me. Insult my peers, mock my desires, or abuse my words, and so help me, I will stab you with your own claws. Show me respect, show my class respect, and return my damned corsage, or I will pull your weaknesses from the roots and leave them to wither. I'll tear through this Chamber and find every fact you seek, and then I'll make you prostrate yourself for them. Do you understand me?"

Malice stares at her, his body pressed against her damp nightgown. For once, he's at a loss for words and not bothering to hide it.

And then a declaration slides out of him—a word she hadn't actually expected to hear given so freely. His jugular bobs as he answers, "Yes."

Wonder blinks. He'd spoken with humility, without a guise, as bare as his flesh. It's a complete departure from a second ago, with a blush sprinting across his jaw and his eyes tripping all over her.

It's the countenance of that boy.

But it's not that boy. It's Malice.

It's her rival, her adversary gazing at her as if he's never been this near to a female, as if he doesn't know what to do. For all his lewdness, Malice's expression scarcely parallels his indecency, nor the slices of eroticism that had slipped between the cracks. Gone is his bravado, leaving behind the vestiges of a well-played fraud.

A harrowing notion drains Wonder of contempt. She loosens her hold on him.

It fills the void until it doesn't, because it tells you only so much about what you like.

Malice's speech clashes with his physical response to her, the hints compiling and pointing toward an unfathomable conclusion. This whole time, he's been mouthing off with dirty innuendoes as if he knows what he's talking about, as if he's experienced.

When in fact, he's...

No, it can't be. Not at his age.

But then, what deities would lust over a hedonistic god, no matter how striking his features? No matter how stimulating they find his diabolism?

Wonder gnaws on her lower lip, a thrill shimmying up her calves when his gaze traces the motion. Curious, tentative, she experiments. She slips a golden lock behind his ear, a gentle ministration that causes him to flinch.

Her mind stutters. Yes, that's it.

For all his profanity, he excels at bluffing. He's nothing but a pretender, a consummate fake who's lived a less promiscuous life than he lets on. By Fates, he's been celibate for almost two centuries.

It's unthinkable. Yet it makes all the difference.

Their gazes collide. He glowers with speechless defiance, all the while molten pupils swallow his irises, and his lids grow hooded. She dismisses the past hour, sweeping aside prudence and rationale in favor of this one sinful morsel.

True, she's had only one male before. But she's frolicked with others enough to know a thing or two.

They trade breaths as she leans in and whispers, "Now where were we?"

Astonishment splashes across his face. It's the only warning she gives as her head veers beneath his jaw, her mouth dragging across the underside to skim his flesh.

Malice goes rigid. "Shit," he hisses.

The exclamation ends on a croak, a naive reflex that provokes a euphoric clench between Wonder's thighs. Her head swirls, drawn into a vortex, her nostrils fueled by the scent of wood and rainfall.

As she nuzzles him, Malice shivers. His fingers grasp her sides, either to shove her away or cling for balance, as if the universe is about to collapse. Marveling breaths skitter from the misfit as her lips pass over him, sketching the softness. His wet flesh yields to her mouth, a delicious bead of salt leaking onto her palate.

The sounds trickling out of him are borne of epiphany, wrought of pure, unsophisticated innocence. Nothing has ever sounded like this, tasted like this, felt like this. Moisture collects at her center, and his length wedges between their hips, impaling itself there for her to chafe against.

She wants more of this friction, needs more of his voice. She's going to take it all, take everything she's been denying herself. She'll consume him like a selfish little goddess, and she doesn't care, and she won't regret it.

The flat of her tongue flicks out. And she licks him, gathering another droplet.

Malice buckles, a full-bodied convulsion as his muscles go lax, reduced to putty in her arms. His head falls against the wall, his eyes rolling to the back of his head. And it's the sweetest surrender.

"Christ," he says on a strangled groan.

"Is that all?" she coos, her mouth sinking to the crook of his throat and shoulder. "That isn't like you, Demon. You say so much, in order to say one thing."

"You say so little, in order to say a hundred things," he grinds out, his head flopping to give her better access. "It drives me crazy. You drive me crazy."

"You were already crazy before we met. And it's the ones who know the least that exhaust their tongues the most."

"Oh, fuck you."

The harsh delivery is a throb inside her, an ache to be filled. It's the word *Fuck* thrusting from his lungs.

They pant against each other, gasping through their confessions. Wonder cranks her head upward, kissing the incline between his lower lip and square chin. Then she swabs the chin itself, speaking against the hard ridge. "I'll do nothing of the sort. I cannot stand you."

"Yes, you can. You've withstood me plenty, so knock it off."

"If you insist."

With that, she twists. Her mouth latches onto the corner of his neck and begins to suck.

Malice dissolves into a moan, velvety and flitting to the rafters. He melts into the *façade* while his talons dig into her, puncturing her ribcage. It's a pleasurable sting that makes her gasp into the nook of his jugular. She works him between her teeth, then laps at the spot, ending with an open-mouthed kiss.

And another. And another.

She devours his neck, rolling kisses across the veins. Her tongue flicks, catching the tempo of his pulse point, then migrates lower, sampling a clavicle with her canines. He likes the twinge of pain, so she pays similar attention to the other slender cylinder until his joints quake.

Wonder cannot think straight because there's so much to ravage, and she's consumed by the serration of his moans, the glorious tremors wracking them both. She feathers the spongy dip between his collarbones with the point of her tongue. His hoarse gulp infatuates her, spurs her on as she strokes him there, inside that receding spot.

Malice hyperventilates as if he wants more, as if he's afraid to want more, as if he doesn't know how to want more.

Wonder mumbles against swell of his Adam's apple. "You've never done this."

His palms clasp her cheeks and force her to meet his gaze, which is contorted with fury. It's not a denial. But his visage is a broken seal, exposing the truth. There's no shame in his status, yet he detests losing this leverage, detests admitting it to her, detests that it's a visible fact.

That he's never done anything, with anyone.

He's ready to pounce on her reaction. His taut lips warn her not to pity him, nor consider this an advantage. But behind the expression is a quaver of the eyebrows, a sliver of timidity.

That's the boy he used to be.

Wonder's heart compresses, because the sight of him putting up a front while at her mercy is too much. She might faint, but she'll take the chance. So she does what she's been dreaming about for decades.

She cups his face and leans in. "Malice, I want your mouth."

His lips part. Again, he's stupefied—not by the request, but by its inflection. Has no one ever lavished him with tenderness?

Certainly not. Why would they?

Gripping her shoulders, his thumbs slide under the nightgown straps, those saber nails sneaking into the garment and grazing her breasts, stopping just shy of her budding nipples. The sensation is a tad sharp, the titillating point of a knife.

She's dizzy, falling against him, brushing his lips with hers. It's madness, and it's rapture. "I want your mouth," she repeats. "Give it to me. Take it from me."

The disorganization of that request is not lost on her, but it's the best her foggy stream of consciousness can do. Because Malice doesn't protest, she shows him what a fine guide she can be, and what an apt pupil he can be.

It starts when she pecks the crook of his mouth, then the other, planting two caresses at the edges of the world. "Now you," she breathes.

His mouth quirks, commas digging into his face. Oh, so he likes being told what to do.

Malice follows her lead, sweeping the corners of her mouth while their hands roam over each other. Skin prickling, Wonder entreats, "Yes, dearest. Just like that."

It continues with another exploration. She instructs him to part wider for her. Once he complies, she sketches the bow of that upper lip with her own, then nibbles on it.

His waist bucks, the solid evidence of success thrusting against her. The result is a flood of her own, which pools for him.

Although she's been dominating this seduction, Malice takes a turn licking the seam of her lips. He learns quickly, because a sob of want streams out of her.

When she spreads her lips for him, their ivories nick and fight for the lead. His incisors skim her, which is too much to endure.

Wonder veers backward. "Give me your tongue," she instructs, which might have come out like an overwhelmed, over-eager purr.

Malice fulfills her request. His tongue pokes out, and their combined strokes nudge her to the ends of the earth. He dabs at her, and she coils against him, and they tease one another.

Their bodies tangle, humming from within. He measures her hips, and she races her fingers up his fletching-and-quill tattoo. The barbs of his nipples shave hers, and what's left of Wonder's restraint fractures. She cinches around that blushing tongue and sucks hard.

He shudders. So does she.

Her eyes moisten, and she's going to cry, and her heart is going to wail, because he's that boy, and he's not that boy. He's Malice and Not Malice. And this is sublime, and it's severe, and it's not about to end.

"Kiss me," she chokes, breaking away.

"Wildflower," he says hoarsely.

"Kiss me like you hate me. Kiss me like you love me—"

On a growl, his mouth slams on to hers.

She gasps. His lips are saturated like the rest of him, and they're pliant, and they're pleats of silk. They slant over her, swooping in and fitting. He folds his mouth with hers, whisking them together at a livid pace.

Malice opens and closes, sloping widely and deeply, so deeply that Wonder's toes curl. Delirious, she mewls into his mouth. Her arms hook over his shoulders, her fingers scrubbing through his hair.

His own palms scoop the back of Wonder's skull, trapping her in place while his tongue flexes into her, flicking moans from her like scattered pebbles. The texture of his groan ripples down her throat. She pries away in order to nip his lips, making indentations there, because yes, yes—

"Fuck, yes," Malice rasps, snatching her mouth again.

His hands surge to her buttocks, hoisting her against his naked body. The kiss erupts into a frenzy. He takes her mouth hectically, like he knows her mouth, like he hates her mouth, like he loves her mouth.

Wonder spreads beneath his kiss, his tongue whipping into her, the contact tingling her spine. It's the motion of consummation, with its drenched intrusion and chasing rhythm. Each synchronized thrust penetrates the apex of her limbs.

He's soaking her. And his nudity magnifies his stiffness, and she wants it inside that dark, blooming place of hers, filling that channel to the brink. She wants him pounding into her with no end in sight.

She's going to shatter, but she can't stop, and he's not stopping. He releases her backside, their intentions synchronizing, their digits threading. Wonder exerts pressure, taking control and pinning his wrists to the wall above his head.

Then their heads bank as they destroy this kiss from a new angle. Her tongue undulates beneath his, their mouths elastic, revolving into one another with fluid motions. The kiss seals in their moans, inaudible to an outsider but detonating like a star from within.

Only when a raindrop cuts down his profile and seeps into her flesh, only when oxygen becomes a struggle, do they wrench apart.

Their mouths dislodge on a collective wheeze.

They slump, his forehead landing atop hers. She's hungover and swollen and damp for him. And after a few great pulls of air, she seeks his lips again with a needy whine, loathe to be away from him.

Malice rumbles, his head tilting for hers. They brush, this time languid and exhausted, on the ledge of something poignant and patient.

Therefore, perilous.

And it's so dear, and he's so dear, and this is so dear.

Just before they connect, she whispers an endearment. And it isn't until she encounters the absence of him that she registers the error—what she'd said.

What she'd called him.

Malice tenses. She has a second to glimpse his stricken features, a single moment before those features corrode.

He pushes her away. The force of it sends her careening, stumbling until a bookshelf across the aisle catches her, breaking her fall.

"What did you say?" he asks through bared teeth.

Wonder straightens. She clamps a hand over her mouth, wanting to take it back, but she cannot. The sight of his wounded expression causes her palm to leave her lips. "I...I...didn't..."

But she did. She'd recited from the letter she'd taken from him, the letter she'd written to him, back when he was somebody else.

Dearest Wayward Star

That's what she had called him.

Is that whom she'd been kissing? Malice, or his ghost?

Raking his hands through his sodden hair, Malice glowers at her like she's a stranger, or like he's been waiting for this. He stalks up to Wonder, and he plants his hands on either side of her, bracketing her in. "Who are you?"

Wonder blinks. "What do you mean?"

"Who. Are. You?" he fumes. "From the moment I met you, you've looked at me like I haunt you, you've checked on me during my nightmares. In the library vault, you glanced at every object like you recognized it. The rocking chair, the telescope, the crate of envelopes. And here, you stole the letter from my saddlebag—"

"You knew?"

"Do I look like a moron? I let you get away with it because from the beginning, something was off. You're too invested, too concerned, and way too shitty at faking it. You came into my room the other night to fight another nightmare that isn't even yours, and it's not because it was ruining your goddamn sleep.

"Why do you care? Why do you look at me like you care? Why do I pass out every night only to end up suffocated by flashes of countryside, of old letters, of a dilapidated library in some backwater town that I've never seen before? Why am I dreaming about envelopes crowding my saddlebag, and my arms bound in straps, and a cell with bars? Why, why, why?"

The straps. He'd looked so traumatized in the Chamber, when she'd pointed out the ancient journals. The texts had been wound in thongs. The sight must have triggered a recollection, a mortal memory of being incapacitated.

He'd had a nightmare on that same evening.

"Why are the visions always the same?" he snarls. "Why do they feel like more than just a vision? You want to know why the fuck I'm here? That's why I'm here. Because from the moment I was born, half of me has felt immortal, the other half not. I've had these nightmares since I was a little shit trying to nock a wooden bow. Why did I choose hickory wood? What dumb-shit deity chooses wood? Why do I remember smells and sounds and tastes that I've never known? Why doesn't my past feel like my actual past?"

He glares at her. "And why do I get the feeling you know something about it? Why else have you acted in a million bizarre ways since you first saw me? That's why I brought you here with me. So I'm going to ask you again, and again, and again: What do you know? Who are you?"

Wonder fumbles for a response. Malice bashes his palms against the books shelved on either side of her head, demanding that she answer him. With a gruff sound of surrender, his face sinks against hers, his eyelids clenching shut.

"For Christ's sake," he pleads. "Don't make me beg."

A guilty cry escapes her. The rims of her eyes glisten from that lovely kiss and the desolation in his tone.

What can she say? What must she conceal?

What does he deserve? What does she owe him?

Nothing. Everything.

"All right," she says.

His body relaxes, and he nods. But when he pulls back, his glower is a fixed point before he stalks to the quiver, the span of his buttocks on full display, along with the wisps of hair down his calves. Fishing out his pants, he wrests the material up his limbs, not bothering to fasten them. They slump low on his waist, leaving his torso bare as he retraces his steps.

At least she doesn't have to do this while he's completely stripped. But where he's discarded his boots is anyone's guess.

Malice slides to the ground, reclining against the opposite bookcase. Steepling his legs, with his toes peeking from the pant hems, he pats the ground.

She's not fooled by the invitation. It's hardly a friendly gesture. From her end of the aisle, she matches his pose, lowering herself to the carpet, her soles scratching the fibers as they face one another across the lane. Her snafu has leached whatever affection he'd begun to feel, the passion of their kiss forgotten.

He waits, and he waits, and he waits. "Tell me," he says.

Wonder inhales. And then she tells him.

15

The Chamber's celestial light bathes the corridors in green. Wonder tucks her legs beneath her as she stares at the countless book spines, taking solace in the foiled titles glistening across the shelves. Since childhood, they've been her source of strength, more than any weapon.

Who are you?

That's a question she has always pondered. From her first memory, musing has been a beloved pastime. So who could have known how dangerous it would become?

She certainly hadn't...

16

There's a star that drifts in the sky. It wanders from constellation to constellation, exploring each celestial arrangement and pondering the shapes they make. It's a curious little traveler, a nomadic firefly of light bathing in moonbeams and trailing comets.

This star changes its course often, overwhelmed by the possibilities. Unable to stay in a single place at a time, it muses from one planet to the next, from one astral attraction to the next. It wants to know, and it wants to ask, and it wants to see, and it wants to do.

Mostly, it longs to think. It yearns to wonder.

Unfortunately, it floats without paying attention to where it's going. On one such occasion, an asteroid bumps into the star and knocks it back to the place where it began, right into its original position. Right back in its cradle.

It wiggles there, restless. That's when the five members of the Fate Court identify it, able to discern its nature now that it finally stands still.

Although they should know better, thinks Harmony, the amused Guide of Wonder, who stands beside them. What other archeress would behave this way?

It can only be her.

The star's future mentor smiles with pride and holds out an open palm. From the canopy of constellations, that celestial firefly sinks and settles into the Guide's hand. It blinks with luminescence as if glancing around, as if it's just found a new place to explore.

―

Sitting atop the hill, Wonder crosses her small limbs, her lap swaddled in a skirt woven from petals, an overflow of blonde pouring from the crown of her head and covering her hips. Because the marigold locks cascade around her, sometimes it's difficult to skip across the grass while collecting flowers.

She cocks her head. At the glen's base, fragments of a landmark peek out of the forest. From this vantage point, a series of towers merge with the beeches and willows.

"You're not paying attention," Harmony scolds affectionately, because this usually happens during morning meditation.

Wonder points to the building, because someday she will get a favorable answer, and she won't stop until she does. "What's in there?"

Her Guide pats Wonder's knobby knee, tucked somewhere beneath all the tresses. "You'll find out soon enough. Save your inquiries."

"But what if I forget my questions?" she questions.

The deity laughs. "Then they weren't that important, and you'll have new ones. There is always something to ask."

Wonder beams as if she's been promised a confection. "And something to discover. And something to daydream about."

Mirthful, the mentor wags a finger. "And plenty of time to do so later."

Dutifully, Wonder closes her eyes and practices emptying her mind and breathing deeply, which lasts until the next breeze stirs her hair and a hyacinth stalk tickles her bare toes.

When she's a little bit older, she earns her bow and quiver of arrows.

Her classmates have been anticipating this moment, but truthfully, Wonder has anticipated so many things, queried so many things, contemplated so many things, that she must have misplaced this excitement. She must have lost it somewhere between one rumination and another.

That's why it takes Wonder longer than any of her peers to choose an element for her weapons. Love favors iron, swapping dirty looks with Anger when he makes the same choice. Envy chooses glass, and Sorrow chooses ice.

After much hemming and hawing, and fantasizing over the endless options, Wonder decides on quartz. She likes the shimmer, which reminds her of drifting stars. And when her Guide mentions that quartz is a healing element, well, there's something precious about that.

There's something crucial about it, as though Wonder will need to heal sometime in the future.

In addition to archery drills, lectures ensue. She and her classmates sit in an enclave, in a misty cove of waterfalls. Gathered in a semicircle, they listen to the Guides and Fate Court explain an important fact: Wonder's class is the most elite and promising archers of the Peaks.

Terms like caliber *and* ethos, humanity *and* destiny, *get bandied about. The latter skips through Wonder's mind because* destiny *is such a pretty word. Wouldn't it look magical scripted in calligraphy?*

Harmony quirks an eyebrow. The silent reprimand causes Wonder to straighten and pay attention, all the while directing covert glances at her peers.

She likes each of them, even if they're a fussy lot.

Anger has tight eyebrows and longish, storm-battered hair. Envy smirks with no shortage of vanity, as if he's made of caramel—delectable and pleasurable. Sorrow gnaws on her lower lip, and her eyes are the color of tears. Love has raven hair and smooth hands, and Anger keeps looking at Love, and she keeps ignoring him.

In fact, Love—who's the first goddess in history to represent that emotion—stops concentrating on the lesson. This makes Anger grumpy, but it makes Wonder feel less strange about her own meandering, which makes her smile.

Usually, whenever Wonder goes off on tangents, Anger loses his patience. Sorrow pinches the bridge of her nose. Envy makes gooey comments targeted at Wonder's blush, since he adores attention and gets crabby when he loses it. Meanwhile, Love either snickers—she enjoys whatever annoys Anger—or minds her own business, too busy contemplating her fingers to care.

During the instruction, it's nice to see another peer lost in thought. It gives Wonder permission to rebel a tad more.

She should be in bed. She should be home, in her house mounted on stilts, above a glossy pool of water. She should be resting in her private refuge where eucalyptus, white stephanotis, and purple peonies dangle from the ceiling, spill from the windowsills, and frame her front door.

But she'd been imagining, thinking, debating. She hadn't been able to sleep or keep still. So why bother?

Being a renegade is ever so much fun!

Resting on her back atop the hill, Wonder consults the galaxy while blades of green tease her earlobes. She greets her birth star—once she locates it flittering aimlessly through the firmament—and then deliberates without constraint.

From her Guide and trips to the mortal realm, she's been learning the textures of imagination, the sounds of uncertainty and bewilderment, the tastes of deliberation and fascination, and the sights of reverence and curiosity. She's been studying the intricacies of awe and the framework of astonishment. She's been mastering how to identify these things, how to measure them in humans, what physical and verbal signs to look for.

But what is the actual essence of wonder? What does it mean to drift?

Is there a limit? Is there an end?

Why do flowers grow from the soil but not from the sky? What would it be like to pluck stars from their roots, the way she plucks primroses?

What's the farthest an arrow has ever flown? What would a bow look like if it were constructed to shoot backwards?

What is fate? Does it have an opposite?

And what's in the building at the bottom of that valley?

Books! It's a galaxy of books!

Wonder halts at the threshold, her mouth hanging ajar. The world beyond is a treasure chest of upright shelves and cases embedded into receding niches, each branded by foil titles and metallic lettering. There are collections of tomes and volumes, scrolls and vellum, and so...many...pages.

It's called the Archives. Tucked within the forest at the basin's core, it's the great, ethereal library of the Fates.

The building is a divinity, a shrine to words, a temple of knowledge and stories and legends. Multiple levels and offices contain study desks and reading chairs. Outside the windows, ancient branches sprout with leaves tipped in amethyst. Inside, it smells of ink and pages.

It's as timeless and sacred as a mausoleum, yet so very alive. Only one other place has ever truly felt like home to Wonder—the hyacinth hill. But here is another haven that spurs an intrinsic reaction in her womb, coupled with a giddy tingle through her fingers.

Inside these bookish halls dwell more questions and mysteries. The sponge of her mind soaks up the cavernous hush of voices, the flipping of parchment sheets, and the scratch of quills. Nearby, a librarian rotates an atlas, and a keeper strides past geography charts, which indicate some kind of cartography section.

Wonder's head whirls with pure elation, and her feet shuffle restlessly. Oh, to be an aficionada of this environment. As much as she appreciates the preordained power to wield awe with her bow, if she could be any goddess, Wonder would be a deity of libraries.

So that shall be her second job. And where to start?

Harmony leans into Wonder and whispers, "Go on. Have a look."

Wonder's smile splits her face in half. She has more than a look as she dashes through the aisles, losing and finding herself.

But not all pages are equally accessible. Some conceal messages that require ingenuity and a malleable mind to decipher their true content.

Even better. If Wonder's anything, she's a wanderer. She's a cura-

tor who appreciates the elusive. That's why snipping particular sentences from a page yields a surprise to Wonder's gaze, as she leans over a desk in the Hollow Chamber. Casting a wary glance around, she deems it safe and then watches the leftover script rearrange itself. The narrative dictates that mixing a seed and blossom creates something called Asterra Flora, which unlocks barriers.

Wonder grins. That night, she's in a rebellious mood. Perhaps it has to do with her new curves—lots of curves to match her height and weight and age.

Beneath the effervescent night, she sneaks into the Archives, breaching the latches by using this illicit blend called Asterra Flora, which she has mixed together herself. All she wants is to stroll in this repository alone, to have it to herself for once.

But that's when she ambles into forbidden territory.

Returning to the Hollow Chamber, she descends upon the restricted section without anyone there to prevent her. The lone telescope points to a wall mural, concealing the entrance. It's a known area, though not a frequented one—not by those permitted to do so.

The Asterra Flora works. The sheer veil appears.

And Wonder steps through.

The first time she sees him, she's hiding in a bush. Sneaking in and out of places has become a hobby, which extends to the mortal realm.

Her Guide would box her ears for this, not that Wonder plans on getting caught. But mortal libraries exist just like the Chamber's forbidden section, like another ripe temptation. She wants to see such a library and refuses to wait the final three years until she's assigned here.

At present, it's the mortal year, 1860. The cusp of war brews in this southern land, yet on a remote prairie hill, it seems far away.

Or perhaps this moment drowns out everything else.

On the outskirts of a ranch, she had been picking lupines when she'd spotted his golden hair. Dropping the stems, she'd plummeted and then crawled through the underbrush, dirt streaking her elbows and pants.

Now she stashes herself in the shrubbery. But really, she's too old for this.

And really, she doesn't have to hide. Humans cannot see or hear her.

However, this unknown figure might be an immortal spy who's caught up to Wonder. She'd thought herself alone, sequestered in this vacant setting. So she nudges the bushes aside, careful since that's something a mortal can detect.

What she sees causes her mouth to part.

It's a young man.

Resting atop a checkered blanket, he gazes at the night sky, at the stars, at her home. He wears black pants speckled in dust. Unkempt blond waves drape around his profile, which is cut like a square and hints at a pair of wiry lips.

It's a kindly face, a human countenance mesmerized by the heavens—skeptical of them, too. He tilts his head, asking a silent question, his brows furrowing with interrogation.

Wonder likes his speculative expression. She likes the book resting on his chest even better. If she were capable, she'd plop beside him, take delight in his shock, and promptly ask what he's reading. She would be impolite and snatch the book to see the title.

She doesn't need to. The gilded spine reveals that it's a mythology text.

Oh, and there's more. This young man is less of the escapist sort, more of the investigative sort. Resting beside a saddlebag, a stack of nonfiction hardcovers awaits his attention. It's an ambitious collection. Is he planning to read all of them in a single evening?

Kinship unfurls in Wonder's belly.

The incense of pomegranates wafts from him. As he resumes reading, he thumbs through the pages, his fingernails filed longer than any mortal male she's observed during her field trips.

In the pasture, a piebald horse grazes, and a trio of hounds give chase around the young man. One of the animals chomps on the boy's book, clamping it between the jowls and darting off.

"Hey!" the mortal chuckles as he lurches to his feet and races after the dog.

Wonder plants a hand over her mouth to quell a laugh before remembering he cannot hear her. Because of that, a pebble of disappointment skitters down her chest, and her shoulders collapse. An inexplicable loss consumes Wonder as she witnesses the scene.

He snatches the book, then kneels to pat the hounds who happily gather at his feet and slobber his cheeks. But it isn't until he hums to the animals that Wonder's palm falls from her lips.

His tenor is beautiful. It's spectral, made of starlight and something buried underground.

That's when she feels an impossible sensation. That's when her heart changes shape. That's when it gives a tight, permanent clench.

The human archive is so quaint!

Wonder prances behind the young man, who attends to the local library. It must be the center of activity in this prairie landscape, considering the town's modest size. The repository stands no bigger than a humble house, with shingles and a pitched roof, the vicinity surrounded by pomegranate trees.

It's nearly closing time, the sun dipping behind the hills. Hints of starlight sprinkle the area, making some of the green-bound books glow like a trail.

Like a trail to an answer, a revelation to an unknown inquiry.

Wonder puzzles at the sight. Is it a mere trick of illumination? Is she projecting? Or is it a prediction? Some type of foreshadowing or sign?

Best guess, it's due to her nomadic tendencies. She blinks out of the trance.

It has taken Wonder a half dozen visits to learn that he's a librarian, a connoisseur like her. And he's good at his job, smiling at patrons, talking with them about the war and about enlisting, blushing at fashionable girls who flaunt their parasols and shimmy their shawls as they pass by.

He's handsome, like a ray of sunshine, and they know it.

One of them has a nose like a peg. Wonder wants to jam it deep into the girl's face, so that it forms a crater. But the young man doesn't indulge the debutante beyond a cute flash of sharp teeth.

The canines startle the peg-nosed girl, and she bustles off. His face slackens, pink slicing across his jaw. And now Wonder really wants to retaliate against the female who has made him feel self-conscious.

Instead, Wonder shadows him.

Over time, she returns, making a habit of it, peeling back layers. He's a respected local who kneels in church pews, tutors children living on the ranch where she first saw him, and rents a room beneath the library. He owns a telescope that peers out the repository's front window. He rides that piebald horse and scratches three sets of floppy hound ears.

He loves knowing secrets, and mysteries, and loopholes. He loves *books. He loves reading.*

And Wonder loves him.

⁓

Isn't that what this is? Isn't it love? Isn't it?

She may be uneducated about this emotion, and it may be nonexistent between deities, but with a human?

Surely, this is what mortals feel. Surely, this is love.

Yes, it must be. So, there. That's that.

But wanting a human is forbidden. It's risky and against celestial law.

Wonder is far too besotted to care. The sentiment is soft, and gentle, and dear. It's a second skin, a private lining stitched under her flesh, insulated from the rules.

After several months of researching methods to contact him, she finds a scroll in the Chamber's restricted section. It says that if a human and a deity fall in love, they'll be bound to each other, and that deity will become mortal, which means they can be together.

Together.

She's never enjoyed the concept of together with someone. What is that like? Is it worth it?

Again, how can she communicate with him? Maybe it's simple.

She uses mortal ink and paper to compose a letter. Drafting what's supposed to be a perfectly structured declaration, she deviates into a stream of consciousness.

He has a name, one that had revealed itself when an elderly schoolmarm and her husband—who's too old to fight in the war—had tipped their bonnet and hat to him.

But Wonder doesn't address the young man that way. She has a lovelier moniker in mind.

Dearest Wayward Star...

Pulse thumping, she smuggles the letter from the Peaks and packs it into his saddlebag.

⌒

His reception is not what she hopes for.

At sunset, orange slashes through clouds. Sitting on the library stoop after closing time, he discovers the envelope in his saddlebag. Beneath a pomegranate tree, Wonder fidgets and watches him scan the contents.

A flush creeps along his throat, which should be a good sign.

It isn't. He glances around, his normally sweet expression crinkling into a glower, as if he thinks somebody's playing a joke on him. His irises flash, resembling scythes. "Very funny," he calls out to the panorama. Crumbling the note, he jams it into his pocket and stomps indoors.

Wonder's heart dries like a flower. She tries to console herself, because at least he hadn't destroyed the note, even if he'd been tempted to.

⌒

Another letter. And another. And another.

She tries, and she tries, and she tries. She offers a hint of who she is, and she tells him that he's magnificent. She adores the sound of his voice and wants to know what his favorite book is.

Why does he like pomegranates with his eggs? Why are his nails tapered?

He never answers. Rather, he studies and then stores the letters in a book.

Befuddlement crosses his features, and apprehension glazes his eyes, growing more pigmented by the day, purple pansies of sleep deprivation leaking from under his lids. He pores through hardbacks with a zealousness that disturbs the library debutantes. He interrogates the ones who'd once fancied him, as if they might be the culprits of this prank.

༄

This hardly bodes well for her duties. She misses every bull's-eye during target practice, squirms during meditation, and snaps at her peers.

It kindles suspicion from her classmates. When Love asks what Wonder thinks touching a human would be like, Wonder merely shrugs. She's not interested in dwelling.

༄

The letters consume him. When he concludes they aren't the product of a wicked stunt, he gets vocal about it, riling up the locals by claiming there's a female specter calling out to him.

Have they heard her, too? Do they know who she is?

One time, he shouts at thin air, calling out for her while wandering the main roads. "Who are you? What are you? Where are you from? Christ, answer me! Why won't you answer me, huh? I said, who are you?"

Wonder cries into his ear, "I'm here! I'm right here!"

Belatedly, it occurs to her that she can write to him in real time while he's watching. However, that would be an even greater peril, since she cannot trust herself not to get more carried away than she already is. She might reveal too much of her world.

He hunts through the prairie-scape until it's no longer tolerable. The townsfolk convene. Fearful, they send for a regiment of physicians who drag the young man across the dust.

"It's true!" he screams at the physicians, thrashing against them and kicking up grit. "It's true! She's real, she's real, she's real! Keep away, let me go! She's real!"

Wonder has read many words in her lifetime. Asylum *is one of them.*

His possessions—including the letters—burn in a pile, smoke puffing from the nexus. They hustle him into a barred wagon while a councilman bolts the library doors.

Wonder begs for them to stop, stop, stop.

"Stop!" she wails, rushing forward. "Release him!"

But before she can rip the lock from the wagon's hinge and free the young man, a pair of mighty hands fasten on to her shoulders and haul her backward.

She fights, even though these aren't the hands of a classmate or Harmony. No, these are the hands of a celestial sovereign.

⌒

Her floundering of late has given her away.

It has caught her peers' attention. And it has caught her Guide's attention. And although they haven't reported a thing, their concern hasn't gone unnoticed by others far more powerful.

While Wonder was busy defying regulation, the Fate Court had ordered a search of her home. That's how they'd found the mortal ink and paper.

Harmony had discovered it first and ordered Wonder to trash the evidence. But Wonder hadn't, even though she'd promised to, and the mentor had believed her.

Wonder confesses everything once they threaten to punish her classmates as well as herself. To that end, the rulers command her peers to carry out the torture, to strap Wonder down and slash those offensive, obstinate hands. In front of the congregation of deities, she struggles against the binds while a blade slices through her skin, blood blooming like petals, as red as pomegranates.

She makes out the shapes of starbursts, a preview of how the scars will look. Is this why she'd chosen quartz for her archery? Because it shall heal her hands later?

The whole time, her friends wear tormented expressions, living vicariously through this introduction to physical pain. They maim her hands, each movement forced. It stings, and it throbs, and she shrieks.

Please, no more. Please, it hurts.

It hurts, it hurts, it hurts!

Tears pierce her temples and seep into her hairline. She imagines the young man, the beloved librarian who owns her heart, the one who will never know her the way she knows him.

Where is he? What are those physicians doing to him?

Her friend, Love, cannot take it anymore and flings herself in front of Wonder, blocking the swing of Envy's knife. For an instant, all four classmates appear relieved by the interruption. But then Anger reluctantly drags Love out of the room while she bucks and screams, the rage god preventing her protest from getting the rest of them into trouble.

At the behest of a Court member, it continues.

Wonder's Guide watches with a trembling chin, periodically glancing at her superiors with glints of fury. Then Harmony meets Wonder's eyes and holds the gaze, schooling Wonder to breathe, to empty her mind like they've practiced.

She can do this. She will survive.

But will that boy?

Anger pounds on her door in the middle of the night. Blearily, Wonder answers and barely has time to process as his mouth crashes onto hers, stealing her breath in a ferocious kiss.

She knows why. Despite delirium, she knows how Anger looks at Love, and how the goddess doesn't look at him.

Wonder knows this unrequited agony. She's attuned to this heartache, this loneliness. So on a desperate moan, she spreads her lips for Anger, letting him ply her with his tongue. She kisses him back, and it feels good, and it feels comforting.

In her mind's eye, she envisions blond curls, blushing cheeks, and ashen irises. A humming tenor and filed fingernails turning a page.

Picturing those wiry lips, she surrenders. Together, they stumble inside her house and slam the door shut.

The next morning, she awakens next to Anger, who rests on his side. They stare at one another until her mouth wobbles, and her eyes blur. The archer's own guilt reflects back at her as he smears the first tear with his thumb.

"I know," he whispers, then holds Wonder while she weeps.

It never happens again.

When she's of age, she serves the mortal realm. By that time, the young man is gone, having perished in the asylum.

Wonder sobs at his grave and traces the name on his headstone.

As the decades pass, she looks for him in the visage of every human male graced with sunny curls. But it's no use, because she'll never find the face she's looking for.

So she gives up.

Fifty years later, during a break from servitude, she returns to the Peaks for an intermission. There, Wonder curls into her reading chair. The Archives aren't busy today, the lull having afforded her time to pursue the Hollow Chamber's restricted area and pilfer a text or two.

On the pretense of innocence, she'd then exited the section and discreetly chosen this seat, tucking into her reading material.

A slant of glittering, rosemary light from the lanterns and the Chamber's overhead sphere wend into the space, dappling a selection of books...like a trail. The spectacle calls to mind a human library, from an era when she'd witnessed a similar effect while spying on a certain young man.

Of all things to recall, why that? She shakes her head, then pauses, her nape prickling with the knowledge of someone's eyes on her.

Glancing up, she scrutinizes the aisles. There's no one around. But she does spot a sudden movement in her periphery, a splash of gilded hair disappearing around the corner, evading her notice.

Her heart twitches. She's about to rise and follow the stranger, but something else catches her eye from the book on her lap. It's a string of words that materialize under the right slant of mystical light.

Wonder straightens. It's another legend—something about a deity winning the heart of another deity.

17

When it's over, Wonder has no breath left, no voice left. Perhaps she doesn't have a heart left, either. She may have just sacrificed it. That's the price of telling the truth—its overgrowth unfurling and spreading like a jungle, the weeds of history choking what's left of buds and petals.

Sitting in this forbidden artery of the Hollow Chamber, Wonder's mind drains, spilling onto the aisle's runner. Her psyche tires of wandering, of scuttling here and there. She only has energy for two emotions: regret and loss. One of them seeps into her pores, and the other digs a ravine into her stomach.

Once, she had uncovered her first legend, a scroll about a human and a deity falling in love. It hadn't worked in her favor.

Initially, she hadn't told any of her peers about that scroll—not until Love met Andrew. Although the legend hadn't helped Wonder, she'd wanted to believe it could aid her classmate.

And it had. It had given Love and Andrew a future.

From that very first discovery, Wonder had acquired a taste for unearthing such marvels. Her passion for it had eventually led to another legend, which had united Anger and Merry.

Across from her, Malice remains quiet. His silence is the loudest noise she's ever heard, more abrasive than his temper, his threats, and his screams during nightmares.

When this god doesn't speak, anything is possible.

When her mind empties, anything can happen.

Yes, if he'd heard about Wonder's torture from other archers, and of the mortal boy she'd risked everything for, he might have connected the dots to his nightmares. Fortunately, as he'd once said, the tale of her indiscretion had never reached him. Him being the bookish rather than the social type—a page turner rather than a gossiper—had worked in her favor there.

Be that as it may, Wonder's gaze makes the steep journey from his bare toes to his knees, from his navel to his slack jaw. At last, she catches his eyes, those ashes whirling, the vortex sucking her in.

His forearms drape loosely atop his knees. Only the writhing furnaces in his pupils contradict the numb expression. This is what he'd wanted, isn't it? Just as he had vented earlier, this is the information he's been searching for: the root of his existence.

Please say something.

Please don't speak.

Malice obliges and refuses. Resting the back of his skull against the shelves, he lifts a finger and rubs it back and forth across his chin. "Sounds like you really did a number on that mate. He must have been one hell of a temptation."

"I loved him," Wonder says.

That finger halts. "What about now?"

"The heart doesn't work like that. It doesn't just stop—not with him."

"You sure it was love? One, we didn't grow up in a sappy world where deities provided monogamous examples for us to learn from. Two, we were raised to believe that deities can't feel love anyhow. Three, you never shared a tangible moment with him. The admiration was one-sided and from a distance, so how do you know what you felt back then?"

"I just *know*," she defends, prickles darting across her cheeks.

"Then it must have been excruciating, seeing your library-god-slash-sweetie-pie hauled off like that, sent to some loony bin."

"Don't call it that." Wonder wraps her arms around her upturned limbs. "I'd have taken his place if I could have."

Malice scrapes his tongue across his teeth, testing the weight and depth of one million plausible replies. At which point, he nods. "So then what happened to me?"

You died.

But he knows that now. That's not what he's asking.

He wants insight into the asylum and what befell him there. Dismissing the details of his untimely death, he wants access to the years of his detainment.

What happened to Malice in that place?

Wonder doesn't know. She feels, rather than hears, herself tell him that. She endures the dull ache in her stomach and the floppy movements of her tongue.

Technically, her response is the truth. Because she'd been caught by the Fate Court, and because she'd been heavily monitored until her assignment in the mortal world, she hadn't been there to see what they did to him behind those walls.

Not the extent of it, at least.

But she does know how it ended.

"You were reincarnated," she says. "You became…"

Malice jabs a thumb at his chest. "I became this."

He was reborn as a deity, yet his past traumas came with him, cursing him in a new way. Whatever monstrosities that befell Malice in purgatory, they continue to plague him in the afterlife, slithering into his nightmares and strapping him down.

So instead of turning into a god, he has morphed into a demon.

There's a rubbery texture to his words, but it lacks accusation. Does he blame her for his fate, the way she blames herself? Does he mourn the life she'd poached from him?

If he does, he's not showing it.

"Hmm," Malice hums. "Can't say any of this jogs my memory, except for the bits and pieces that crawl through dreams. Now it's clear why I became a fan of the Archives and then parked my ass in the Celestial City's library. They both felt safe—the only places that made sense, where I felt most like myself.

"When the Fates banished me, and I found my new home, away from home, away from home, I conjured my saddlebag, the rocking chair, and the antique telescope, and I used them to outfit the library vault. I thought making replicas from the flashbacks would help me figure things out in my head, connect the dots—not that they did. I must've been channeling my mortal roots without realizing it.

"Ah, and the envelopes. Those were easier to conjure, not so easy to fill in the blank pages. It took a while to replay the nightmares and recall each sentence you wrote, but when a deviant's got eternity to transcribe—" he flings up his arms "—what is time?"

Wonder curls a lock of hair behind her ear and notices his own waves scattered around his face, mussed and just as slow to dry as her tresses. "If I'd known what would happen, I would have never written to you."

"I guess you found the bibliophile in me irresistible. Back atcha."

"So you've chosen sarcasm."

"You want me to have an episode instead? Just say the word,

and you'll get a sample of what's going on under my skin. If I were you, I'd take a compliment over the alternative. Compliments are complimentary. And I wasn't being sarcastic. As enticing as I find your hips, it'd be lazy of me to salivate over your beauty instead of your intellect, which is more delectable. I'm pretty sure that's the key to your heart."

"Malice—"

"Am I right? I like being right."

Of course, he's right. "Malice—"

"That's me," he confirms, resentment tainting the words. "Glad to know you're still aware of it."

Wonder flinches. "What is that supposed to mean?"

"The locals sent me to that hellhole, not you. You didn't kill me."

He's wrong. There's more she hasn't shared, an addendum to the tale, a detail that she cannot bear to admit. Her selfishness won't let her.

Along the cases, engravings introduce stories, and fonts present chronicles. It's a collision of texts, flanking Wonder and Malice within this aisle.

It's fitting that she has bared herself here, protected within the Chamber walls. It's her confessional, her saving grace.

It's her life. And it's his.

It's an existence of wrongdoings on both sides. She detests him for using her friends as pawns and then trying to eradicate them. But he wouldn't have done that if he hadn't been reborn, and he wouldn't have been reborn if she hadn't meddled in his universe, entitling herself to it, branding it with immortal influence.

Perhaps being tainted with the residue of a deity had trapped him in between worlds, and that's why he'd transformed after death. Perhaps it had linked him to the immortal world, to an unforeseen afterlife. Either way, she had played her part, and she should apologize to her peers for the domino effect.

But they're not the only ones.

Wonder whispers, "I'm sorry."

When Malice just stares at her, she drags herself to her feet. In their current moods, they need to be alone. He needs to absorb this backstory, as does she.

Pausing outside the aisle, she glances over her shoulder. He probably hadn't expected her to do that, because she catches the tick of his jaw, his flippancy replaced by a glower aimed at the spot where she'd been sitting.

His body twitches when she speaks. "You asked me once. I didn't answer then, but I will now: Yes."

"'Yes.' Such a bold and permanent word," he remarks without facing her. "Yes, what? I'm all ears, Wildflower."

"Yes, you were worth the scars."

He blinks. The pleats across his forehead vanish, as do the faint commas around his mouth, his entire face losing its crease. It's a raw and rare profile, one of vulnerability.

And yes, she sees it. And yes, he lets her.

And yes, yes, yes. She doubts that he's ever heard that single word used in conjunction with him.

Wonder pads away, strolling past banks of knowledge. The farther she gets, the more her journey through forbidden territory fortifies her. She's a tree shedding its leaves, making room for new foliage that will sprout and reach for the moon.

She covers every inch of this place, traipsing deeper into the Chamber's restricted roots. By the time oxygen returns to her in reassuring lungfuls, her nightgown is dry, and only the tips of her locks remain damp. How quizzical that she feels the most at home amidst revolutionary and scandalous texts. She's not the only one, and as she thinks about it, her eyes prickle with the need for release.

Wonder traces each volume. Here's where she found the solution to Love and Andrew's happiness, and the key to Anger and Merry's future. The reminder fills her with amazement, as well as jealousy and sadness.

When will it be her turn? Does she need anybody to call her own? She has survived this long without a partner, hasn't she?

Some of the books are square, some rectangular, some circular. Who first thought to shape them this way? Who first thought to bind them in leather and sketch titles along the spines?

If she were a book, which kind would she be? What secrets or revelations would she contain? What words would she tuck inside herself?

And how long has she been ambling?

Quite a while, because she hears him coming, crashing his way through the lanes. She whips around. Rounding the corner, Malice stalks toward Wonder. With his eyes pinned to hers, he knocks a misplaced reading chair out of his path, sending it crashing to the floor.

She barely has time to foster another thought before he's on her, snatching her by the waist and hoisting her against him. "Fuck this," he growls.

And then his lips smash against hers.

Wonder gasps, or maybe it's a sob, and maybe he hadn't been the only one reaching out for an embrace. In that millisecond before he'd captured her, maybe her arms had already risen for him, desperate to repent or surrender, or both.

Whatever craggy sound she makes, it causes her mouth to open, and it causes his mouth to split. And right then, they work in tandem. They slant and fit, their lips clutching. And more grating noises twist out of them, conducive to one another, an entanglement of confusion and fury and guilt and desire.

This pent-up kiss is a lifeline and a punishment. It's a refuge and an abduction.

It's hatred and perhaps a seed of the opposite—a perplexing enigma that deities aren't supposed to feel. Perhaps this is something that hides in a crevice between the past and future, something that has to do with the heart. No matter how broken, somehow that organ still functions—still pounds, pounds, pounds.

Her pulse is utterly alive. It's wild, slamming from her chest into his.

The tip of Malice's wet, infuriating tongue flicks the crook of Wonder's lips. In response, she unfurls under that hungry mouth, spreading for him, for herself, for this. His tongue probes her with swift, frenzied strokes, and her hands rip into his hair, seizing the roots and holding on as though he's a ledge, as though she's dangling over a bottomless pit—if she lets go, she'll fall for eternity.

Then she matches his pace, her own tongue curling, setting a rhythm.

A passionate groan travels from Malice's throat to hers. It reminds Wonder of elusive heat, an element that's impossible for them to feel, even though hints writhe along their bodies, emitting thick swatches of air, radiating especially from their groins. The density of it swirls at the center of her thighs, which mash against his.

He's erect, straining against her navel, and she likes it.

No, she adores it. That she affects him this way incites pride and possessiveness.

What else can she draw from him? What else can she give herself? What else can bodies do for each other?

In how many ways? For how long?

In the throes of ecstasy, does he sound the same as his mortal self? Does it matter?

Consumed by these questions, she gyrates into his body, curves fitting into muscles. Frustrated with everything, with herself, with him, she lets go. Her reservations dissolve, and the books dissolve, and the room dissolves, all of them replaced by his palms roughly claiming her waist, his mouth latching on to hers. She yields to a century and a half of yearning, of wishing things had been different.

When she does, power floods her veins. It soaks her like a tempest to soil.

Malice's saber nails prick into her sides, which makes her yelp against his lips, which makes him grin into hers. He's likely poked holes in the nightgown and broken her skin. Though, his attack hadn't hurt more than a second, with a bolt of pleasure tingling up her spine—flesh prickling from her bare soles to the back of her skull. It had felt good, so incredibly, pertinently good.

How she'd like to bite him for that. So she does, yanking her mouth away and snaring his bottom lip with her teeth, hard enough to draw blood, the copper tang of it leaking across her tongue. There, now they've made one another bleed.

They're even.

As if reading her mind, Malice half-winces, half-sniggers. He grabs her cheeks and takes her lips again, but his amusement alters the slope of his tongue, the tip sliding across the roof of her mouth. It tickles and vexes, a smattering of the two in quick succession.

Oh, stars. She's kissing him, and he's kissing her, and it's nothing like she'd imagined. No, it's better. The kiss keeps going, and widening, and deepening.

Malice flings his head away from her. They pant for breath, and their hands cling, digging in. His chest heaves while her lungs thrash, gusts of oxygen sawing through her.

His delirious eyes find hers, and he rasps, "Yes or no?"

She's given him *yes* after *yes* tonight. But there's one more left.

Wonder nods, mouthing her reply, and it's enough.

Malice walks her backward, striding so fast that her rump bangs into a bookcase, causing the structure to teeter. As it regains balance, he grips her backside and hauls her off the ground.

Her legs bend on either side of his hips, her heels finding purchase on the rim of a shelf, shoving books farther into the recess. A few other titles dislodge and plummet on either side of Wonder and Malice, the ancient texts smacking the floor in clouds of green stardust.

Everlasting Fates! They might have damaged some of the precious volumes!

Wonder feels compelled to reprimand Malice, but then his forehead presses against hers, his irises swallowing her vision. The nightgown bunches up around her. His pelvis rouses the nexus in between her split thighs, the coarse jeans rubbing her sensitive, uncovered flesh, creating a friction that pulls another gasp from her.

For someone with no experience, his actions bespeak confidence and instinct. She can relate. It's awakening, this craving that deities know how to satisfy.

Nevertheless, she's created a monster. Though, it certainly isn't the first time.

Which is why Malice hooks on to the scoop of her bodice—and wrenches it. In one rough motion, the garment tears, sheared down the middle from neckline to hem. He's overdone it, because he staggers from the effort, almost dropping her.

Wonder instinctively clutches the nape of his neck. Her amazement reflects in his pupils, arousal shooting right through her, pooling low in her body. Her breasts and the folds of her belly jiggle against his pectorals and abdomen. Appraising the torn material dangling off her shoulders, his gaze darkens as it skims the column of naked skin. The considerable span of her thighs flares around his waist, clenching the low-hanging pants.

Malice looks like he wants to devour her. Like he will.

His mouth plunges to the crook of her neck, marking it with open kisses, swathing his tongue against her pulse. Wonder arches, her scalp hitting the shelf above, a whine skittering off her lips as he sketches her clavicles with his teeth. Her fingers yank on his golden curls, and he shudders, and she realizes that he enjoys it—just as much as he enjoys her breasts.

Her lips part on a silent cry the instant his head sinks. While nuzzling and nipping the cove of her breasts, the blades of his talons trace the circumference of her nipples, a slight tease that wracks through her bloodstream, so that she contorts into him. Her nipples stiffen, pleasure quivering from the peaks as he scrapes them gently.

Wonder balls her fist into her mouth, stifling the octave of her response.

Cursing, Malice pries away her wrist, unblocking the sound. And why shouldn't she be loud? There's no one else here.

And then his mouth dives, purses around a nipple, and sucks.

Wonder unleashes, her moans swirling to the rafters. It provokes Malice to sample her harder, drawing her peak into the tight, drenched channel of his mouth, his tongue flicking the nub.

Then he moves to the other breast, and she's nothing but sound, which accelerates with every exquisite pull.

She's damp, more so than she's ever been. She's ready.

And now it's her turn. Breathing shallowly, Wonder reaches down, working on his jeans. Malice drags his mouth from her nipple, his face slack with rapture. He helps her, their fingers fumbling in a hurry.

As the material buckles around his waist, they maneuver the jeans down enough to free him. Malice's length extends from the pants, rising for her, tensing for her.

Recently, Wonder had been privy to a glimpse of it. But now she savors the view, when he's about to fill her, to conceal himself inside her.

For an instant, mutual self-consciousness creeps in. Yet she's still wet, and he's still hard. And at the first accidental shift of their hips, his tip nudges through her curls, snuffing out hesitation like a candle.

An inarticulate word bubbles from her mouth. A stunned one slips from his.

They lock eyes while rolling their pelvises into position, needing a few subtle adjustments. Malice's heart smashes into her breasts, and her pulse hammers into his torso. A maelstrom of nervousness and anxiousness and selfishness spirals up her limbs and dashes through her stomach.

It's a preview of more excessive things to come.

Wonder grieves and celebrates.

And then she bends her knees, her legs splaying farther to accommodate his body, her heels bolstered on the bookcase. Malice claims her wrists, lifts her arms above her head, and shackles her hands there.

He braces himself, his shaft on the cusp of her entrance. His tongue strums along her ear, then he murmurs, "I'm going to throttle you deep into these books."

"I'm going to let you," she whispers.

Malice gives her a fiendish look, not quite a grin, nor a glare. It's all or nothing.

They lurch at the same time. He snaps his hips, just as she jolts hers. His length pitches up into her, and she buries him whole. They flex against the bookcase, their mouths unhinging, hanging ajar from the penetration as two shocked moans collide.

With his joints trembling, Malice runs his lips against her jaw. "Are you all right?"

"I am now," she says.

He nods. "Good."

And then he thrusts.

Wonder shouts, her body vaulting upward. Malice growls something against her mouth.

Oh, Fates, he's inside her. So deep inside her.

She cannot help but rock her hips, demanding more. Without preamble, he obliges, setting a primal, whipping tempo. He churns against her without calculation.

And he moves like a virgin, proving that he's never done this before—but also giving the impression that he has. Because what Malice lacks in synchronicity, he makes up for in stamina, eagerness, and intuition. He measures the signs rolling across her face and listens to her reactions. Glancing between their flushed bodies, he watches himself disappearing within her, then checks Wonder's countenance yet again.

She aides him, signaling the depth and angle and cadence that make her whimpers crest. And crest, they do. And because they do, Malice swells even more.

He catches on. His ministrations grow bolder, forging ahead

and locating the carnal spots. His backside pumps, whisking his pelvis into her, infusing them both with adrenaline and a flurry of sensation.

Lost in the rapid juts of his body, her mind dissolves.

And that's when they really get loud.

His groans express awe and artlessness, which fizz in her blood, lacing it like a drug. Wonder shuts her eyes as iridescent lights whirl behind the lids. At this intense rate, she's going to burst like a star and detonate the galaxy.

Or they're going to wreck the poor bookcase.

A string of encouraging sounds tumbles from her, though she cannot identify them. All she knows is that Malice likes what he hears.

He grates, "That's right, Wildflower. Take it from me."

"Malice," she mewls. "Keep doing that."

"What? This?"

When he jabs at a particular spot, she pleads, "Yes. More."

"How much more? What would you like?"

She cannot answer, not on the brink of a spasm. Constantly, he rushes at that spot, a button that has them chanting. With each punch of his hips, their cries amplify.

It's hectic, the way he charges into her. And it's wanton, how she floods him.

Every time she calls his name, in tune to his thrusts, Malice increases the pace. He goes rampant, gets stiffer. It's as though hearing her like this fuels him.

Wonder seizes his mouth and kisses him, tasting his moans. The thrust of her tongue accentuates the thrust of his waist, working in tandem as they ride each other.

Oh, but he'd better not stop. She'll pummel him if he does.

It's not until Malice chuckles huskily that Wonder realizes

she has spoken aloud. Glancing at his wicked face, she laughs with him. To find anything funny at a time like this, while on the precipice of climax, stuns her. Their shared humor is winded, partly labored, partly diverted. Only with this misfit can she fathom such a transition.

Just like that, the mirth stutters into restless whimpers as they gyrate across the shelves. Because exertion rather than implausible heat causes deities to sweat, condensation beads across their skin, turning into mist.

At some point, their digits lace overhead. Whereas he'd pegged her to the shelves before, she takes the lead and squeezes his hands, fastening them to her.

Wonder loves the intimate sensation of her breasts pressed into him. She loves discovering a beauty mark on his elbow, the way a single curl flops across his forehead when he moves a certain way, and how exhilarating it is to feel the fine plumes of hair trailing from his abdomen to his pelvis.

She loves knowing that she's the only one who has ever heard him like this, drained of intellect and malevolence. She loves that he doesn't care whether she dominates him, or whether he dominates her. She loves her thighs flanking his waist as it revolves into her. She loves how they fit together.

She loves that it's taking forever to get *there*. She loves his impatience.

Malice sucks in a breath. "Come on, Wonder."

The demon speeds up, pushing them to a cliff's edge, or to the edge of a planet. Venting in pleasure, Wonder splays her fingers. She lets him go, allowing him to grip her backside and hold her in place, the better to enter her.

Pinioned like this heightens the experience, enabling her to concentrate thoroughly on his thrusts. Blindly, Wonder grapples overhead, her nails embedding into leather anthologies. Once secure, she begins to shout.

And so does he.

All at once, this ambitiousness catches up with them, turning their bodies into the universe. A meteor shower of release sprints through Wonder, swarming from her core to the tips of her being. It's the onslaught of a shooting star, the magic of flapping pages.

Malice freezes, going still inside her. His mouth searches and finds hers—and then with a violent jerk, he shatters like glass, his holler splintering into a hundred fragments that cut through her moans, piercing her heart.

Because now she knows what making love feels like.

If only once.

18

They slump against the bookcase. Malice's head lands on her shoulder, and her cheek lands on his temple, and his palms cup her backside, and her digits glide through his mussed hair. She wants to touch him everywhere, wants to be touched everywhere.

The shelves refract lunar lights, akin to lambent strands from a pool of water. It turns the room into someplace fluid, as though Wonder and Malice are floating in a sea of stars. While she'd relish having him atop a bed of flowers, she likes consummating while surrounded by books.

Consummating. Malice would hardly call it that. He'd used a rowdier word.

Not Wonder, which creates a lovely balance between them. She appreciates that.

She's also boneless. Though unlike the last time she did this, it's hardly satiating. Like a bunny in heat, she wants him again.

Time is fleeting, so she seeks out his rear, savoring its rounded shape and firm texture, the dimples caving into the sides.

Malice's shoulders ripple with humor, and he speaks breathlessly against her collarbone. "Did I say…you could…fondle my ass?"

Her sole travels down the column of his calf. Her voice is just as winded as his, heaving through a reply. "I'm in…the mood…to be a goddess."

"Keep it up and I'll be in the mood to fuck one."

She feels a blush sneak up her throat. "You've just done that."

"Hmm, that's true." He heaves, drawing in air. "Was it nice?"

"It was eternally nice."

"I like being nice to you. Tell me more, be specific about your siren needs. I want to know everything."

"I'm not that experienced, remember?"

"I'm planning to change that. I'll negotiate more noise, more anarchy, out of that plush mouth."

Wonder cannot help the bittersweet lump in her throat. He still has *that* face, but he no longer has *that* soul, yet slices of the past linger when she considers his adoration for all things scripted across pages. There's still that.

And that one day in the forest, when she'd glimpsed him playing with the adolescent dragonflies, teasing them as they capered around his head. Yes, he hasn't lost his affection for animals, his respect for nature, or his singing voice.

Notwithstanding his mercurial flaws, this reborn outcast lives in the moment, acts boldly without being foolish, and never assumes he's wiser than anyone else. He licks his lips after chewing on berries, doesn't make excuses for his behavior, doesn't engage in self-pity, and wants to belong. She had noticed the latter, from the times when he'd observed the camaraderie among her peers.

He's a mosaic, a portrait made of chipped pieces, distorted up close but beautiful as a whole, once you step back and give him space.

Wonder's muscles ache in a profound way. How extravagant to be wrapped in joy and melancholy. She may as well have deflowered two people at once, giving them her heart with one moan, cheating on them with one gasp.

All the same, she giggles as the pads of Malice's fingers locate a ticklish spot beneath her triceps. He gets sneakier, nipping her shoulder while prodding the creases and folds of her body, hunting for the areas that make her yelp. This is new, learning that he's playful after mating, even while they're slick with perspiration.

Also, he remains firm, the length of him fixed within her. In the aftermath, she had anticipated his departure from her body. She had foreseen her own panic and withdrawal, expecting them to come to their senses.

Hearing that he craves a second romp provokes a traitorous thrill. She traces his tattoo, skimming the fletching and the quill's inky tip.

Malice lifts his unruly head and leans in for a kiss. She veers back, happy to tease but likewise curious. "When did you get this marking?"

"Have a thing for my tat?" He grins, flashing chiseled incisors. "I fancy what you fancy."

Wonder sweeps hair from his forehead. "Since when?"

"Isn't that obvious?"

His flirty tone makes it clear to what he's referring. The fact that he's rooted inside her has everything to do with it.

He pecks her lips and shifts, readjusting her position in his arms, bringing her closer. "Can we talk about the fact that you've stolen my virginity in a forbidden domain? This takes trespassing in a restricted section to a whole new level. How edgy of you."

Wonder chuckles. "I did not steal it, you scoundrel."

"No, you've stolen other things."

His sultry tone darkens. He might mean the letter from his

saddlebag, but his answer seems directed elsewhere.

Wonder would ask him to elaborate, but then Malice casts his ink a sideways glance. "Some archers in the Peaks are mighty talented artists. I got this one after my first nightmare."

"Oh…" Wonder hesitates at the design. "Did it hurt?"

"Always worried about everyone more than yourself." Affection and residual pleasure douse the inferno in his irises, revealing glossy rings of gray. "I'm betting it didn't hurt as much as your scars. Whenever I look at them, I get pissed off at the universe. Say the word, and I'll claw out the Courts' innards."

"You'd do that without me having to say a thing. Not that I approve."

"Don't underestimate me, Wildflower. Your approval means more than you know." He traces her jawline with his nose. "It didn't hurt as much as the nightmare." He sets a pinky against her lips, preventing her from waxing sympathetic. "Shush. It takes more than a verbal reference to trigger me."

"No, it does not. It takes a syllable."

"Okay, sure, but I'd rather screw you senseless again than have a meltdown. But that means being at my full capacity."

"This is an awfully sudden change of heart."

"Is it?" he counters. "Angst is an aphrodisiac. We've been at this foreplay ever since you showed up in the Celestial City, looking like some magnificent meringue palace, all whipped curves and sugar. You'd fixate on me like I actually meant something to you. I'd never raged so much in my life or gotten so randy."

Wonder suppresses a smile. "You scarcely knew me."

"And that matters because…" When she gives him an evident look, he says, "You don't put much stock in the sex appeal of animosity, much less your gorgeous intelligence. Besides, I could echo the same about not knowing me. By the way? Echoing is fun, listening to yourself reverberate down a chasm." He howls, the sound quavering through the Chamber, diving into the floor and soaring to the ceiling. "Heard that? You should try it."

"To say the least, my lungs have been depleted."

"Speaking of depletion, I've got an idea."

"Sleep," she translates.

Malice gives her neck a love bite. "You read my mind."

He carries Wonder from the aisle, cradling her to him while traveling naked from the Hollow Chamber. It's anarchy, but she's too startled to protest.

Her nightgown may be a tattered swatch hanging from her shoulders, but she's not about to discard it here, and they shouldn't leave his clothes behind, either. And what about their archery? The disarray of books?

"Malice," she chides. "I can walk."

"Wow." His eyes widen with mock discovery. "So can I."

"The weapons—"

"I'll get them later."

"You cannot possibly make it to the tower while you're still—"

"Oh, you'd better believe I can. If you don't mind, I'll stay like this for the rest of the night. It's so cozy inside you. I might relax and read a book."

Her mouth plummets open—and then she barks with laughter. One moment, she can predict to the consonant what he'll say. The next, most decidedly not.

This is insane, leaving behind proof of their residence, but Malice's indifference has as much to do with reason as it does with carelessness. What are the odds that anyone will turn up during Stellar Worship? What are the chances that somebody will visit the Archives, much less the Chamber's restricted section?

Malice lugs her from the area, migrates across walkways, and hikes stairs, emerging into the Archives' main foyer. Their nudity, plus the fact that he's lodged inside her, causes Wonder's chortles to double.

Her forehead drops onto his shoulder, her joints loosening, her body shaking with scandalized humor. This journey is ridiculous, comical, and rather sweet. She cannot believe they're doing this, nor can she fathom what's happened over the past few hours.

In between chuckles, the trip causes her to jostle against him, the friction inducing groans from Malice, whimpers from Wonder. They make it as far as a velvet couch amidst written retellings of dreams. They bounce onto the cushions, Wonder throwing her head back and tittering as he devours her neck. She scrapes through his curls, arching her back and shivering under his mouth until exhaustion forces them to slump. That's when Malice withdraws from her, the intimate place that he'd filled suddenly empty.

She divests herself of the torn nightgown, letting it fall to the floor. Together, they twist, entangling their limbs like vines. She burrows her face into his throat, and his lips mash into the crown of her head, all of which inspires another sentimental gulp.

Safety. That's what this feels like.

Something phenomenal has happened tonight. Many infinite somethings.

She dreads where this will lead in the morning. But for now, she sinks into the cushions, her toes pressing against his.

His breath stirs her hair as he mumbles, "Your mind is a kaleidoscope, spinning and tossing prisms all over this world. You can pull a dozen unanswerable questions from a single moment. You dance with dragonflies and dote on your friends, because you're loyal and find happiness through others. Your eyes change tint depending on what book you're reading. You're the smartest person I've ever met."

Wonder exhales. It seems that he's been measuring her more than she had thought. From the onset, just as she'd been compiling details about him, he'd been doing the same about her.

"What do you want more than anything?" he asks. "Don't hold back, or I'll know."

"To forgive myself." There's no response as they let the answer simply exist. And then she whispers, "You?"

"To know myself."

"And what are you most afraid of?"

Malice's smooth chest rises and falls. "Same thing."

Wonder nods. "Yes."

The very same thing.

⁓

Her eyelids beat like wings. The space around her is a watercolor of imagery without borders, rippling at first and then finally solidifying into furniture.

Wonder pats the couch, skimming the pads of plump velvet. Then her eyelids flip open. Naked and on her back, she gapes at the ceiling and experiences a flutter of panic.

Had it been a dream?

The soreness between her legs testifies that it hadn't been, prompting Wonder to cup her mouth. There's additional evidence in the form of a thicker limb against hers, extending from the opposite side of the sofa. The other leg pitches like a roof, its masculine foot flattened on the cushion.

Wonder balances on her elbows and scans the bookcases,

midday yawning through the windows. She notes her longbow and quiver propped against a bookshelf.

When had Malice collected the weapons?

He lounges across from her, his back resting on the couch's arm. Absently, he sketches her toes while an open book rests in his free palm, his head tipped toward the pages. It's a mouthwatering sight, that bare torso and those tousled waves. He narrates aloud, uttering in low tones to the assembly of juvenile dragonflies flitting around him.

Reading. He's reading to them as if they understand.

Wonder mashes her lips together, stifling a grin as she gets another flashback of him play-chasing three dogs across a prairie hill, then rubbing the flank of his horse and feeding it an apple.

She cranes her neck toward the title.

Not in time, because his fiendish grin swings toward her, and he whispers to his guests, "Fina-fucking-lly. She's awake, mates."

Without another greeting, he continues reading. *"History says that a star once wandered in the sky, searching for its devious, wayward match. At last when they met within the galaxy, their collision woke up a shit ton of drowsy, hungover constellations, and then—"*

"That is not what the book says."

"Details, details."

"Let me guess. The genesis of destiny and deities?"

"I like to remind myself how it all started. Now let *me* guess." He licks his thumb and turns the pages. "Your favorite part is page one thousand and one?"

Wonder laughs as he dramatically clears his voice. *"Some attribute the dawn of the Fates to a meteor shower. When it smashed into the dormant stars, they shook from their eternal slumber, blinking in surprise and breaking open like rifts in the darkness. Their radiance spilled into the galaxy, splashing through the universe, brighter than any planet.*

"And it was their unparalleled light that gave them agency. And it was their agency that gave them authority. So marked the beginning of an era—the stars evolving with the capacity for thought and intention. They began to wonder, was this planned? And so began the concept of destiny..."

Wonder curls onto her side like a snail and listens to the rest. It would be eons before deities came into being, a solution forged once the stars began to anticipate a turning of the celestial tides: the impending rise of humanity.

Because she's read this text dozens of times, her mind changes course and resurrects last night. She and Malice had performed a ravishing act, disturbing one another's bodies to the point that it strikes her dumb. Already, her limbs hum as she pictures his hips in between her thighs.

Is this healthy? Is this common?

She should meditate, but she cannot. And as a goddess, moreover as promiscuous Envy's classmate, she should know the answers. Wonder has been privy to plenty of graphic stories aside from her own limited experience. But hearing about orgasms versus actually recovering from a mind-bending one is another matter.

She clenches in too many private areas to count. Malice would be delighted with himself, but he wouldn't have gotten there if it hadn't been for her. She started that first kiss by instructing him, and he had shut up quickly, collapsing into her like mush.

Huff. Is she keeping tally of who'd dominated whom? This

isn't another rivalry.

It's blissful. It's stressful.

This morning? It's intimately simple, maybe a tad bashful since they keep glancing at one another and looking away. Maybe they need this breather.

Done reading, Malice twists, his muscles rippling as he plucks a chronicle from a stack on the floor. Wonder appraises the selection. Knowing him, he'd gathered this stash from the Chamber's forbidden level, each candidate a perceptive choice. He had been considerate of her research methodologies, as well as his own.

Though each option appeals to Wonder, she selects a circular book and sprawls nude. Hours pass, lethargic and unrefined. At some point, the platinum dragonflies scatter, hardly entertained by silence.

Malice's eyes scan the chronicle while Wonder folds and unfolds a particular page, mindful of the book's spine. Limited by the vellum binding, she tests whether some variation of origami might alter the content and yield a mystery. Then she tries holding the book to the window from endless angles, in case clandestine words are embedded in the paper.

Her wrist gets a cramp, and without looking away from his book, Malice massages the offensive spot for her. Lowering the tome, Wonder peeks over the rim and studies him. Like his facial features, he has retained other traits from his past, such as his inability to read aloud for long without his vocal cords giving out; a common god would not suffer such an ailment, much less any other ailment, for that matter. Deities are not born with impairments, nor are they susceptible.

Then there's Andrew, who still limps despite his immortality. He might not be a deity, but he and Malice live as the products of two worlds.

"Isn't it sucky when vellum-bound books play tricks on you?" Malice remarks, aware that he's being watched.

"I know the signs," Wonder says. "I've tried exposing the page to light, a gust of breath, and even this." She indicates the fold lines from her origami disaster. "But there's nothing."

"Then move on."

"The stardust ink changes tint halfway down the page."

"That doesn't guarantee shit. It could be a fluke."

"Ink doesn't change like that unless there's a chink in the paper, which could indicate a secret."

"Or it could be a common trickle of light. It could be nothing."

A trickle of light. That brings to mind the glowing trail that she has witnessed twice in her existence, in two other libraries: in Malice's past life and in the Celestial City.

"What are you reading, smarty-pants?" Wonder asks.

"An oral history of fucking," Malice answers.

Aghast—and intrigued—she leaps forward and snatches his book, pouring over diagrams of genitalia, in addition to erotic positions that would baffle a contortionist. "Where in the Chamber did you find this? Amongst the texts on primitive celestial psychology?"

Malice retrieves the title from her, his gullet producing a grating buzzer sound, as though she has lost a point. "It wasn't with the 'head case' books. Tsk, tsk."

Wonder narrows her eyes. "Astral social behaviors."

"Warmer."

"Eternal anatomy and physiology."

"Very warm. Impressively warm."

"Mythic anthropology."

"Hot. Hades hot."

Wonder bubbles with mirth. She would ask how Malice knows what "hot" is, but then she remembers that he does know. He used to know very well.

For a second, she had almost forgotten this.

Nevertheless, on some intrinsic level, he still comprehends the sensation of warmth. She makes a mental note to inquire about temperature later. To know what heat is to Malice? That intelligence would be a delicacy.

Actually, she doesn't wait. "What does it feel like?"

Malice's visage rises, angling toward her. Uh-oh. He cannot be serious!

Again?

He chucks the book over his shoulder, the hardback landing with a wallop. "Why read or talk about heat when you can demonstrate it?"

Wonder chortles as he crawls across the sofa and tackles her. Her arms and legs welcome him, relishing the weight of his body atop hers. His tongue licks the seam of her mouth, then sweeps inside, flicking against hers until she's disorientated.

The vellum book also hits the floor. Yet that's when Malice pulls away, so soon after they'd begun. Far too soon for Wonder's liking.

Hovering over her, he stares down, his face the epitome of wicked intent. He's happy, as if a weight has been lifted.

He's also aroused, his hungry pupils eclipsing the gray as he scoops her backside in his hands. "Soooooo, recap?"

Wonder cannot keep her hands off him, her touch wandering over skin and bone. After everything they've done, her friends would be appalled, offended. But her heart is another matter, rioting inside her chest because she loves what they did, and she dreads what they did.

She hesitates. "We should—"

"No, we shouldn't," he growls.

"Everything I confessed last night, everything you learned…the past…the present…and we have the legends to figure out…a mission to accomplish."

"Christ, Wildflower. You can't even wait until I have coffee?"

They've been up for a while, and there's no coffee in the Peaks.

All the same, Wonder backpedals. "No nightmares?"

He swirls a lock of her marigold hair around his pinky. "None."

"How do you feel? Did anything I said ring a bell? Any clear memories?"

That isn't what she would call pacing herself. It topples out because now that he knows who he was, maybe he'll recollect more.

Deliberately, slowly, Malice unwinds the yellow strand from around his digit. He lifts himself higher above her, his knees punching craters into the velvet. And then he cocks his head, which isn't good.

His voice slices like a blade. "Are you hoping to cure me or resurrect him?"

At the tip of that blade is resentment. And the truth is, she cannot answer him.

Malice sees as much. His jaw ticks as he disentangles himself from her.

Wonder jolts upright and seizes his arm. It takes effort, but she wrings him around to face her, then clasps his disgruntled face. "Are you hoping to punish or redefine me?"

Her parry has the desired effect. Malice's nostrils flare, then shrink back to normal. "I'd call that a draw."

"What are we doing?" she inquires as his forehead lands against hers.

Malice traces her lips with his. "We're making a deal."

19

But with Malice, words are never about what they appear to be about. And with Wonder, thoughts are never stagnant, nor are interpretations.

So it's not a deal. It's a declaration.

It's a benediction. It's elemental—as penetrating as wind and rain and hail, as intense as firelight, as deep as water. It has come out of nowhere, without warning, yet it's been brewing for ages, taking centuries to manifest.

It's give and give, take and take. That's how they've always worked, without a medium, digressing from one extreme to the next.

They resume their previous positions on the couch, her legs extending from one end, his from the other, entwining in the center. Wonder stretches naked while Malice's pants drape low over his hips. He rubs her calf when she shivers for no reason, then he retrieves the decadent book and reads aloud again, having regained his voice. And she pokes his side with her toe, and she listens.

Soon enough, they switch roles as his voice strains once more, which is an awfully cute sound…awfully mortal.

After finishing the chapter, he gets comfortable addressing his former life, and she gets comfortable recounting incidents from her upbringing, plucking them randomly from memory. Their recollections work in tandem, supporting one another like crossbeams.

When he shares a secret, she shares one back, from the grand to the simple. When she expresses a favorite or least favorite—color, book, drink, flower—he reciprocates. When Malice accepts a confession from Wonder, she accepts a confession from him.

And when he tosses the book for a second time, she spreads her arms.

And when he hunches over her with a groan, she arches with a sigh.

And while sucking in each other's breaths, they whisper, "Yes."

The *yes*ing continues.

During this interlude, Wonder is agog. At one point, she eases away to stare at his swollen mouth and hooded eyes. She and this demon god had been insatiable for half the previous evening. They cannot possibly have more to express physically, at least not until tonight.

Truly, they need to work. They need to calm down.

She grabs his jaw and yanks him back to her.

They don't make love, but they do try everything short of it, until they wear themselves out.

It goes like this as the days bleed into one another. They've been here for two weeks, a blink of time, the halfway point before Stellar Worship ends. Thus, their window of opportunity is shrinking, leaving only a fortnight's width of space.

They make the most of it in dutiful and reckless ways, a fusion of rationale and utter stupidity—sober and drunk on this deal, this declaration, this whatever-it-is.

Keeping their distance is inconceivable, as much as keeping their clothes on. That barricade is down, a pile of rubble in its wake.

In the mornings, they rummage through the repository, searching for fossils of information. In the evenings, they cavort nude through the Archives, racing to see who can get to a designated section first. They fashion a scavenger hunt, assigning one another the most obscure titles and then darting in opposite directions.

Usually, these competitions segue. Malice dismisses his quest and prowls in search of Wonder, and she outsmarts him, knowing the optimal places to hide or mislead him. But somehow, somewhere in this haven, it always culminates with them finding each other. These games end with Malice hoisting her in his arms and splaying her across a table, her legs clenched around his waist, or with Wonder shoving him into a chair and straddling him.

That's not all. They like to stun one another.

One afternoon, she's studious and diligent at a table when someone's head nudges her knees apart beneath the furnishing. Wonder tenses in shock—and then she squeezes the chronicle she'd been researching, as Malice sidles under her pine-colored gown and slips between her thighs. His curls tickle her skin, and his curious tongue flicks into a valley of sensation, and Wonder is gone. Automatically, her legs hook over his shoulders and droop across his back, and she grips the chronicle, its contents spread open to the ceiling—just like her.

Wonder's spine curls, her head flinging back, her mouth uncontrollable. The chair creaks, and it's too loud in this hall, but nowhere near as loud as she.

By the time Malice is done with her, she's wheezing, and his gleaming eyes surface from under the table.

She plots revenge, sneaking up on him later, in very much the same manner, her knees burrowing into the floor's plush runner. Malice is scanning a journal, but the page-turning ceases once she grabs ahold of his jean buttons. He drops the book, the hardback hitting wood with a boom. She hears a speechless gulp, which grates into something feral the instant her lips find purchase. He tastes immoral, and it's as though she feels what he's feeling, understands the high-pitched groans. Amazed, delirious, she encourages him with each lap of her tongue, each mouthful of pressure around him.

The intoxication prevails in multiple areas of the Hollow Chamber, plus a few in the Archives. Yet they rarely feel sated. There's too much to learn and discover with their bodies.

It's a novel form of tutelage. His filthy vocabulary enhances their antics, but it never veers into lewd territory. Rather, it's enticing, naughty how Malice recites what he plans on doing to do to her. It's attractive how easily she silences him by taking his lips, splitting him wide and coiling her tongue with his. She'd never imagined herself capable of this, never perceived joining with someone like this, wild and wandering through the halls, exposed to danger and hidden from it.

They shouldn't be doing this.

They shouldn't be doing anything else.

Their escapades lead to snippets of affection. Malice takes her hand and laces their fingers as they walk down a stairwell. Wonder brushes her palm across the small of his back as she passes him. These random strokes of intimacy, touches and kisses and lovemaking, slip between the cracks of their mission.

However, their bouts of intimacy don't override their dedication. If anything, these dalliances enhance productivity.

When he can't find a book, she procures it for him.

When she can't remember a fact, he reminds her.

When one of them locates a potential detail that might explain why Malice was reincarnated—how exactly had it happened? why did the stars allow it to happen?—they inform the other.

Unmistakably, the Fate Court hadn't known about Malice's past life. Otherwise, they would have banished him earlier, for that reason alone. To their kind, humans are inferior. Not to Wonder, Malice, or her friends, but to many others. Even if Malice is no longer mortal, his rulers would have seen his existence an insult, an accident of birth. Unless the stars commanded the Court otherwise, they would have tossed Malice from the Peaks without a second thought.

Malice and Wonder alternate between finding answers for him and answers for her. When they each have a theory about fate and free will, about deities and humans, about life and death, they compare notes. Historical accounts of their culture, analyses of combat, the strengths and weakness of immortality and mortality, their union with the stars, and maps of the Peaks.

Most of it, they already know and seek to review, in case they've missed a sliver of information during their upbringing. And some of it reveals hidden gems, such as techniques for targeting, the essence of compromise, and the choreography of negotiation.

But there's a loophole missing, a key ingredient they've yet to sniff out.

Their days are comprised of gasps and quarrels and debates and chuckles. Wonder meditates, Malice breaks something in a fit of frustration. She drifts off, he calculates. She chides, he gets sarcastic. She puts him in his place, he makes her guffaw.

They hike into the Chamber's abyss. They resurface, scouring the Archives. They come up for air, practicing archery in the forest or making each other climax against a tree.

And always, always, always they have something to say to each other.

～

She whines while rigged against the balustrade overlooking the acquisitions quarter, her backside rolling into Malice's groin.

He bites the bell of her earlobe. "Like that?" he inquires, oxygen puffing from his lips and sliding across her nape.

To emphasize, he slants his movements at such an incline that Wonder goes breathless. "Like that," she verifies, her thighs inching farther apart to accommodate each entry and withdrawal.

From behind, he brackets Wonder in, his arms flanking hers while grinding. His knuckles flex at either side of her hands, both of their grips choking the railing. The tempo of their bodies agonizes her, a prolonged exploration when it's usually a passionate rush, as though they'll run out of arousal or lose hold of each other any second—as though such rhapsody will never occur again. Their hips revolve into figure eights, pacing themselves and taking the conscious approach, searching one another like enigmas, gathering knowledge with every thrust.

Him, filling her. Her, surrounding him.

Planting her right heel on the balustrade's lower rung enables him to vary the penetration, striking delicate areas that make her chant, her voice shivering across the repository. His torso rubs her spine, and her head lolls against his collarbones, her breasts pushing upward.

He murmurs, "Look at you, so happy. Can I make you happier? Hmm?"

In spite of the confident words, Malice is on tenterhooks for the answer. He likes being instructed, likes questing inside her, pulling these sounds from her.

She likes doing the same to him, so she beats her hips backward, inciting a raspy moan. His forehead lands against her neck in supplication, that tenor jostling from his tongue and sinking into her head. He hunches over, wrestling to keep his grip on the rail while pitching his hips forward, matching the leisurely glide of her own form.

Immortality fortifies them. Case in point, they've been at this escapade for an industrious thirty minutes, and they're going strong enough that Wonder prepares herself for another hour or two of this madness.

"Please," he begs into her flesh. "Please tell me."

"Yes," she says. "Yes, like that."

That spurs him on, and he cups her breasts. And they keep doing *that*, and *that*, and *that*.

Soon, they'll need to eat and drink—and calm the Fates down. Not yet, though. Their cries convulse as a breeze slips through the hall, buffeting curtains and lanterns.

Public displays are common within casual settings of the Peaks, but not within formal institutions. Malice and Wonder would be flayed, degraded, judged. They would be deemed degenerates, misfits.

They would be called flawed. They would be likened to humans, with their imperfections and double standards…and hearts.

Fine by Wonder. She's not giving up this version of her soul.

But she does vow to cleanse the balustrade with a cloth later. She'll make Malice help her, as she's done in every nook and cranny they've corrupted.

Outside the glass panes, constellations glitter, celebrating the day's end. It had been a productive one in the arts and recreation section until Malice had given her that look. Or maybe Wonder had been the culprit, when she appraised his figure as he'd combed through his hair, the action pulling his shirt taut across the bluff of his chest. Maybe it had been when he'd caught her admiring him like that.

"That wandering gaze," he'd complimented, tossing aside his choice of reading material.

And this is the result.

In between mewls, Wonder voices a wish. "At some point… we need…to do this…in a bed."

Malice lifts his head, a smile curling through his voice. "Now where's—"

"—the fun in that?" she finishes.

On a grunt of feigned outrage, he changes his mind. Wonder yips as he pulls out of her, encircles her middle, and hauls her against his torso. He proceeds to carry her back to the dormitory like this, her legs flopping, her laughter ringing through the corridors while Malice's gifted tenor hums an impish tune in her ears.

In her room, they plummet onto the mattress in a fit of hysterics. Wonder lands atop Malice, her limbs astride his waist, their stomachs pumping. Her tresses spill all over his damp skin, and their hands clasp on either side of Malice's head.

Wonder drinks him in. She counts the ways in which this demon has become dear to her, like when he produces books on topics that she muses about, or when he spoils her with blackberries in the mornings, as they've taken to sharing her bed.

He hasn't had a nightmare since. And she sleeps through the night.

In defiance of their nature, they rest every evening, sleeping bare and fastened together. Once, she'd awakened to his mouth on her breast. Another dawn, he'd awakened to her mounting his abdomen. So much teasing and temptation in this room.

However, those specific events hadn't led to consummation. They have exerted themselves in numerous corners, except in their chambers.

Until now.

Celestials trickle into the dorm and sprinkle the linens. Wonder inhales the perfume of the wisteria headband cinched in her hair, the only item that she's wearing.

"I'm addicted to you," he says, grabbing her face and plying her with restless kisses at her temple. "Your mind." The inside of her bicep. "Your nerve." The pulp of her scars. "Your resilience."

Wonder pecks his lips. "Your daring. Your candor. Your humor." Then she inches backward to gaze at him. "I wish you could see where I lived here. My home across the glen, over the tranquil pools. My favorite meditation spot, where my Guide taught me the art of breath. I wish that I could see where you lived here, too. All the places that matter to you."

"Really?" Malice asks. "You mean that?"

Of course. Why wouldn't she?

On a branch outside the window, the likeness of a mortal nightingale chirps a melody.

Malice's ashen eyes jump all over Wonder, not like cinders but rather embers—desperate and erratic in their movements. He hunts for a sign from her countenance, some type of verification.

Those irises glint, making a decision. Slinking out from under her, Malice vacates the room and returns with the saddlebag dangling off his shoulder. Wonder sits upright, curling her legs sideways as he dumps the bag onto the blanket. Sitting on the mattress's ledge, he pushes the carrier toward her.

Wonder glances at him, dubious.

He nuzzles her jaw, his voice muffled. "You'll just read them behind my back."

Her pulse races. With regard to the stolen letter, she hasn't returned it yet, and neither has he asked for it.

The same can be said about her corsage.

Malice watches her with a flat expression. It's void of vitriol or protectiveness, yet he teeters on the brink of a conclusion.

Her lungs expand and release. With shaky fingers, she flips open the bag and withdraws the sepia-stained envelopes. She starts at the beginning, on the day she first haunted him. Fishing out the worn paper, she unfolds it, the sound slicing through the room.

Malice winces. He scoots closer, their shoulders touching.

Wonder's teeth ache, and her chest aches, and so much aches. But this reaction is fair, and she wants to oblige, because she wants to hear herself recite the words that she'd once written. She'd never gotten the chance to speak them aloud.

Thinking on it, eagerness skips through her. But for some reason, Malice's face falls when he notices.

"Dearest Wayward Star...," she begins. *"I've been wandering, wandering this universe, searching for a destiny that I might call my own."*

"At last, I suspect that I may have found it," Malice says from memory, as if he hadn't asked her to narrate at all. *"I suspect that I may have found it in you."*

She blushes at the letter's presumption. As the words tremor into the room, she tumbles into the past. Her, sitting at home and composing this note, her desires leaking onto the page. It was her and not her, writing to a boy who was there and not there.

The composition is puerile, or perhaps naive is a better assessment. But it's alive and unapologetic, each sentence surging into the next. The emotions have no veneer, no artifice, so intensely do they exist.

Yet it's not precisely how Wonder recalls having felt. It's slightly lackluster compared with the cyclone of responses that she has since experienced around him.

She lowers the letter and also recites from memory. "*You don't know me, nor do I know you, but I hope that may change.*"

"*Let this be a wish fulfilled rather than lost,*" Malice adds, then takes the missive from her and sets it on the nightstand. "*I could not bear it otherwise.*"

"*I fear that I've spoken too quickly,*" Wonder says to him. "*Please continue, so that I might introduce myself. I'm an invisible dweller, thus you cannot see me as I can see you.*"

"*Yet the sight of your life has brought me to heights.*" He crawls toward her, and she reclines beneath him.

"*I've been hiding, watching you*," she sighs, parting her limbs.

"*But do not be frightened,*" Malice intones, his lids heavy as he hitches her thighs around his waist and positions his length at her entrance. "*I won't harm you.*"

Wonder arches, releasing a pleasured whine as he thrusts in slowly, executing a single, patient stroke. "*I would never...,*" she moans to the ceiling. "*I would never do that.*"

"*Believe me,*" he insists, their hips riding a sensual tempo.

"*I'm not shy. But invisibility is tedious, and so I'm reduced to this letter...,*" she gasps as his length searches her, sliding to the hilt. "*...and hope to express my admiration, to tell you that I'm here, that I* *share your love of books and reading, even if I'm different, even if I'm a divine being and you're a human, even if we come from separate realms."* She clings to his backside, spurring him faster. *"You're magnificent, and I adore the sound of your voice, and I should like to know your favorite book, and I should like to tell you mine. I long to know about your world. I yearn to be your friend."*

"Your ally," he pants.

"Your confidante," she keens.

"Your star."

"Your fate."

Breathless, she kisses his lips. Tireless, he kisses back.

They groan, on the verge of bursting when he hits a narrow spot, which accelerates their rhythm and pushes the depths of entry.

"Answer this letter," he rasps, plunging inside her, *"and I shall tell you more, and you shall know more, and we shall fuse worlds."*

"Me and you."

"A wandering star."

"And a wayward star," she cries out.

He stills. Suspended above her, his body locks in place as if lashed by a whip.

The sudden break jolts Wonder out of her delirium. "Malice?" she heaves, gazing up at him. "Malice, what is it?"

His head plummets into the crook of her neck, then instantly lurches upward. He clutches her face, partly glaring, partly pleading as the embers dash from his eyes, leaving behind a surface cleansed of debris. Those aren't the pupils of the demon she has come to know.

They're the eyes of someone else.

She freezes as clarity stares back. Malice gazes at Wonder as if seeing her for the first time, or from a different angle, in a different slope of starlight.

"I remember," he says.

20

Once the words are spoken, they cannot be unspoken. And while Malice should be relieved to utter them, and while Wonder should be relieved to hear them, they gawk at one another in turmoil.

I remember.

Attached to his announcement is a ligament of knowledge. They listen to the lingering margins of each syllable, a reverberation of sound permeating the room to its bones.

To say nothing of Wonder's internal distress. The sight of his resurrected memory clearing the film in his eyes and peeling a layer from his visage should be a triumph. And it can be, depending on which recollections surface.

Or it can be a travesty, if other visions recover themselves.

Malice is still inside her.

Both he and that other boy are inside her. Truly, he's one and the same, no longer separated by lost pictures or abstract sensations.

Wonder's limbs remain knotted around his naked hips, which have long ceased their quest for that zenith of pleasure. Her palms grip his rear, her breasts tip against his torso, and their breathing labors. Strapped to each other like this, they shiver.

Wonder finds a stitch of time in which to muse. Did their nudity summon this turn of events? Is it felicitous? Is it by chance?

"How?" she queries, for once not trusting herself to unravel the answer.

Malice's flummoxed expression lingers on her. His fingernails puncture the linens on either side of her head, the tips stabbing the mattress and creating slits. As if some innate power exists within him, or as if he just knows, he says, "Because I heard you."

Is that it? Unlike his mortal self, he can hear her. So did this happen because he'd finally listened to her narrating aloud the scandals and desires of their past? Had that done it?

Had her verbal recitation triggered this resurrection, the writing and her voice working in tandem to activate the change? Had that combination become a magical force, thereby reaching its hand into the wellspring of Malice's mind and yanking out the deepest roots?

It must be. After all, it's the missing link between Malice and Wonder. It's the one effort she'd made and failed at back then: communication.

Her, speaking the words. Him, absorbing them.

She ventures to touch the side of his face. On reflex, he twitches from the contact, so she withdraws, her hands landing carefully on his waist.

"What do you remember?" she asks.

"Everything," he seethes, shoving out the response, getting the task over with.

The atrocity of his tone isn't directed at her, but at the facts. He remembers everything, all that had happened during her attempt to woo him.

And all that befell him afterward.

It's now or never.

Malice shifts, a reminder that they're still intimately joined. He withdraws but remains above Wonder, entwined with her as he lightly drags a thumbnail over her cheekbone.

She swallows, making that digit lurch. "What happened to you?"

Inconceivable images flash before him, his inhalations growing shallow until she grasps his waist hard, stifling the onslaught. Despite the tension in his joints, his body settles against hers.

"The cell was dark," he says. "As damp as shit. And the sounds were a clusterfuck. I heard people shrieking, so many people shrieking." Air skates through his teeth. "And then I was shrieking, too, because they were tying me down, harnessing me in, buckling me in. And I couldn't get out of it. I wept…I-I fought back, scratching them and wishing I had claws to destroy them."

"Them, who?"

"The doctors." He twitches in thought. "No, not them…the guards. Their faces blurred together, and they bound me to a bed. For days, people prodded me until I stopped kicking. They asked questions, so many questions, and some of them tried to be nice, tried to listen, but they didn't understand, and that made me furious. I kept telling them you were real, you were so real, if they would just look at your letters. But of course, they couldn't, because I'd hidden the envelopes in a book."

And that book had been thrown by the townsfolk into the flaming pile, right before the asylum wagon had come to collect him.

His voice cracks. "For an instant, I'd forgotten that."

A sob tumbles out of Wonder. "Malice."

"Let me finish. I need to finish." His eyes glaze over. "Not all of the doctors were detached, and not all of the guards were brutal. Some cared, some brought me blankets and spoke kindly. But still, there were a handful who glowered at what they couldn't understand or control. The longer I was there, the more I feared. The more I feared, the more I raged. The more I raged, the more I hurt them back. The more I did, the more often they called me a devil possessed. The more they said it, the more I believed them.

"They pumped shit—I don't know what—down my throat. For weeks, for months. And all I kept thinking was, what happened to the library? What happened to my dogs and my horse? What happened to you? Where were you? Where did you go? I bellowed for them to take off the bindings. I wanted to go home; that's what I kept saying. 'There's a library goddess, and I'm a library god, and I want to go home.'"

"I-I'm sorry," Wonder weeps, the words scrawny and unstable to her ears. "I'm so sorry."

"What the hell for?"

"I wrote those letters. I terrified you. I contaminated your mind."

"Fucking listen to me! Your letters didn't send me away!" He snatches her face. "Mine did."

Wonder tenses in his arms. His...what?

Malice nods. "Think, my wandering Wildflower. I was a master researcher even back then. I wasn't afraid or disgusted by you...all right, maybe at first. But after? No. And why? Because I figured out who you were. Even then, I liked figuring out things."

"That's impossible. There's no text remotely close to uncovering the true mythology."

"I'm reincarnated," he states blandly. "Love had a quick stint as a human, Andrew's fallen down the rabbit hole of immortality,

Anger rebooted his power, Merry survived a failed love-goddess birth, and Sorrow's willingly humping Envy. Talk to me about impossible.

"Knowledge was my crack from the beginning. I got the gist, read between your lines, and had an obsession with the stars. I cobbled out enough to know you were harmless, somehow part of the sky yet real on earth. So it wasn't your letters that did me in, Wildflower. It was the letter I wrote back to you."

He'd written to her?

All this time, she'd thought him repulsed and petrified by her antics. And while he may have been at the onset, his feelings had changed. In the end, he had wanted to know her, to contact her in return.

Malice holds her gaze. *"Dear Wandering Star, it's a pleasure to make your acquaintance. That is, it wasn't a pleasure at first, but I get now that you're real, and I'm not spooked anymore. Though I gotta say, it's a damn shame that I can't see you, the way you can see me. I'm figuring I can't hear you, either, since I've been hollering but getting nothing back. Doesn't seem fair. But stories always begin when things aren't fair, don't they?*

"So what's it like to be an invisible divine being? I mean, besides tedious like you said. Can you feel the wind? Can you hold a book in your hands?

"You mentioned loving to read, right? If you've been watching me for a while, I guess that means you've been tailing me in the library. I'll tell you my favorite book, if you tell me yours first.

"Oh, and if you fill me in on this other realm you're from. I'd sure like to know more. I like knowing things.

"I'll take one guess that you're immortal. I wouldn't mind trying that out, living forever. Maybe the stars will align, and it'll happen one day.

"Or maybe you can help me out with that.

"But anyhow, yeah. I'll be your friend.

"Just please write back,

Your Wayward Star."

Wonder balls a hand and presses it to her mouth, quelling the shock as Malice recalls placing that one and only missive in his saddlebag, hoping she would find it.

Instead, troublemaking children got their hands on it while fixing to loot the bag for money or whiskey. One of the youths had been the mayor's son. That, and the spectacle Malice had already been making of himself in town ever since Wonder entered his world, had motivated the townsfolk into action.

His became the only surviving letter. It had been handed over as proof of his insanity, while everything else had burned in that pile.

Wonder focuses on her weapons, then the wash of hydrangea light in the room, the curl of nature outside the window, the scent of pomegranates and old books. Her fist abandons her mouth, her heart crashing into her breastbone. "Even if my letters didn't send you there, even if I didn't send you to the asylum—I still kept you there. Because I tried to save you."

Malice pauses, his golden hair blazing around his face.

Wonder explains. After her indiscretion and subsequent torture, the Court had her under close surveillance. However, she did find a sliver of time to steal away, intent on freeing Malice. The nearest asylum was in a city, some twenty miles outside of town. She'd concluded that Malice must have been taken there.

But her heroics only made things worse. Locating his cell, she had spied him through the bars. Wonder hadn't known what they'd done to Malice up until that point, but upon her arrival, she saw the pallor of his complexion, the bruises on his exposed skin, and the vacancy in his eyes as he stared at the ceiling from his cot.

The sight of a dozen buckles and straps had nearly eradicated her.

Malice had been locked up for three years by then.

Wonder had wrenched open the door and tore his bindings as easily as paper. Malice hadn't flinched despite her invisibility, nor the fact that his restraints had yielded presumably out of nowhere.

She knelt, whispering entreaties and endearments. His pupils had flickered, seeming to sense her very presence, and his hand had lifted as though to touch what he couldn't see.

An alarm had sounded. Wonder got back to work liberating him. But within seconds, the wardens appeared in time for them to witness the bindings come off at lightning speed and ostensibly by magic—or satanism.

Wonder acted impulsively, not giving herself the advantage of planning. She hadn't devised a means to actually harness Malice, her fingers slipping through him like water.

Rashness had made her sloppy, causing her downfall. Inanimate objects are fair game to deities; humans themselves are not. Therefore, the room had lacked tangible gadgets that she could have used as a weapon, and she hadn't been able to throttle the wardens or medics with her bare hands. She just kept passing through them.

Her archery had been temporarily confiscated by the Court, so she couldn't shoot the mortals with a dose of awe to distract them. Before she could race into the hall and seize a makeshift alternative—a pipe, a shard of glass—the orderlies had swarmed Malice.

That's when he'd snapped out of his trance and begun to

struggle. It should have taken Wonder milliseconds to locate a suitable method of defense in the corridor. However, desperation had impaired her faculties, deterring her from acting swiftly enough.

So when that prairie librarian who'd stolen her heart attempted to do his captors bodily harm, they retaliated. The pocketknife would have inconvenienced a goddess. To a frail mortal, it did much worse.

Malice's blood coated the handle, the blade lodged in his stomach as he slumped in the casket of the guards' arms. If Wonder had been in possession of her archery, she'd have dropped it. Instead, she'd plummeted to her knees and watched him die.

The guards had left him, dashing from the room to avoid getting caught by their superiors. Shrieking, Wonder had pawed at his face to no avail. She'd tried, but she hadn't been able to cradle Malice, hadn't been able to comfort him in death.

Well...he hadn't been called Malice. Not back then.

Emptying herself of the story, Wonder sinks into the bed while Malice studies her. "I remember a warm breeze and sparkling light when it happened," he reflects. "Like a guardian had knelt in front of me. It was the same feeling I'd gotten every time I reread your letters."

He recalls the slice through his belly, the slick coat of crimson, and a metallic scent. "Despite all that crap, I felt you there with me," he says, stroking Wonder's tears. "I felt you there, not wanting to let go."

Indeed, she had burdened him instead of letting him rest in peace. As she'd suspected before, the tether had been strung too tightly. He'd died inexplicably linked with a deity and without closure.

Yet he doesn't look furious that she had interfered, nor accusatory that she'd sealed his fate. Matter of fact, the forks and trenches of Malice's face scarcely attribute his demise to her. "Tell me who I was," he prompts.

Wonder's so tired that it comes out effortlessly. "You were a tenant of the prairies in the nineteenth century, living on the brink of war. You ran a library surrounded by pomegranate trees, with a telescope aiming out of the window. You were kind to patrons, and you lived below level, in a room with a rocking chair. You liked reading about birth and death and legends, and I remember thinking, 'Oh, how his eyes glow for myths.' You had three hounds and one horse, whom you adored. You carried a saddlebag over the right shoulder, but you wrote with the left hand. You had a gravelly singing voice."

She kisses the inside of his wrist. "And your name was Quill."

"Quill," he repeats. "Yeah, that's it. Except you never told me your own name."

"I tried to save you."

"I tried to answer you."

"But we're here now. We're right here."

"Are we?" he draws out. "And who am I? Right here?"

Wonder considers him. "You're..."

She may know the details of who he used to be, but she'd never gotten to know that boy. Not like she knows him today.

So this request should be simple to fulfill. Nonetheless, Wonder stammers, and Malice's gaze darkens. "Tongue-tied, eh? How about a simpler question: Who do you want? Me or him?"

Again, her mouth goes numb.

And with a slit of his eyes, Malice shears her silence down to the cartilage. "That's what I thought."

Just like that, his weight is gone, and his scent is gone, and his voice is gone. But it's only when the door slams shut that Wonder realizes he'd gotten dressed and evicted himself from the room, his absence producing a mishmash of emotions that hardly correspond. Her womb cramps, and her fingers bend at the knuckles, forming steep inclines. Lastly, a suffocating density fumes in her cheeks.

Perhaps it's akin to heat, a visceral and vicarious blend of him and her. It's Wonder's sorrow, Malice's envy, and their anger.

Every moment she delays is one step closer to losing him all over again.

Him, who? Malice or Quill? The past or the present?

No matter which, he cares about her response more than she can fathom.

Wonder pulls herself together and leaps from the mattress, making a beeline for her wardrobe, where she stabs her arms through an off-the-shoulder blouse and harem pants, then stomps into boots. She collects her archery for no other reason than to catch his attention. If need be, she'll shoot a quartz arrow past him, if it means he'll give her a second to process—a second to be heard.

By the way, it would mollify Wonder to target him for putting her through six thousand dramas since his reincarnation, then expecting her to worship him the way she had worshipped his predecessor. Because of what? A few carnal romps?

Her heart aches, each pump a percussion of shame and longing. Their interludes hadn't been meaningless. Not a single one.

Wonder descends from the dormitories. Along the corridors, lanterns twitch while fears and affections and resentments curdle within her, so that she's unable to reconcile his question and her reticence. She cannot perceive Malice and Quill as separate.

Then again, neither does she think of them as equals.

She had cherished yet harmed Quill.

She had hated yet bedded Malice.

Tenderness and angst and worry clash. Malice has only just remembered the horrors of his past. He's in no condition to handle any reply from her, not when the mystery of his existence has barely sunk in.

What can she say to him? What does she need in return?

Forgiveness? An apology? Both? Neither?

Is he all right?

Strobes of ethereal green embellish the Hollow Chamber, and the abyss suspends its breath. Engraved titles cut through book spines, the script flashing. Wonder follows the pungent sulphur of discontent, the ginger palate of a grudge, which barricades the slick, underlying texture of hurt.

Are these sensations pouring from her or him?

Wonder increases her pace, striding into the restricted section. She heads for the spot where they had collided, where everything had changed between them, where he'd stood naked after a rainstorm, and she'd exposed their secrets, and they'd taken each other to unprecedented heights.

She spots Malice prowling down that aisle. Bracketed by enigmas and loopholes, he paces ahead without a destination.

"Malice!" she barks—or cries. It's a little of each.

He stops, the plates of his shoulders fixing in place as if her words have nailed him that way. He's partially clothed, his feet unshod, his chest uncovered, and his jeans slumping across his waist.

Like her, Malice carries his weapons, the hickory bow and quiver knocking against his spine. Had he collected the archery from his room for the same purpose? To target or hinder her? To catch her attention, as if he's never done so before?

All she knows is that it works on both accounts. Because at the same instant he whips around, his arrow nocked and fixed on her, she's got him in her line of sight, the quartz arrowhead aimed at his heart.

They stare at one another, her grip shaking as visibly as his.

According to the legend, if he remembers, that means he's restored his heart. Doesn't it?

So why does it feel like everything and nothing has changed?

They lower their weapons. When Wonder opens her mouth, Malice's wiry lips compress. Harnessing his archery, he turns and continues striding away, retreating under the starlit lanterns.

"Malice, no," Wonder says, her voice cracking as she pitches aside her bow. "No, wait, please. Please, don't go!"

He stills, his muscles strained. She sweeps up to him, startled to find his eyes clenched shut. Surging to her toes, she flings her arms around him, because if she cannot reply to his inquiry, she can at least show him that the answer matters just as much to her.

Malice flinches when her mouth crushes against his—and then he grabs her, his palms seizing the back of her skull as their lips fuse. On a hoarse groan, his tongue strokes against hers, and Wonder keens into his mouth. She pulls on the gilded waves as he kisses madly into her, and she into him.

But before she can fully ride the kiss, basking in the tart curl of his tongue, Malice veers back. He swallows, hissing against her mouth, "Now stand aside, Wildflower. Before I say something I'll regret."

"Why not say my name instead?" she asks. "Have you ever done so?"

Once, he had. Once, in the midst of ecstasy, right in this spot. Not before, nor since. Yet he isn't the only one who'd like to be known for who he is.

Malice's ashen irises slice through her with grief. His talons graze her cheeks, then he lets her go, his touch falling away.

Wonder is about to protest when she notes the direction of his gaze over her shoulder. She spins, her head cocking sideways. She hasn't revisited this particular aisle since they first surrendered to their mutual craving, not since the first time they made love.

Books had fallen from the shelves during their union. True to his word, Malice had tidied the area afterward, piling the evidence back into the cases. However, he must have restocked them out of order, because one book is glowing—not that texts ever do that to indicate disarray or disorganization.

Their impulsive night together had dislodged something. Evidently, they'd overlooked this during the aftermath.

Wonder and Malice swap a look, then step closer to the volume, its spine flickering like a rosemary-hued constellation. She presses her fingers to the book, which causes another title to flare green.

Frowning, Malice repeats the action with the next book, invoking yet another volume to blaze from across the aisle. Wonder's pulse escalates as she recollects previous incidents when she'd experienced such spectacles, in which winks of light had animated a path of books.

Twice, in human libraries. Never here.

She had deemed those events optical illusions. And maybe they had been.

But not this one.

"It's a trail," she says.

They rush from text to text. Throughout the restricted section, each spine ignites a partner the moment either Malice or

Wonder makes contact. Although these random titles fail to make sense as a unity, the result is a route leading to...where?

At a shelf carved into the wall, they reach the final tome. Wonder grasps it, and beside her, Malice stalls.

Footsteps stampede in their direction.

Malice's gaze traces the sound, then lands on her. "It's not a trail."

No, Wonder realizes. No, it's not a trail.

It's a trap.

21

The book trail they'd left behind gleams, its luminescence splashing into the lane, marking a phosphorescent path to its occupants. It's an ethereal and silent alarm gracefully sneaking up on them. Presumably, the visual has been designed to captivate, mesmerizing viewers to the point where they forget to flee.

Can alerts really enchant? Can they dismantle one's consciousness?

Is there beauty in capture? What other traps exist in this funnel? How have they avoided this, neglected to know about this?

Who devised the first trap in history? Had it been the stars?

Are traps fated or made by one's own hand? Why—

"For Christ's sake," Malice utters under his breath. "Stop that."

The hushed words snap Wonder out of the trance. A legion of feet flies through the Chamber, the pace unanimous. In the human realm—where every natural foundation is less equipped to handle it—this would cause landmarks to convulse.

In the Peaks, the environment is far more robust, able to withstand the charge. The impending ambush reverberates, woven of starlight and comprised of figures on the prowl.

Wonder and Malice spring into action. He snatches the

volume from her hand and punches it back into the shelf. She clamps on to his wrist and yanks him down the nearest lane, which snakes deeper into the area. As they dash past colonies of vellum and sequences of plating, his fingers weave with hers, his grip practically crushing her bones. She squeezes him back, not about to let him maintain the tighter hold, much less take the lead.

His profile creases into a glower. She would laugh at the absurdity of this moment because, to say the least, their rivalry over heroism is out of proportion to the moment. Not to mention, it's plain idiotic. Squabbling over who gets to save whom has no place while they're being chased.

Certainly, the pursuers will identify Wonder. Foolishly, she'd left her archery behind.

Malice's hickory weapons smash against his back. And if he's forced to exercise the longbow, their pursuers will know with whom she's been in cahoots.

Wonder measures the kinetics of those on their tail, each attacker possessing unique qualities. Butterfly agility, and ramming soles, and offended exhalations, and lethal amusement, and unflappable focus.

Her pulse goes wild, battering her flesh. She knows who's after them.

So does Malice, because his talons puncture Wonder's flesh and urge her faster, or maybe he's reacting to her acceleration. She can no longer differentiate.

Malice swears under his breath. "Fuck me."

"Must you?" Wonder scolds, because they'll hear the unmistakable abrasion of his tenor. Besides, profanities accomplish nothing except squandering oxygen.

However, he's Malice. That's why he responds to her lecture

with an infuriated cackle, the sound busting open its shackles and lurching from his throat. In rebuttal, Wonder thumps his narrow hip with her substantial one.

Which way to go?

As they surge ahead, they lean toward different passages, tugging on one another and trading I'm-right-you're-wrong glances. *This way* and *No, this way* and *Trust me* and *I know what I'm talking about* and *Listen, for once*.

At an impasse, they align themselves.

What's the meaning of this? Since when does the restricted section bear traps?

This area had been conceived by the original Fate Court, to stash secrets they didn't want the populace to discover. The stars may have permitted it, seeing as the Court had acted chiefly out of protection, yet the stars also planted their own mysteries here. The disparity is the latter mysteries were meant to be found, so it makes no sense for the constellations to designate a trap.

But it does make sense for the Court to do so, especially after Wonder and Malice's previous exploits. The rulers must have designed this snare as an additional precaution, and only those with access must know how to avoid the trap.

Thusly, the books had triggered a mystical siren.

Assessing the sector's geography, Malice and Wonder consult one another. Pumping their limbs, they pivot toward a cul-de-sac, then plummet into a hip-slide across the ground, hunkering as they propel toward the bottom shelf of a built-in bookcase that swallows them whole. They pass through and shoot along a horizontal channel. All too quickly, they skate to a halt, the artery depositing them within an inlaid room.

Leaping upright, they barrel past cases of illuminated manuscripts, pigments of clover and iris shining through the shadows.

It's a secret gallery with pages of prohibitive and notorious texts, whose lower corners are stamped with emblems of authenticity.

Want to know the most successful way to slander a ruler unfairly? Interested in tormenting mortals? Eager to find out how to cheat at target practice?

One may gauge the answers here.

The slip and slide of unwelcomed guests is enough to get Wonder and Malice hurdling across the divide. So much for outwitting assailants.

A door leading back to the upper levels stands at the opposite end of the gallery. As they jet toward it, Wonder's ears perk at the zing of an arrow. Without looking back, she pirouettes from its path, dodging the projectile, which shatters a casement, glass exploding into diamonds.

Her heels skitter. Every inch of the Archives is sacred; to defile the structure or its contents borders on sacrilege. How dare they!

The azurite arrowhead that vanishes on impact confirms the enemies' identities. The twang of a bowstring has Malice cursing. He whips around and lets a hickory arrow fly, his eyes laced with wrath.

His arrow spears through the room, intercepting the azurite's renewed path. Unfortunately, he's too caught up blocking one flight to notice the other zooming toward him.

Wonder pounds into Malice, her weight thudding into his, her joints smacking the ground and her teeth clattering. They crash, their limbs tangling, a manuscript display shielding them from the firing squad.

Malice scrambles to a sitting position, his back propped against the case's pedestal while Wonder squats in front of him. Air saws through her lungs as she assesses the situation, glancing from her would-be-soul-mate to her would-be captors.

A man with hawk features and long braids stalks beside an ebony-skinned beauty in a butterfly gossamer gown. An androgynous female in frothy lace approaches, hemmed in by another goddess with purple locks similar to Sorrow's hair, and a cloaked male with slanted brows.

All five members of the Fate Court enter the gallery, brandishing arrows of azurite, pearl, crystal, purple agate, and lava rock. Weapons that, unlike those of lower deities, can kill.

The Court must have suspected this might happen, that Malice or Wonder would defy logic—as well as sanity—and procure the means to return here. Either that, or the rulers had increased security out of reflex. Whatever the reason, they had accomplished this cleverly, installing the type of snare that waits until offenders have their defenses down.

There are two ways out of here. Back through the channel or via the door, the latter of which Wonder and Malice had been counting on. If they destroy the encasements to startle the Court, they can make it. They just have to—

"Not gonna work," Malice pants, his breath sliding across her jaw.

Wonder's gaze skates from the ruthless spectacle to the private one before her. His chest beats to the rhythm of his exhalations, another sign that he's not as robust as a common immortal. The human ghost lurking within him makes itself plain in moments like these. Although Wonder's panting as well, her demon is doubly fatigued.

He grits his teeth. "When it comes to distractions, one is better than two, especially with these mates. Problem is, they'll expect us to head for the door."

She shakes her head. "What, then?"

"Backtrack. It'll stunt their aim, since they won't be expecting it."

"Their reflexes will atone for that."

He smirks. "Not if someone is a decoy."

Her eyes widen. "Malice—"

"Do you know how long I've wanted you?" And now he looks venomous, his face scrunching like a wad of cloth. "From the first moment I saw you in the Celestial City, my body screamed and bawled. I didn't know what the hell was happening to me. Ever since then, every time you've walked into a room, I've wanted to shout at you and kiss you, make you bleed and make you come. I wanted to punish you and hold you, like I was two different people."

The soft contours of his confession clash with the battery acid taste of it. "You're still on my shit list for substituting me for him. I'm still on your shit list for being a son of a bitch. If we weren't being hunted, I'd still walk away from you, just like you should walk away from me. But it looks like only one of us'll be doing any leaving."

"Malice, no—"

"I hate these," he says, taking her hand and pressing his lips to the starburst scars. "Hate them so much." He glances sideways at her. "Now fuck off."

"No!" she screams, leaping forward to steal his bow, take his place, rob him of free will and, hence, seal his fate for the better this time.

Malice may be a former human, and he may carry some of that residual vulnerability with him, but in that second, he's faster than she. Barreling from behind the encasement, he targets and shoots, causing glass shards to detonate in the Court's path and blind them.

This is the part where she's supposed to run, flee to safety. This is the part where she's supposed to honor his choice, so it's not in vain. This is the part where she loses him again.

Wonder thrusts herself into the maelstrom of glass and arrows, dismissing the door and pitching toward the channel threshold from which they'd come.

But the thing is, she has never been good at listening to Malice. Or to anyone.

Once she passes the rulers, Wonder doubles back. She skids behind the gossamer goddess and rams a booted foot into the female's tailbone.

On the goddess's way down, Wonder swipes the pearl longbow, its arrow still nocked. The weapon is heavier than Wonder's, forcing her arms to slip momentarily.

The room becomes a prism, a spinning kaleidoscope as glass splinters. It's a wave crashing ashore, translucent fragments sparkling like droplets. The effect flings particles of gem colors across the space and illuminates bursting scraps of clover and iris paper.

Attack or be attacked. Sacrifice texts or be sacrificed.

The Court has made their decision. Though debatable, these taboo relics are supposedly less valuable than all others in the main Archives. Sovereigns of history have stashed them away, but they can be rewritten if need be.

Their people cannot be replaced as easily. The Court believes Wonder and Malice are here for a traitorous purpose: treason against their superiors, anarchy against their kind. To these rulers, the two of them are dangerous.

Still, the literary carnage is a mournful visual that sets Wonder's ivories. Then, beyond the minefield of glass, there are flickers of Malice's hair, his tattoo, his bow. Relying on adrenaline, he deflects a series of strikes.

Saturated in glittering crusts of blue, an azurite arrow flies toward her demon god. Wonder growls and aims. The bow is foreign, forcing her to adjust, making her feel like an amateur.

She has no time to collect herself fully. Her shot breaks through the azurite projectile, severing its length in half. The weapon's hawk-nosed owner flounders and then rounds on her, gobsmacked until he realizes that it's Wonder instead of his comrade.

They gawk.

She dives for the fallen goddess's pearl quiver, surges upright on a bent knee, and lets loose as he targets her. His strike aims to disembowel Wonder, but she gains her feet and arches into a backflip, propelling herself over a casement that's blessedly still intact—for a second.

Then more glass shrieks, slicing the air.

Wonder lands and ducks an arrow of lava rock, swinging her upper body beneath its trajectory. She whisks to the right and blocks an agate arrow, then a crystal one. Suddenly, she's the primary target of every ruler present. Throwing herself to the ground, she somersaults and comes up, her elbow cocked and ramming into the jugular of the pale female in lace. The goddess goes down, bowling into the cloaked god as Wonder yelps, glass biting into her side.

Where's Malice?

An agate arrow explodes behind her, blocked by a hickory weapon, sparing Wonder from taking the hit. Wherever that misfit is, he's got her in his periphery. He sees her, even if she has lost sight of him.

Wonder retrieves another arrow but grunts as the dark female in butterfly gossamer hauls her backward, pitching Wonder to the ground. Pages crush beneath her weight, and the quiver shudders from the impact. The goddess's mouth peels back to reveal incensed canines.

Wonder rolls over, averting the ruler's fist, which punches through a mound of parchment instead. Flicking her limbs forward, Wonder catapults to her feet and blocks another blow from the goddess, who manages to brawl without shredding her gown. It's surreal, the confounding vision of this female charging her, when she'd once encouraged Wonder to have faith in her abilities. All of these sovereigns and illustrious servants of the stars had once supported her.

Perhaps that wound appears on Wonder's face, because the goddess pauses, twitching in hesitation as they face off. There's a millisecond of regret that kin have become enemies. And for that millisecond, Wonder muses how it has come to this.

Why must it continue this way? None of them want to fight, and these dearest rulers have never known war. Theirs has been a peaceful mythology for eons, however prepared they are for the opposite.

The goddess blinks, then swerves her bow toward Wonder.

What have these figures taught her? What have her Guide and peers taught her?

To endure.

A second twang resounds from behind, a weapon forged of hickory. Waiting until the pearl arrow is about to spear her, Wonder rotates sideways, letting it bolt past her nose and crack into flashing pieces as Malice's hickory arrow guts through it.

Pirouetting, the back of Wonder's arm jabs into the goddess's profile, causing the female to drop the longbow. Wonder catches it and aims toward the cloaked god homing in on Malice.

"I wouldn't," a feminine voice cautions.

Staying the weapon, Wonder's eyes dart toward the androgynous ruler in frosted lace. Stationed behind Malice, she nocks her crystal arrow at the nape of his neck, a placid expression on her face. Meanwhile the gossamer goddess festers, and the hawkish god with braids aims at Wonder, alongside the female whose hair compliments the purple agate of her archery.

Malice's hickory weapon lies on the floor, amidst the gallery's casualties. His chin locks, and his annoyed eyes lift heavenward, but whether he's vexed at Wonder or the figure imprisoning him remains to be seen. Red slashes cross his chest and arms and throat and cheeks, red leaking from the strips in his skin.

Wonder tenses, her side stinging. Under her ripped blouse, she feels her waist oozing from the casement piece that had pierced her.

Her grip trembles. Is the pale goddess bluffing?

"Cease, Goddess of Wonder," the sovereign commands. "I'm quite serious."

No, she's not. The compartments of Malice's brain are too important to do away with, at least until they have sifted through him for answers.

Wonder slits her gaze, fixing the pearl longbow on the cloaked god. How stubborn of her, yet the corner of Malice's mouth creeps upward.

Nevertheless, Wonder should know better. The goddess imprisoning him cants her head, issuing a silent but crucial reminder: They might not kill Malice, now that they have him contained.

But that doesn't mean they won't do damage.

Without looking away, the female uses the flat of her arrowhead to smack a blade of glass protruding from Malice's chest.

The blade sinks halfway into his flesh, below his heart. On a guttural howl, he seizes up, his furious eyes rolling back.

Somehow, he remains standing, shaking with effort.

Pandemonium crawls up Wonder's throat, but she mashes her lips to stifle the protest. Her arms plummet as she lowers the bow, chucking it to the floor. The gossamer ruler swipes it off the ground and inspects the nicks within its pearl limb.

At which point, the goddess's palm crashes against the side of Wonder's face.

22

In her two centuries, Wonder has been the recipient of precisely three slaps.

Once by Hope, because Wonder had been daydreaming while strolling straight into the archeress's line of fire during another class's training session. Needless to say, Wonder's stream of consciousness had directed her into an opal arrow's path, disrupting Hope's aim and causing the female to accidentally shoot her own Guide, inadvertently blasting the mentor off his feet and knocking the wind from him.

Another time, it had been Wonder's Guide, right after Wonder had reappeared from one of her unsanctioned excursions to the mortal realm. Harmony had been waiting as Wonder floated on a cloud into her home. To say the mentor's expression toggled between livid and terrified is an understatement. The elder who'd educated and inspired Wonder since her inception had known what her charge had been up to, though not by intuition. No, it was because Wonder had left a trail of evidence in her house: drafts of her letters to the human named Quill.

Startled, Wonder had opened her mouth to explain. The crack of Harmony's palm had silenced her, and the shimmer of reprimanding guilt in the mentor's eyes afterward had kept Wonder silent. "Did you think I wouldn't recognize your moves?" the female had said, then pointed a solitary finger. "Never again."

Wonder had nodded while holding her cheek, knowing that she wouldn't keep her word.

And here in this gallery of desecrated manuscripts, she experiences her third shockwave. It's one thing to be struck by a fellow archeress or a Guide. It's another thing entirely to be the recipient of a ruler's hand.

Former episodes had slung Wonder's head sideways. But this smack knocks the skeleton out of alignment, rattling her ribcage and jostling her mandible. It turns her face into an exploding star, baubles of light popping before her eyes, her body twisting under the force.

She staggers but catches her balance, righting herself as soon as the spots ebb from her vision. In the background, a protest tears through the space, the voice stripped through a cheese grater and peeling apart at the ends.

Wonder focuses on Malice. With his face scrunched in pain from the glass wedged in his chest, he spews nonsensical venom, his eyes murderous toward the gossamer goddess who'd hit Wonder.

The female pays him no heed, only waits for Wonder to compose herself. It's not a long intermission, because Wonder understands why the ruler had lashed out. It's a grave offense to handle the weapon of another deity, graver still when it's a Court member's bow, punishable in too many vile ways to tally.

Wonder may as well have spit on the goddess.

That's why Wonder inclines her head, acknowledging the error. She may disagree with these rulers, may abhor them for defacing the Chamber and extending violence toward those whom she cares about, but she hasn't lost her respect for their weapons.

The ebony beauty pauses, her profile tilting as she regards Wonder. A spark of intrigue rips through the female's copper irises, unlike anything Wonder has previously seen from her. Following this, a subtle film of regret coats the ruler's eyes.

Wonder knows the signs of inquiry, the moment when unforeseen questions simmer to the surface of one's cranium, be they random or formerly dormant. This female is known to sing lullabies to immortal youths who cannot sleep. Despite her vicious reaction to Wonder, she has an empathetic side. And prior to her ascension, she'd held a different title.

She used to be the Guide of Wonder. That is, until she advanced to the role of ruler, with Harmony taking the goddess's place. Such is the hierarchical evolution of the Peaks.

Once upon a time, this grand figure had been a mentor. Before that, she'd been an archeress like Wonder.

She'd *been* Wonder.

Glass clinks, nudged by the purple-haired goddess. Glass crackles, collapsing beneath the weight of the braided god's foot. Glass tumbles, bumped by the cloaked god, as well as the frosted female pointing her crystal arrow at Malice.

In the semidark, paper flutters as though pushed by a breeze, painted images and texts twinkling, alive despite having been shredded.

Surrounded by the mess, everyone waits, debating how to proceed. For some reason, Wonder suspects they hadn't anticipated capturing their quarry. They had expected a cunning sleight of hand and an escape.

Have Wonder and Malice frazzled them that much? Is that remotely possible of any archer?

"What a pity," the purple goddess says, observing the scene.

"It's damned reprehensible, is what it is," the cloaked god

grumbles, his brows taking a steep turn for the worse. "If you two weren't enemies, we would congratulate your proficiency."

"Never in our existence have we...," the braided god cuts himself off, his hawk nostrils flaring. "It seems our dispute with you and your peers last year hasn't dwindled. We should have known it wouldn't end in that mortal library, however much we'd hoped you would see reason."

"On that score...," the frosted goddess hints, pricking Malice's flesh with the tip of her arrowhead, to which he squints, "finally, he's learned to be silent. However did you manage that, Wonder?"

"You credit me too soon," Wonder predicts.

Because three, two, one: "Go to hell, mate," Malice grits out to the ruler, right on cue.

The goddess moves to impale him, render him mute.

But she halts when the gossamer goddess stares at Wonder. "Are you in love?"

The question thrusts from the ruler and spears through the room, staying everyone's tongues. The word is a force unto itself, ill-fitting in the sovereign's mouth, too large for her to bear, too massive for her companions to catch. Coming from her, it has an alien shape, a slippery texture, and a translucent body, lacking visible composition.

The braided god balks. The cloaked god scowls. The purple goddess is aghast, her eyes jumping between the gallery's occupants. The frosted goddess hikes a single brow that fails to reach her hairline, as though she's gazing through a lens, searching for an object that isn't there.

Wonder's heart lashes against her breastbone.

Is she in love? With whom?

Because it's such an inconceivable query coming from a sovereign, Wonder fails to apply it to anyone. That a Court member would ask borders on acknowledgment, a willingness to believe that such an emotion might be possible amidst their kind. Or this goddess is just toying with Wonder.

The word dangles off a hook. It waits to be plucked, to be claimed by a courageous soul.

Battered and bruised and bleeding, Wonder snatches the word and clasps it tightly. Is she in love? With him?

Him, him, him?

Which *him*?

It's the same thing Malice had asked her. *Me or him?*

She feels the brushfire of his gaze. Her eyes cut over to the demon god, the scholarly satyr, the maddened outcast who has become her friend and lover.

Malice, who thinks her intelligence is beautiful. Malice, who inspires her to darkness as well as lightness. Malice, who treats each of her thoughts like books, individual and infinite. Malice, who doesn't hold back.

Malice, who makes her scream. Malice, who makes her laugh.

His eyes flare like furnaces, as though he doesn't want her to answer. Wonder's gaze trickles over his features, slipping to the rapid pulse in his throat. She'd give anything to see that pulse beat for eternity.

Her attention slides back to his wiry lips withholding breath—and belief. He thinks he knows what she'll say, how she'll answer, because how can she reply any other way? Who would love a black soul like his?

Are you in love?

Meeting his eyes, Wonder whispers, "I..."

"Too flustered to answer? That's fine," the goddess says.

"Because I wasn't asking you."

Wonder falters, goggling at the sovereign. Then whom had this female been addressing?

Oh. That's whom.

The goddess maintains a steady gaze on Wonder, but her query shifts toward the only other exile in the room. Malice's lips split, parting in confusion. He screws up his face as if he doesn't understand.

But it makes sense. Whatever the deities believe about love, they would deem Wonder susceptible. She's part of the elite class that had included the first love goddess in history; as time has gone by, her peers have been revealing a penchant for sentimentally. The Fates either assume that it's due to Love's influence or because each member of her class—Anger, Envy, Sorrow, and Wonder—is a fundamental component of the emotion.

But Malice isn't part of Love's class. Between him and Wonder, he's the one less likely to emit that breed of affection.

Wonder watches him reach the same conclusion, a snarl curling from his mouth. Those gray orbs waver, wrestling with the notion.

"Sorry. I didn't get the question," he lies, and for his trouble, the crystal arrow presses into him. The weapon's about to break skin, urging him to show obedience, so he offers a scant crank of the head, a brief nod.

"Pardon me?" the gossamer goddess says. "I did not hear that."

At last, he speaks, averting his gaze from Wonder. "Yes," he bites out.

Wonder's mouth falls open, landing somewhere on the floor.

Malice loves her.

Certainly, the hate has evaporated, replaced by camaraderie, respect, and desire. But this?

Joy and fear take root in her body. She should be insulted that he can only confess his feelings at the point of an arrow—but this is Malice. He would rather saw off his tongue in slow motion, or donate his cerebral cortex to research, than to expose a vulnerability.

Or is there another reason? Wonder has a hunch, which causes a twinge in her chest, in her hands, in her everything.

From the rulers, repulsion and denial knot together. Only the goddess draped in butterfly gossamer watches the scene steadily. She stays that way, lost in thought while the Court members shove Wonder and Malice against the only two podiums left standing.

Clearing the debris, the rulers push them to the floor and bind them to the fixtures. They use tethers instead of star-dusted manacles, but no matter. These harnesses are just as impervious to a deity's strength.

The gossamer goddess suggests a conference, and the others agree. They leave their prisoners mounted to the encasements, surrounded by dunes of glass and manuscripts.

Wonder takes a guess. The Fate Court will allow them to live, then pry their psyches for information, particularly any secrets unearthed from the Chamber, plus whatever revolutionary plans Wonder's class has devised.

The rulers will prepare themselves for Malice's mind games, his smarmy half-truths, and his pornographic lexicon. They'll appeal to Wonder's nomadic frame of mind and take advantage of Malice's feelings for her.

Whether or not the Court believes in love, that's immaterial. The point is that Malice does. Against his will, he's handed the Fates a bargaining chip, a means to keep him in line. If it comes down to it, they shall torture Wonder in order to pull answers from him.

They might do the same to him, make him watch while they surround her. Regardless if these affections are recognizable to the Court, Wonder and Malice's actions imply caring and connection. In this room, they had tried to protect one another, and not out of duty.

After the Court's departure, the quiet grows spectacularly loud. Across from her, Malice glares at a spot over her shoulder. His chest injury oozes, but at least the frosted goddess had ripped out the glass shortly before vacating the gallery.

All the same, Malice winces, blood spritzing from the wound. He drags his tongue over his teeth, stained with dots of crimson as though he's been gorging on pomegranates.

From opposite ends, their feet brush in the middle, her boot soles against his bare soles. Wonder fixes on the sight while the most vital organ inside her goes wild. If she doesn't spit it out, she'll second-guess herself.

She asks, "Did you mean it?"

"I told you to fuck off and take off," he mutters. "Didn't I?"

"Haven't you heard, dearest? I'm not good at following orders."

"If you had, you'd be long gone."

"If I had, you'd be long dead."

"I've already been dead once. I can handle it."

What he can't handle are the bindings. Malice struggles against them, his breathing rampant because they'd restrained his arms. He might panic soon, revolt against the universe, and hurt himself even more.

Gently, she rubs her foot against his until he sags, his skull thunking the podium, his inhalations evening out. After a few moments, she's certain he won't have a meltdown. Though to keep it that way, he shall need a distraction.

Wonder whispers, "Malice, look at me."

He does, narrowing his gaze. "What?"

"Did. You. Mean. It?"

"You'll have to be more specific. I mean lots of things, and I mean lots of nothings, too. I'm chock-full of meanings. I like meanings."

She grins fondly, sadly, because she knows what he's doing. "You meant it."

"Meant what? What do you care?"

"I do ca—"

"Oh, I'm sure you do."

His drawl points right to the past—to Quill, not to him. Is his assumption correct? If the goddess had requested an answer from Wonder instead of Malice, what would she have said? Yes or no?

Loving Quill isn't the same as craving him.

Craving Malice isn't the same as loving him.

So which is it? Which incarnation?

Pain creases Malice's visage, either from her refrain or his injury. His neck bobs as he swerves away, giving her his profile. "I guess sharing you with my ghost is okay."

"Malice—"

"I mean, far be it from me to deny a voluptuous goddess her ménage à trois. It'll be like doing the nasty with twins," he improvises. "Or we can split our schedules. You can have me on the weekends, and then you can live it up with my deceased doppelgänger during the week. Of course, touching him will be a problem."

"Malice—"

"Fucking him, an even bigger problem, in addition to the reek. I've heard corpses smell funky, and who knows what condition my former cock is in. But huh, maybe we'll find a legend to rectify that, something that resurrects dead bodies and repairs erectile decay. Or we can try a seance."

"Malice—"

"Unless you want to go really crazy and add former lovers to the mix. I'm sure Merry won't mind if Anger answers your siren call. What's a little reverse harem between friends?"

"Malice!"

"Wonder?"

She gasps at shape of her name on his lips. Despite his artless eyes and sarcastic tone, he's only acknowledged her thusly once before. How she longs to hear that sound again, and again, and again.

And just like that, Wonder knows. She's been misinterpreting her heart for two centuries, all because she comes from a world that doesn't know better, has grown up with people who have never identified with it, much less valued it. Even while witnessing the bonds between her friends, Wonder hadn't learned.

She understands now. There had been affection, admiration, and atonement on her part.

But it hadn't been the grandest of emotions, after all. Not back then.

She smiles at Malice. "I love you."

All signs of mockery drop from Malice's face. His features crumble, and his brows knit.

Is the declaration too much for him?

"I'm sorry," she rushes out. "I thought...in my room, you asked me...I thought you wanted to know."

Because he makes no reply, she begins to twist her head away, until his voice reaches her. "Say it again," he murmurs.

The plea is faint but haggard. Wonder's pulse stutters as she traces the contours of him, all the shadows and highlights. All of him.

She says it again. "I love you, Malice."

"Are you sure?"

"Are you?"

Doubt lingers in his tenor. Yet he glances down, and his lips twitch, the hint of a dimple imprinting in his cheek.

Oh, to hell with captivity. In defiance of their bindings, this bleak fate, and a spike of foreboding, she likes this moment so very much. Matter of fact, it's probably her favorite of all time.

When did he first feel the stirrings? And how? And why?

"You have some explaining to do," Wonder says, elation tangling with apprehension.

Malice peeks at her from beneath his curls. "First, we have some escaping to do."

"Need I remind you, we're weaponless and shackled."

"Hmm, there is that. But guess what? Rumor has it that I got my memory back. You know what that means? It means I can do this." He gives a serpentine tug, and the bindings come loose, his arms flopping freely at his sides.

The tethers are not broken, since that's impossible for any deity. Rather, they're untangled.

Standing and swiping his hands, Malice says, "Apparently, I've got experience with restraints, and asylums, and escape attempts. Call me an industrious patient when I wasn't otherwise sedated." He wiggles his taloned fingers. "Also, these help. They're good for undoing knots."

Wonder gawks. An astounded—and appalled—chuckle

stumbles out of her. Of course! The straps used on them may be immune to a deity's strength, but not to a deity's logic. In another life, Malice had learned how to maneuver out of such restraints; not that it had rescued him in the end, but perhaps it shall today.

He kneels before her. "Say pretty please."

"Untie me," she commands. "Now."

"So much for kink."

Wonder laughs as he releases her, and together, they rise. The ascent happens so swiftly that they bump into one another. Grabbing each other's forearms and steadying themselves, they fall into a staring contest. Wonder cranes her head up, and he angles his head down, and it's a different kind of gaze, stripped to the core, with no layers left. She explores his features, as he embarks on his own quest. Tattered and bleeding, they abandon rivalry. Moreover, they dispense with animosity, guilt, and blame.

Eyes stinging, she gives a quick chuckle, which he matches.

This is what it feels like to look at someone you love.

This is what it feels like to be loved back.

They never uncovered a loophole or secret to aid their campaign for free will, but at least they found this. And perhaps that, in and of itself, is a strength. Like Love and Andrew, and Anger and Merry, this bond might supply Wonder and Malice with power.

If they're fortunate, and if the stars support them, and if they work together, they might live through this. They might survive long enough to research more. And from that, they'll put up an even greater fight.

Searching her expression, Malice plucks a few tiny shards of glass from her locks. In return, Wonder untucks her blouse and tears the length of its hem, then winds it around his chest, feeling his gaze caress her bent head.

His body flinches when it hurts, so Wonder's careful. And when she glances at him, she recognizes the enraptured expression, having been trained to recognize it.

"No one's ever done that," he says.

She swallows the bulb in her throat. "Now someone has."

The experience is mutual for her. With any hope, they'll flee. And then they'll have plenty of future chances to dress each other's wounds, introducing each other to tenderness, learning what it's like to be cared for and how to return the gesture.

Malice seizes her around the waist. Hauling her against him, he crushes her lips with his, kissing her hastily before letting go. Thinking twice, he surges in for another kiss, but Wonder leans back. As much as she wants to taste him thoroughly, they'll have to wait.

Later. Soon.

The way they'd entered this gallery will dump them into the Court's lap. Possibly, others have joined the rulers, keepers and archers having scattered throughout the Archives when the hunt began.

She collects spears of glass, snatches his hand, and barrels through second exit, across the door's threshold. It leads into a tunnel of lanterns, which they sprint across, then race up a stairwell. Ahead, another door waits at the landing, so they bolt—then slam into the partition, staggering from the impact.

Malice jostles the knob, using brute force to try and pop it from the socket. When that fails, he slams a hand against the edifice. "What the fuck?"

"They must have taken precautions," Wonder surmises.

Above, rosemary pours from the lanterns. Malice slumps against the corridor wall and bows his head, grasping his curls and yanking them from the roots—not exactly one of his default responses during moments of severe calculation. He must be at a loss.

Wonder paces the narrow landing. *Think, think, think.*

She pauses, snapping her fingers. "What if we—"

"—back up," Malice says, tackling her to the opposite wall as the door groans.

They brace themselves as the exit unhinges. Malice whips around, blocking Wonder. In protest, she skitters to his side, refusing to be shielded, brandishing the glass shards that she'd collected.

The door glides open, a spectrum of light flooding the interior. From the beyond the veil, ivory archery and a curtain of sage hair emerges, followed by an older face that gazes upon Wonder with a mixture of reproach, exasperation—and pride.

It's the same countenance from decades of training and meditating. The last time Wonder had seen it, she'd been sneaking through the forest to the Archives, and she had attacked this female, not recognizing the opponent until she had rendered the female unconscious.

Her Guide holds up a set of quartz archery. "You forgot this."

The glass spear hits the ground, the makeshift weapon slipping from Wonder's hand. She leaps forward and throws her arms around the elder, wrapping her in a suffocating hug. "Harmony!"

"Wonder," the mentor says, embracing her and then pulling back to offer Wonder the longbow and quiver. "I found it before the Court did."

"How did you know..."

Mild amusement shines in Harmony's features as she speaks familiar words. "Did you think I wouldn't recognize your moves?"

During the forest battle, Wonder and Harmony had wavered, vaguely registering the singularities of one another's fighting tactics. After Wonder had stuffed that bloom down the Harmony's mouth, the Guide should have awakened thinking she'd hallucinated.

Wonder should have known better, not to underestimate her mentor. At some point, the elder must have concluded who had attacked her.

"I wanted to convince myself otherwise," the Guide says in a rush. "But the alert verified what I'd suspected after you knocked me out. A breach in the Chamber during Stellar Worship could only be you." She glances at Malice. "I don't believe we've ever crossed paths, yet you look familiar. Best to save explanations for later, though. It's a marvel they didn't hear you attempting to break down the door."

Wonder straps on her weapons. "We didn't have—"

"—this?" Harmony holds up a capsule of seed-and-blossom fluid.

Quickly, the mentor explains that the Court had called upon her, trusting that she'd be able to scout for Wonder more successfully than anyone, should Wonder turn out to be the trespasser. Harmony had found the liquid while scouring the dorms, pretending to hunt along with everyone else.

Rapidly and briefly, Wonder divulges that Malice had created the Asterra Flora, enabling them to breach the Archives.

"Perceptive concoction," the elder compliments, handing the blend to Malice.

"I do like perception." He swings his gaze to Wonder. "Your Guide's the one you laid out in the forest?"

"Did I forget to mention that?" Wonder inquires.

Footfalls rush across the level, punctuated by hollers.

Indeed, the details can wait. Wonder, Malice, and Harmony spill into the stacks, two levels above the restricted section. They hustle through the aisles just as a voice yells and the first bowstring vibrates.

23

They command Wonder and her companions to halt. They roar warnings and entreaties, because enough damage has been done to sacred ground. To escalate this conflict rather than surrender further endangers the Archives.

How dutiful of them to finally remember this landmark's worth.

It's hypocritical after leaving the illuminated manuscript gallery in shambles. Nonetheless, that episode had been an isolated affair, not full-blown mutiny. Perhaps the Court does not wish to put this area at additional peril and now strives for a peaceful result, to preserve the environment as best as possible.

Wonder agrees. And she would obey if her peers weren't counting on her, if she didn't know what would happen to Malice and Harmony if caught.

She dashes past compartments full of books, foils and engravings flashing a million letters on either side. Within the labyrinthine funnel, that first bowstring vibration perks Wonder's ears. The reverberation hisses through the lanes, enhanced by footfalls charging with the speed of asteroids.

The nocked weapon seethes like a smoldering object. It's the noise of a lava rock arrow teeming with life. As Wonder hurdles over a chair, she spots the cloaked ruler in her periphery, his longbow taking aim.

She dives, evading the projectile as it skims the air. Somersaulting alongside her mentor, they surge onto their bent knees and fire, a synchronization of quartz and ivory arrows that block more blows and knock two souls off their haunches.

Agate lances across the distance, striking from the sidelines. An iron table leg swings into the arrow's path, smashing it off course from Wonder and Harmony. Malice skids in front of them, wielding the broken furniture limb like a club, spinning it in his hands and then crooking his free fingers at the enemy, beckoning them to try again. His leer teeters on the edge of sanity, baiting the legion of Court members and keepers and archers.

Wonder does a quick count, her gaze hopping from one face to the next. She recognizes the repository warden who always showed her where to find the best maps and reading nooks.

And there's Hope and Joy, whom she's known since youth, who must be in the Peaks for an intermission from servitude. That accounts for her classmates' inability to approach and recruit them as originally planned. That explains why her peers had called out to both and received no reply.

The archeresses wear tunics of starlight and leggings of moonlight, embellishments of leaves and gems woven in their hair. They brace themselves, hedging before exercising their archery.

The Court has chosen this means of defense selectively, enlisting subjects with whom Wonder has a connection, those whom it would pain her to battle against. And while the sight produces a hitch in her gut, it also pumps her veins with defiant energy.

Surging to her feet, Wonder yanks on the waistband of Malice's jeans until he twists. They keep running with Harmony, dodging relentless arrows of lava rock, agate, crystal, azurite, pearl, marble, copper, and a dozen other sources. The Chamber spasms from top to bottom, with titles beating against one another.

Ahead, the lane splits into three like the prongs of a fork. On instinct and lacking the time to choose, each of them takes a different route. Wonder races down the center aisle while damning the breach. Why hadn't they just stayed together?

Vaulting into the quarter housing books about the ethics of constellations, she steers her assailants west. Arriving at the correct passage of stacks, she jerks on a sequence of titles, the order of which causes the bookcases to rotate like doors, rearranging their positions and changing the surrounding layout.

Based on the grunts, she has caught her adversaries by surprise, hemming them in with unexpected dead ends. Although they must know this trick, they hadn't anticipated it.

Wonder pumps her limbs, flying down the new route. Assailants glide in and out of her vision, shadows brandishing weapons of longbows and crossbows and blades. Spotting their quarry, they chant orders and cry out directions.

She cannot hear over the fuss. No echoes of a grated tenor or meditative flight. No throbbing gait or graceful exodus.

Where are they? Where's Malice? Where's Harmony?

An unrecognizable archer-in-training rounds a corner, blocking Wonder's path. She darts toward him, then slides on her hip, uprooting the archer from his stance before he looses his arrow. The male topples, and so does his archery, which doesn't belong to him.

Wonder whisks to her feet and swipes the weapons just as Malice materializes. Having emerged from his route, he catches the hickory bow and quiver when Wonder tosses them his way, then he scans the arrows' turkey fletching. Had the Court given it to this unknown archer for safekeeping, or to taunt Malice until he got angry enough to make a mistake?

Humming in appreciation, Malice mashes his heel into the male's jugular. "Nice try, mate. But you messed with the wrong wildflower goddess."

"My pleasure," Wonder says.

Arrows rain from below and above. Malice grabs Wonder's hand, and they make haste...for another shelf? Why?

Stumbling in front of a cylindrical bookcase, he rearranges three titles, causing steps to jut from the furnishing and form a staircase that winds around the column. The ascent leads to the network of bridges in the funnel's center.

Later, Wonder will remind him to clarify how he discovered this. In the meantime, she experiences a sweep of gratitude and a prickle of envy. And he must see it, because he favors her with a smug grin, to which she makes a face.

"You'd better not be keeping score," she declares.

"Who? Me?" he asks, guileless, as he plants a hand on his chest, his fingers splayed. He jerks his head toward the book steps. "C'mon."

"No," she quails, resisting his grasp. "Harmony. I won't leave her!"

"And I won't fucking leave you! Move!"

Another bout of arrows forces her into action. They drive up the book steps and cannon across a bridge, the ramp leading to other stairways and levels. Moving in tune with each other, they swerve and duck and block attacks. A crystal arrow hits Malice's wound, reopening it so that he growls. An azurite one slices past Wonder's cheek, etching across her flesh. And damn the rulers' arrows, the only ones capable of piercing flesh when shot from a bow.

Wonder and Malice make it to the top level. Abreast of the exit, they notice the Fate Court standing vigil across the distance, each member posted along the circumference of the funnel railings.

Blast. They've got us surrounded.

The sovereigns draw. A circle of arrows arc in warning.

Wonder and Malice attempt to run, which prompts the sovereigns to shoot, which forces another crossfire. It had been worth a try. Stopping and positioning themselves back-to-back, they loose their own projectiles, quartz and hickory flying and blocking. Then they switch positions, bowing and aligning their spines again, continuing to hinder incoming strikes. At every short gap in conflict, they maneuver closer to the exit.

The gossamer goddess catches Wonder's eye with that ever-present gleam of intrigue. The female isn't firing as aggressively as the others, nor as swiftly.

Does she want to fail?

Wonder's frantic gaze breaks free, rummaging through the abyss speckled in green light from the overhead sphere.

Where's Harmony? Where is she?

Wonder catches a glint of ivory, the longbow poised in her mentor's grip. On aerial feet, the elder steals behind the cloaked god, cranking her arm in position to thwart the ruler—to protect Wonder.

What Harmony doesn't see is the ruler's eyes slanting downward in awareness. Wonder feels her lids bulge. No, not her!

The male spins, his longbow primed and ready. Wonder looses her arrow before the god has fully rounded on Harmony, the quartz tip vaulting into the male's tailbone. While the arrow cannot cut through him, its magnitude knocks him off balance.

His chest thrusts outward, and his spine snaps into an arc, the collision flinging his arms up and backward as he releases the arrow.

The bow swings, sending the lava rock projectile into vertical flight. It's a shooting star, darting up, up, up. Everything ceases, including the movements of all combatants, dozens of heads tilting to follow the arrow's trajectory.

If it were an archer's weapon, it mightn't be of consequence. But as a Court member's arrow, infused with greater power, it's dire.

Wonder and Malice aim their bows to strike, to derail the projectile, but it's too late. They watch, helpless as the lava rock sails into the astral sphere's heart and disappears with a flare.

Wonder and Malice grab for each other. They shove one another across the bridge and dive for the landing, smacking the ground as the Chamber shimmies—then quakes.

The world explodes in a prism of starlight and lunar light, prismatic filaments sparking from the overhead globe. The Chamber rumbles, with bookcases capsizing and secrets crashing to the ground. The ceiling cracks, causing chunks to plummet while levels buckle, splitting and roaring.

A taloned hand seizes hers just as the floor vanishes beneath them.

24

She skips on bare feet through a blooming hill of hyacinths, their sweetness permeating the air. Her fingers reach out and pluck dainty stems, harvesting blossoms until she has a posy, a compact nest of buds that she cradles in her hands. What a glorious day to be picking flowers, with the hemisphere twinkling and the dewy grass glistening.

Can mortal flowers cohabitate with immortal ones, of the earth and Peaks, of sunshine and starlight? Is that possible? Can those blooms inhale the same air, thrive beneath the same sky, take root in the same soil?

As she ponders this, the hill blurs and then solidifies anew, transforming from one realm to another. Now the cliff becomes a prairie pasture, the elevation dropping while the hyacinths mutate into lupines.

Another addition is the pomegranate tree, with globes of blushing fruit drooping from the branches, and the leaves clapping like tambourines. From somewhere in the distance, horses whinny, and hounds bark, and dragonfly wings patter against the current.

Stars prick into the firmament, shards of glass winking with mysteries, the planets swelling in the galaxy as if about to burst. Everything appears close enough to touch, but that shouldn't be feasible here. It's a mystical illusion indeed. Isn't it?

If she asks the constellations where she is, they won't answer. They've brought her to this place, but now she must figure out the rest for herself. What a generous gesture, an embrace between fate and free will, two worlds uniting.

But how? How have these realms achieved this?

Somewhere nearby, pages flap as a person thumbs through a book, the actions nimble and zealous.

Only one deplorable soul reads a text that way.

She whips around, but he's nowhere to be seen. She hollers his name, but no one answers.

She's calling out the right name, isn't she? Is she shouting for the right person? The right name? His name?

The heavens blacken, blotting out the stars. The more she yells for him, the darker it becomes—obsidian burying the murk of night. Her voice tears a rift in the plains. Lupines jostle as the ground opens and burrows into the summit, a pocket of nothing spreading beneath her. It happens so fast that she screams, unable to leap for safety.

The cavity swallows her whole, the wind lashing at her as she plummets into a bottomless pit, an underworld of shredded paper and ash. She claws at the air, failing to find purchase, to stop the fall.

Vaguely, she recalls a mortal tale reminiscent of this moment, something mythical yet unmythical. She expects a figure garbed in ebony to materialize and capture her, dragging her with him while he cackles and forces her into another universe. Some god who will feed her tart seeds and make her believe that she wants to be with him, robbing her of free will.

But no, he wouldn't do that. Not anymore.

And she wouldn't let him. Because she'd take him first.

Jagged, onyx terrain rises out of nowhere, surging toward her—or waiting for her to land. Just before she smacks into the ground, her eyes flap open.

Wonder coughs. She gapes at a torn ceiling, her arms and limbs akimbo, her body distorted upon a knoll of paper and vellum. Tilting her head produces a throbbing skull and shrieking joints. When she sucks in air, stardust slips down her throat, melting away the dryness.

Wonder contemplates the rafters. And she remembers.

The lava rock arrow. The astral sphere. The Hollow Chamber.

It had caved in. They had fallen.

"Malice," she croaks in panic.

A set of knuckles strokes her temple, then the blade of a fingernail gently outlines her cheekbone. Twisting her head, she blinks as a face shivers into view.

Those intelligent cinder eyes and deceptive golden waves. That wiry, foul mouth.

Malice stares down at her, his eyes scrambled with worry. "Shh. I'm here, Wildflower."

Wonder leaps to a sitting position, hurling her arms around him. His bare arms envelop her, holding on while she shakes. Pulling back, she inspects the gashes and bruises splotched across his body, but he's in one piece.

Wiggling her fingers and toes verifies she's also intact, albeit bloody. Not far off, quartz and hickory weapons lay scattered, cracked in parts but repairable.

That's when it hits her, dread and grief slamming into her chest. "No," she cries out, staggering to her feet.

What she sees wipes thought and speech from her soul. Her mouth parts, and her eyes mist at the sight.

Malice rises as well. Together, they gawk at the haphazard

levels and sloped walkways, at the green glaze of stardust and the debris of parchment. It's a wasteland of legends. Stashed between the outdated and prohibited, they had hidden themselves, waiting to be found.

Now there is only ruin, detritus of paper and ink. Bits of the central sphere rest in various areas, each flickering with wane lights like hearts fighting to beat. Amidst the destruction, pieces of the globe struggle to survive.

Wonder's hand shoots to her mouth, her shoulders lurching on a single sob. The Hollow Chamber is a sunken ship, a fallen city of knowledge.

It's the end.

But where is Harmony?

Where are the keepers? Where are Hope and Joy?

Wonder longs to holler, to call out for her mentor, if not by voice then via the stars. But she has no vocal cords, and she has no power. Those privileges have vanished beneath the carnage, because it's too much, so much.

Her knees buckle. She lands on the ground, pages fluttering around her. She scavenges, plucking leaflets and scraps like flowers, trying to reassemble them, to rebind them into hardbacks. Her movements increase, hectic and rushed, picking through the mess. She has to fix this, she needs to fix this, she will fix this.

Malice speaks to her, but she shakes her head. She can put everything back together. She can do this.

Squatting, he takes her hands, balling them with his own. "Look at me."

He knows this crazed feeling, and she has wielded arrows against this crazed feeling. Wonder slumps, the salvaged items tumbling from her hands. She hunches over and begins to rock back and forth, strapping her arms around her knees.

No, it cannot be. Not this place.

If she weeps, it will be true.

Malice hunkers behind her, wrapping her into himself. His forehead presses to her nape, his muscles convulsing. And together, they keep rocking.

In her peripheral vision, a rosemary-tinted dot hops across the ruins. Wonder glances up, sweeping the hair from her face. She traces the illumination, the path of which leads to a surviving book spread atop a pile, its contents displayed.

It's the same book that they'd discovered hours ago, the one that had initiated the others to ignite, to trigger the trap. It's one of the books that had gotten displaced when she and Malice made love against the shelves.

It pulses, invoking a familiar spark of sensations inside her. "Malice."

She doesn't have to say more. He follows her gaze.

Salvaging and then harnessing her weapons, she crawls toward the book, and the moment she sets her fingers on it, another glow pops out of the rubble, coming from farther away. It's the trap, still active.

Or is it something else?

Wonder stumbles to her feet. The same process repeats, with her and Malice attending to the sequence of books, hobbling over chunks of wood and iron and glass and paper. When they come to the spot that had once been the restricted section, they encounter the same final book, tattered but still bound like the others.

It gleams as if having anticipated them. And of all candidates, Wonder and Malice shouldn't have underestimated the star-granted power of these books. Yes, they had formed a trap at the hands of the Fate Court.

But that's not all.

"It *is* a trail," Wonder breathes.

She glances at Malice, who shrugs. "What the hell do we have left to lose?"

She picks up the brittle yet bright tome. The text sparkles, random passages and sentences highlighting, becoming more saturated than the rest, standing out to reveal...a legend.

Wonder scans the contents, with Malice reading over her shoulder. Their heads bank upward at the same time, reaching the same conclusion. A flicker of hope sprouts in her womb, because this is it.

"This is...," she begins.

"...the way to win," he finishes.

It's the answer they have been looking for. The solution to their expedition, the way to balance fate and free will. And the answer is so obvious, so simple that her mouth lifts into a teary grin despite the desolation.

Malice's lips crook, mirroring her smile. His eyes drift past her as the sound of rubble shifting draws his attention. Wonder stiffens, sensing the aura of disillusion just as Malice detects the aura of rage.

Horror floods his gaze. He seizes Wonder's waist and spins her around, the rotation cut off by a clean whoosh of air.

Malice jerks hard into her. His body snaps, caving like a bowstring. He stares at Wonder, his nails digging into her hips as if she's the only thing holding him upright.

Confused, Wonder searches his dazed features. One of her palms rests on his lower spine, where thick fluid leaks over her knuckles. It's a slow-drip—from the arrowhead lancing clear into his back, a shot meant for her.

Its tip protrudes from Malice's chest, right through his heart.

25

The weapon is made of lava rock, ejected from the longbow of a superior: a shot that can pierce.

Poppy red coats the arrowhead, ravines drizzling like paint down Malice's torso and puddling where Wonder's navel presses against his. From there, the fluid weeps through her blouse and pants, spreading into wide blooms.

The projectile vanishes at last, reappearing clean in its ruler's quiver. At which point, three entities drop to the ground.

The first is the lava archery, the longbow sliding from the ruler's hands, his slanted brows flattening in shock, because it isn't every day that a superior fatally wounds an inferior, be the victim an exile, or a rebel, or an archer. In fact, it's never happened during the reign of this Court.

The Hollow Chamber is a ruin, and anarchy abounds, and so the god had sought retribution. Yet his face goes slack, horrified by his own fury. It's one thing to fire in defense of oneself, of the Peaks, of their world. It's another to strike an unarmed archer in the back, a young one who's less than two-hundred years old.

The second entity to topple is the book in Wonder's grasp. Because Malice crumples, she needs both hands in order to balance him against her. As a result, the glowing volume hits the debris, a beacon spotlighting them.

It takes Wonder a second to process his lack of balance, her sloppy grip, and the blood sprayed across her clothes and face. "Malice...?"

His eyes roam hers, awash in affection, the ashen irises beginning to dull.

Terror seizes her sternum, fear splitting her mouth open. "Malice!"

The third entity to fall is him. She yelps when he resists her hold and plummets harder into her. They collapse to the floor, huddling above the wreckage.

He slumps in her lap, his head bolstered by the crook of her arm, more red dribbling from his lips. Frantic, Wonder mops blood from his chin and chest, but there's so much, too much, and it just won't stop.

Whimpering, she rips the sleeve of her blouse, her panicked movements failing to staunch the hemorrhage. "No!" she pleads through her teeth. "Malice, no!"

He just stares at her, gaging on that horrible color, his lungs congested with it.

As the seconds hammer by, footsteps approach. The conscious pace of her Guide is accompanied by the tentative gait of her rulers. Wonder snarls a warning, a string of threats that are audible to them, but not to her. Her ears are clogged, as if stuffed with cotton, so that she cannot hear herself clearly.

But she doesn't care, so long as they back the Fates off.

Taloned fingers etch her jawline, the quavering touch bringing her back to him. Malice's spastic features wince in pain, his nostrils splaying for air. He puffs through the injury, "Shit, that... hurt."

"You'll be all right, you'll be fine, I promise." She changes course and appeals to the somber faces encircling her. "Help!"

she begs. "Please, h-help h-him!"

The entreaty ends on a heaving cry, a sound that tumbles across the ruins. A shadow swims beside her, its shape expanding as Harmony kneels, still keeping a respectful distance. The female catches Wonder's desperate, terrified gaze and gently shakes her head.

Death is out of a deity's hands, no matter how supreme his or her power. Wonder sees the black truth of it on every ruler's expression, their heads bowed in a collective ceasefire.

Wonder whips her head back and forth in denial. Her mouth braces to withhold a response, a screech clawing across her tongue. No, no, no, no, no, this isn't happening. This cannot be happening!

They've only just found each other, they've only just begun to know one another. They're supposed to have time now, so much time.

Malice struggles to fish the Asterra Flora from his pocket, where he'd tucked it after her mentor gave it to him. Shoving it into Wonder's hand, he labors through the words, "I want my home…away from home…away from home."

Wonder nods rapidly, then glances at Harmony, who inclines her head. She will follow. But first, she indicates a beam of starlight filtering through the broken ceiling, coming from the Archive's main level.

Malice must travel on his own, but with his failing strength, he'll need help reaching out. Working quickly, Wonder slathers the liquid onto her and Malice's hands, then threads their fingers and holds them up to the portal.

The world spins into a disc of moons and stars, lurching them upward until the suction ceases. They jolt, still on the ground, except this floor stretches across a foyer with a model globe at its center. The scene wobbles into view, bookcases and circulation desks covered in ivy, titles wrapped in plastic, computers lining a wall, and a half-finished puzzle scattered across a communal table.

The return is seamless compared to Wonder and Malice's previous departure. The Celestial City's library encases them in the scent of mortality—coffee and furniture polish. It's nighttime, the doors locked. But it's not vacant, because a figure with mussed white hair rushes toward them, then skids to a halt.

"Holy shit," Andrew hisses. "Love!"

The goddess is beside him in a millisecond. She gapes at Wonder and Malice prostrate on the floor, their clothes bloody and shredded. Love is about to spring forth to assist them, but Wonder squawks, "Don't!"

Love's gaze shimmers with inexplicable pity and explicable shock, but she obeys. Glancing out the window, she closes her eyes. Minutes later, their class appears, brandishing weapons but lowering them once they reach the scene. There's astonishment but no room for relief.

Anger's lips part in confusion. Merry covers her mouth with her hands, her eyes pooling. Andrew grasps Love's shoulders from behind, anchoring her. Envy's aghast, the hubris wiped from his face. Sorrow's mouth turns down, because she knows this feeling better than anyone.

She knows what anguish feels like.

Wonder cannot pay them further attention. Not when Malice skims her earlobe, then extracts something from behind it. In his fingers, he holds a slit of torn paper for her inspection, a souvenir from the Hollow Chamber's collapse.

"You have...a legend in your hair," he gasps.

"Malice," she croaks. "Malice, don't."

"Tell me…" He licks his lips. "Tell me who I am."

She draws in a breath, sweeping golden curls from his brows. "You're an outcast and a scholar, a villain and a hero. You carry a bow of hickory wood and the scent of old books. You're cagey, and you're funny. You read to dragonflies and have a sketch inked into your arm. You like the taste of pomegranate seeds, and you live in libraries. You're my f-friend," she sobs. "And I love y-you."

He sighs, worn out. "That's what I hoped."

That's what he knows now, and she knows it, too. Once, they'd asked each other what they wanted and feared most. He'd said to know himself, and she'd said to forgive herself.

It's those weaknesses and errors, those strengths and redeeming moments that they've faced. She'd never truly comprehended the puncture and press of love until now. It only became possible when she accepted herself, loved herself.

Such a simple rule, one that doesn't need legends or myths. One can find it embedded within a million books, a million kinships. Yet it's so difficult to achieve.

It's a remarkable similarity between deities and humans.

And now Wonder deciphers the meaning of the legend. To release her heart means forgiving herself for the past. And in order to do so, she must esteem herself.

And finally, she has.

She has forgiven herself for what she did to Quill.

Through imperfect love, she has touched her own worth. She has bid farewell to history and embraced the present, letting go of one boy and opening her arms to another.

And Malice? Recovering his heart doesn't mean questioning or tapping into who he once was. No, it means valuing who he is today. And he does.

They gaze at each other, sharing this realization, sharing it far too late.

Her body shouts to the stars, please don't take him, don't take him from her. But destiny cannot answer that wish any more than free will can.

Malice's lips crinkle, his sharp incisors poking out. Wonder freezes, watching with wide eyes as his own float from her face to the nearest window, to a view of the constellations. "Wonder..." He drags her fist to his mouth and speaks against the starburst scars. "I see my star."

Then his eyes cease to move, and they glaze over, and the light leaves them. Those orbs dim, the pupils winking out. He relaxes in her arms, his body giving like a feather. His expression stills, seeing nothing.

And then his grip loosens, releasing her hand.

From the crescent of archers around them, someone yelps, another moans, and another curses. The rest remain helpless and mournfully silent. In her periphery, they set down their weapons and create a kneeling ring around Wonder and Malice.

She gawks, and gawks, and gawks at his lifeless face, at his vacant eyes. She shakes him tenderly, violently. It makes no difference, because there's no cure for this, no legend to reverse it, no second resurrection to rely on.

He's gone.

They have succeeded in their mission, but he's gone. They have revealed the answer to this battle, but he's gone. They fell in love, but he's gone.

That arrow had been intended for her, but he's gone.

There's no one else she wants, but he's gone.

A silent scream pries her mouth apart, suspended for an instant. Then she sucks in air and lets it out, the disjointed sound pouring from her womb, from her ribs, from her throat, from her soul.

Wonder's heart shatters across her tongue. Her wail hits the roof.

The noise is full-bodied and relentless, streaming out of her over and over and over. "No!" she howls. "No...no...no!" Tears slice down her face as she heaves over Malice, rocking his head to her chest.

Guttural sobs tear through the atmosphere, knocking the stars from their vigils. Pitching forward and backward, Wonder depletes herself of noise. All the while, she mashes her weeping mouth into his gilded waves, inhaling wildflowers and pomegranates.

And the eternal scent of books.

26

She doesn't stop when the bellows sting her lungs. She doesn't stop when her protests fail to bring him back. No, she only stops when her throat dries, her howls ebbing to short swatches of breath.

However, she does keep rocking. She rests her head against Malice's chest, muffling the sounds of archers talking, either to her or amongst themselves, it doesn't matter. Then she begins to chant things Malice cannot hear, to whisper secret legends, to mumble the notes they'd written in the Archives and texts they'd scanned in the Chamber.

Perhaps she sounds like a maddened goddess. Perhaps that's fine.

Wonder recites into his ear, which is still soft and malleable. His skin retains its flush as if he's alive. But it's a lie, and she hates the deception.

The discussion around her amplifies. Her peers call out, beseeching, questioning, cautioning. Let them exert themselves, for all she cares.

When she makes no reply, footsteps approach, boot heels thunking against the library floor. The echo resounds down the aisles, across the demon god's home.

His home, away from home, away from home.

It shall be her home, too. She will live here, haunt this place as he did.

Those stubborn footsteps proceed, even as she recoils from the vibration. A specter intrudes, tall and windswept. Hunkering beside Wonder and Malice, the male silhouette darkens the already dark foyer, daring to blot out the specks of starlight.

Wonder's head leaps up, and she bares her teeth. "You keep away from him!" she growls at Anger. "You don't touch him!"

Anger's soul mate tugs him back. Even bittersweet Merry, along with sentimental Love and empathetic Sorrow, have the sense to stay away.

Who knows what Andrew and Envy are doing? Wonder suspects the latter is shaking his head to further discourage Anger. The former mortal has experience with bereavement, having lost his mother. Whereas Envy is unequivocally at a loss, because he has never valued anything but his own reflection.

Yet for all intents and purposes, they care about Wonder.

Wonder. Not Malice.

None of them will mourn him, because he'd been horrid to them. The notion fills Wonder's mouth with bile, her palate assaulted by a briny aftertaste.

The air whisks, jostling the stars that shine through the windows. Another vision approaches, along with another set of feet. Wonder perceives the distinction: the aerial gait and contemplative dismay. She glimpses the one who taught her so much—how to aim, how to ponder, how to muse, how to study, how to discover.

But not how to love someone, nor how to lose them.

Harmony kneels. In a shaft of moonlight, sympathy crinkles the mentor's brows, understanding glistening in her eyes. The instant their gazes meet, Wonder heaves into another sob, letting the elder embrace her, because it's okay to feel this, it's okay to unleash.

How do humans stand this feeling? How do their hearts keep beating? How do they endure? How can any soul be this strong?

Why must it hurt? Why so much? Can't it go away?

Please, make it go away.

But her mentor cannot do that, nor can the stars. That's not how magic works.

The goddess withdraws, staring until Wonder's able to straighten on her own. All the while, she refuses to let go of Malice, tucking him nearer.

Silently, Harmony presents a few items, setting them beside Wonder. These include the book she'd dropped in the Chamber—the answer to their campaign—along with archery crafted of hickory wood.

Upon returning to the mortal realm, Wonder hadn't thought to bring anything but Malice's Asterra Flora. That, and her own weapons, purely because the quartz archery had been strapped to her back.

Unable to resist, Wonder reaches out. Dreading and hoping she's right, her hand steals into the quiver of arrows, from which she retrieves a sepia envelope containing a corsage. It's a sprig of eucalyptus, white stephanotis, and a single purple peony, preserved with the replica of a letter she'd once written to him.

The first foolish, selfish, shameless missive Wonder had ever scribed to Malice. The one they had recited to each other while rocking across her sheets.

The rest of the letters had been left behind in the dorms, including the note she'd pilfered from him, but not this one. He'd stuffed this lone letter into his archery during their impasse in her room, before she'd chased after him. He'd kept the note close, so close to the posy of florals, so close to him.

Countless reactions whirl inside her, four most of all: wonder, for the time they'd shared; envy of the time they'd lost; love, from knowing him; sorrow, bereft of him.

Then a fifth emotion tightens like a vice around her wrists, flaring her nostrils and locking her jaw. A mirror reflection of her venomous, vengeful expression appears in the Guide's pupils. Any second, Wonder will crush the corsage in her grip.

Carefully, she presses the blossoms and envelope into Malice's limp hands and settles him on the ground. She moves with ceremony, making a shaky fist before she can bear to sweep his eyelids closed, shutting them forever. Then her knuckles brush the curls from his face and the blood from his cheek.

Finished, she kisses his obstinate chin.

Then she surges to her feet.

Without needing to guess, Wonder knows how she looks. Since she has never worn such a murderous countenance, it's possible her features stun everyone into immobility. So before they can stop her, she stalks across the library with hooded eyes and a livid pulse. While yanking the seed and blossom capsule from her pocket, her mind focuses on only one thing, one purpose, one retribution. She hammers toward a beam of starlight, ready to smear the mixture on her palm and return to the enemy. The rulers who took happiness from her.

A flurry of activity ensues from behind. Her peers shout, roar, holler.

"Wonder! Wonder, stop!"

"Wonder, don't!"

"Wonder!"

The world jolts as Envy's arm slings around her waist. "Ah-

ah-ah. Not so fast, my nymph."

"Get off me!" she spews. "Get the fuck off! They took him! They took him from me!"

"Hun, this isn't the way," the god grunts, wrestling with her. "You of all people know this. Come on now, we need you."

"I had him!" she shrieks. "I had him, and he's gone!"

It's pandemonium, everyone issuing declarations and lobbing warnings, all of it overlapping into nonsense. Envy secures Wonder while she thrashes, so that anyone who goes near her receives a scratch, or a kick, or glob of spittle.

Harmony skids in front of her. "Look at me," the female instructs, grasping Wonder's wheezing face. "Look at me, Wonder. Look at me, and remember who you are. Remember who he loved. Try to remember."

Wonder seethes, but she looks, and looks, and looks.

And at last, she remembers.

Three hours later, Malice's body rests across the wooden surface of a long study table. Flanked by bookcases, he still holds the flowers and envelope to his chest, but Wonder has surrounded him with more blooms from outside, and she has set his archery by his hip.

He needs everything close, all of it in reach, just in case he requires them. He might wish to smell the flowers or plot to steal them from her. He might ask her to reread the letter, so he'll want that as well. Or he might crave a book, or he might wish to trace one of his hickory arrows.

She deliberates whether to change his clothes, but that would conceal the way he'd died, and he would despise that.

As for herself, she had freshened up—with the help of Merry, Love, and Sorrow—once she'd calmed down. Unable to stomach wearing his blood, Wonder had conjured a soft green gown to replace her soiled garments, and she'd chosen bare feet over boots.

At present, the anger gushes out of her, leaving blessed numbness in its wake. She perches on the table's edge, constantly rearranging Malice's wildflowers, unable to get them right. If only she could get the bouquets right.

Perhaps she should start again.

Bodies crowd her, a ring of stars drawing near. Love and Andrew, Anger and Merry, Envy and Sorrow. And Harmony.

They stand in solidarity with her. They stand and wait.

Burdened by their attention, Wonder glowers at them, and when she does, her eyes water. Among them, she sees memories and friendship. Beyond that, she sees compassion.

Merry, with her sentimental eyes. Love, with her steadfast chin. Andrew, with his selfless visage. Anger, with his turbulent loyalty. Envy, with his smooth tenacity. Sorrow, with her grim resilience. And Harmony, with her soothing patience.

They hadn't known the rest of Malice. Nor will they truly know him, if Wonder doesn't share what happened in the Archives. There's so much to say, and they're here to listen.

So Wonder tells them her story, his story, their story.

At the end of it, they understand a bit more. Andrew, who knows bereavement. Love, who knows metamorphosis. Sorrow, who knows deprivation. Envy, who knows rivalry. Merry, who knows alienation. Anger, who knows disruption.

Harmony, who knows her pupil.

Yes, and it had ended painfully. But it had been worth it.

Hearing the myth of Malice's evolution from mortal to immortal, of his redemption, of his sacrifice for Wonder, the deities bow their heads, because they'd never gotten a chance to meet the person she loves. And when each archer adds a flower with star-shaped petals to the arrangement, it finally looks right.

A deity's body doesn't wither as a mortal's does. Thusly, Malice's complexion remains tinted with vibrancy, waiting for a ray of starlight to draw him in, to take him wherever immortals go from this point. Based on the firmament and the location where they've put him to rest amidst the books, a few hours remain for the light to shift in his direction.

After that, he will simply fade.

They could relocate him into a full beam and expedite the farewell, but he deserves to lull in peace, and Wonder longs for this interval. Alone, she watches over Malice, feasting on his sleeping face until then. He can rest without nightmares, without needing her to keep them at bay.

She vows to stay right here until he goes. But her ears perk at the tension coming from the religion section, where her companions have convened in a flurry of discord. When she'd told them about her and Malice's time in the Archives, she had imparted the details of this new legend, the one she discovered prior to that lava rock arrow...prior to Malice...

She evicts the vision from her mind, yearning to rip it out with her fingernails.

Evidently, her classmates and Guide have resurrected the subject, too restless to delay. Wonder resigns herself to let them hash it out, however Envy's growls rise another decibel and clash with Sorrow's snort of derision, at which everyone shushes the pair. An ensuing scuffle implies that Andrew and Merry are attempting to corral the group outside, out of Wonder's earshot.

At this rate, they shall misinterpret Wonder and Malice's findings. Without her there to make sure, they might recall the facts wrong, mutilating and misrepresenting the details, thoroughly botching the legend. Won't they?

In exchange for that text, Wonder has sacrificed love. If they hadn't followed that trail, Malice would be alive.

But then, they wouldn't have found the answer. His life had better not be in vain, starting with getting the particulars correct. Besides, he hates loose ends and inaccuracies.

Just like her.

Wonder checks the sky, assuring herself this will only take a moment. Leaning over, she toys with his golden curls, then kisses his lips. "I'll be right back," she promises. "Don't go anywhere."

She locates her friends in the two hundreds, in the mythology stacks. Envy and Sorrow have planted themselves at opposite ends of the space, wedging everyone else between them. Based on the would-be couple's crossed arms, they haven't taken the news well.

Anger had once made a pertinent point: Perhaps when more deities learn to love, fate will bridge with free will.

He's right. Universal love is the answer. In all its guises and forms, in all its capacities and tropes, from each angle and root, it's the ultimate inspiration.

The next question is this: Where does it start? How does it start? With whom?

Love and Andrew's match had been the spark for revolution, which has since grown through Anger and Merry. And now, it thrives from the bond between a villainous outcast god and a wandering floral goddess.

How to proceed from there? That's depends upon Envy and

Sorrow.

According to this new legend, if two deities can choose love over lust, they'll become a force of influence, along with those closest to them.

As members of the elite class, the first ring of emotions that has included love itself, the original five archers are a foundation. Initially, they're the souls most capable of feeling love.

Envy and Sorrow are the only two remaining. If they can progress to something more meaningful, their relationship will seal that link.

Strangers to lovers, friends to lovers, enemies to lovers, allies to lovers.

It's love from numerous angles and the final step to empowering their rebellious group, the compounding of which will create an awakening, one that will stimulate many to consider something remarkable.

They will begin to say, *What if...*

What if all deities can feel love? What if they aren't so different from humans after all? What if they're similar at heart? And what if that means they're equal?

How will that inform fate and free will? How will that change the balance?

If enough immortals consider this, they might start to believe. And if they believe, the dynamics will shift, as will the roles and powers of all beings.

But will inspiration magically happen? Will people simply take action and thus change?

Or will Wonder's class be obligated to solidify the inspiration somehow? Will they need to take one more cumulative step? What will that step be?

In the meantime, what if it still comes to battle?

That's what they shall be ready for.

Harmony seeks to control the argument as voices collide, each person snapping out vital points. Andrew accuses Envy and Sorrow of being selfish. They accuse him of being a former mortal. Love bristles at them for insulting her beau, hence tasking Andrew to calm her down.

Merry whistles for them to stop, while Anger barks for them to be quiet. Both tactics work in tandem, cutting off the commotion.

Because free will is as messy as fate, Envy has one ultimate response. "It ain't happening," he riots. "Me and her? Ain't happening outside of fucking."

"You can say that again," Sorrow grunts.

"For Fate's sake, Merry," Envy groans to the pouting, disappointed goddess. "Stop looking at me like that."

"But it's tragic," Merry laments. "How much you're missing."

"Hun, how's about a refresher? And listen up good, because I'll only say this once: I've got nothing against fluff, but the only person I'm interested in loving is myself."

"Anyway, we can't control how we feel," Sorrow adds. "And no one has the right to make us feel anything."

Wonder leans against a bookcase and clears her throat, causing all seven heads to swerve her way. "Did you hear what you just said?" she counters.

They stare at Wonder. Across each face, creases of worry smooth out, illustrating relief at her arrival and calm demeanor. But there's only one expression that she would give anything to see—a fiendish smirk agreeing with her.

For a moment, Wonder's chest aches from her own comment.

Because it's something Malice would have said.

27

And it's true. Envy and Sorrow are correct. Whether or not by the strike of an arrow, no one can control feelings. It's not a choice, but it's also not destiny.

Regardless, they just might learn to love each other, no matter how much they resist. Everyone hopes so, because a great many futures ride on that. It isn't fair to the couple in question, but that's the price of who they are.

Nonetheless, what one can control is how one reacts to such feelings, so long as comrades stay out of the way. Which is precisely why none may tell Envy and Sorrow how, or when, or why to change. Their class can encourage it, but in the end, it's up to the pair.

Mostly, it's up to them. That's fate and free will.

For the sake of both realms, they can at least try and see what emotions surface from their relationship. That had been Wonder's point. Unfortunately, it doesn't yield the desired effect, because after the group finishes giving Wonder consolatory looks, the argument resumes, picking up where it left off.

As much as Anger bristles and Love stomps her foot, ready to wallop the couple upside their heads, that will accomplish zilch. Envy and Sorrow continue to object, and the class continues to gang up on them, and Wonder continues to observe.

Anger's hoop earring swings in irritation. Merry's fluffy dress glitters like a chandelier dangling over her sneakers, her pink ponytail jumping in place. Love's white shift is a little oversized, in defiance of the short garment she used to wear. Andrew reclines against a bookshelf and folds his arms, muttering ironies and mild obscenities.

Vain as ever, Envy snaps his swanky suspenders. Sorrow readjusts a safety pin on her vest, her purple-painted lips set in a pout.

Wonder reflects. For all their centuries of living, she and her friends are so young. Yet to arm them with the power of emotions, to assume they know anything about these emotions simply by learning techniques and sensory signals, to believe that's the necessary extent of their training and experience? It's a significant flaw of their kind. To conclude that's all it takes to understand humanity, much less themselves, is a selfish failure.

For this equilibrium between fate and free will to manifest, it needs diversity. Not just from immortals like her class and former mortals like Andrew. Not merely from active archers and exiles like Merry.

But from age. From youths to elders.

Therefore, she's glad to have Harmony here. During such proceedings, the Guide would normally interject and share her wisdom. Be that as it may, she has another chief concern. Letting the archers work this out—to *learn* how to work this out—the mentor sidles toward Wonder, concern etched in her visage.

"It would be pretentious to advise you on this sort of recovery," she murmurs while the others bicker. "However, I have faith in one truth: Someday, you will be well again."

"Someday," Wonder echoes, even though she doubts it, even though she believes it.

Someday, she might recognize the value of this path, crafted of her actions and life's twists. Would she do it all over again, just to have that fleeting time with Malice? Of course, she would. Even if she couldn't change a thing, she would.

So yes, that's a union of destiny and choice as well.

Wonder joins hands with Harmony, squeezing their fingers together. As they do, the goddess's attention directs itself elsewhere, her features slackening, then lifting in renewed fortification. "Someday," she breathes. "Meanwhile, today..."

She inclines her chin, and Wonder turns, following the motion. The class's dispute tapers into awestruck silence. From each corner and around numerous bends, figures appear with archery harnessed to their backs and their heads banked inquisitively. Longbows and crossbows of the earth and sky, of limestone and marble, of stones and gems, and of other varied treasures.

Some faces are soft and flushed with youth, others chiseled and polished with maturity. Some wear circlets of leaves, others wear braids or metal clips. Their star-woven cloaks, liquid gowns, and supple, moon-threaded leathers shift with their movements. The visitors glow like lunar beams while bringing with them the scents of misted caves and blooming cliffs.

The fragrances of the Peaks.

Around Wonder, her class gathers, watching the deities' approach. The newcomers pause, a handful gazing about in curiosity, because they aren't old enough to know the mortal realm yet, others hardly sparing the library a passing glance, because they have served plenty of human landscapes.

Among the guests—some unrecognizable—is Hope and Joy, each female nodding toward Wonder and her class.

"This is...," Anger trails off, knowing as well as any of them what this is.

At last, it's what they've been striving for. It's what they've been campaigning for.

Wonder examines these faces, and she thinks of the Archives combat, and the Hollow Chamber's destruction, and the unarmed death of an outcast. With that, the clench on her soul eases, if only for this moment.

She speaks from her heart, from the place where Malice resides. "This is an alliance."

⌒

That's what this is. These gods and goddesses from the Peaks have journeyed here, defying the Fates in order to side with a small band of celestial rebels.

Although Hope had been present to witness it, neither she nor Joy had to report a word; yet news of recent events had traveled quickly. A substantial population of the Peaks spurn Wonder and Malice for trespassing on sacred ground during Stellar Worship. By the same token, the populace blames them for Chamber's downfall.

Whereas others—who were already questioning their positions, especially after hearing the infamous tales of Love and Anger's respective romances—condemn the Fate Court for taking down an indefensible god. No matter how anarchistic Malice had been, to target a disarmed deity and shoot him in the back is dishonorable.

Over the past year, Wonder's class had beseeched allies, making progress with outcasts in the Celestial City. As for residents of the Peaks, they hadn't recruited as many, the majority of the candidates either hedging or not answering the call.

But now, this. Standing behind Hope and Joy are dozens of archers, those who have heard the tales of love and destiny and choice. Realities that may be possible for all.

There is much to impart. At Anger's suggestion, the convocation elects to change location, agreeing upon Stargazer Hill, where the participants can spread around the sycamore tree, under twilight and amidst a sleeping Carnival of Stars.

Wonder chooses to remain behind with Malice. She'll join the assembly later, once he has faded.

On their way out, they pay respect to the fallen exile, passing Malice's table and inclining their heads. The sight peels tears from Wonder's ducts. As she escorts the masses out and then pauses on the library's backdoor threshold, Harmony kisses her cheek, Merry gives her a hug, and Wonder receives nods of support from the rest. She watches them travel into the Celestial City, a collection of renegades bleeding in with the night and heading for the twinkling theme park.

Her chest flutters. The air shifts, along with the sky's inky light.

Awareness and dread pierce through her. She rushes down the aisles, dashing past books and vines of ivy. Rounding the corner, her feet slam to a halt, a lamentation climbing to the rims of her mouth.

Malice is gone.

Now she knows what loss feels like.

Her bare feet sink into the earth, the high grass tickles her ankles, and petals brush her calves. And when a breeze rustles her gown—dyed the green of a calla lily stem—the little pirouette of air billows the material, the hem flapping in a farewell gesture.

Something akin to *Good-bye*.

Of all the forbidden words that she's ever written, she has never penned that one. She's never had a reason to do so. Not until today.

Lupines sprout across the vista, a landscape not of her childhood, nor of adulthood. It's a realm caught somewhere in between, a pasture of budding fruit rather than flowers, of moon beams rather than sun beams. Hence, it's not her place.

No, this is his place. Or this used to be his place, back when she hardly knew him.

Back when she hardly knew herself.

He'd once growled an inquiry at her, demanding a truth that she hadn't been able to grasp.

Who are you?

It has taken a long time, but she knows the answer.

Yet it's too late. He's too far from her, too far away.

What she wouldn't give to have that demon back, to tell him she wants the lightness and darkness. She yearns for that angel's face and devil's heart. She wishes to tell him the past doesn't matter as much as the present.

She wants to call him by his name and mean it.

But she can't. She cannot even scribe these things on paper for him, because he'll never read those words, never any words from her. Not ever again.

Because he's gone.

He's gone because of her.

And this time, he's not coming back.

She bends and picks a miniature flower from the lupine stalk, watching the petals skip against the current. Closing her eyes, she inhales a pomegranate and an old book. And she realizes, he might hear her, after all.

If she speaks, he just might hear. "Malice," she whispers.

But what she doesn't expect is a response. "You remembered," a voice says from behind.

28

The bloom flutters from her hand and floats to the ground. Like a quill or fletching, it sails and then lands, caught by the high grass that sways across the pasture, the brush of green blades and lupines creating a wave.

Wonder's unshod toes splay in the fresh soil, cushioned into the earth. Yet the world tilts like a planet knocked off its axis, floral hues splashing color and dimension everywhere. She ponders if her feet might grow roots and burrow here, and if that's possible, and how long it might take.

Perhaps she's becoming a wildflower or a pomegranate tree. Or perhaps she's going mad like he once had, because she cannot have heard that voice. Not so clearly, nor so near.

How strong is the imagination? How fierce?

Do illusions ever become real?

A shadow touches hers on the hill, the harsh edges of him blending with the curves of her, their silhouettes merging beneath the gauzy outlines of drifting clouds. The masculine form behind her kneels to retrieve the bit of fallen lupine. Rising, he skims the petals along the rim of her lobe, causing a chain reaction down her spine.

"You'd better concentrate," he coos, tucking the flower behind her ear. "Or you'll lose something delicate."

His breath skates across her shoulders, his raspy tenor scooping out her heart. Wonder's eyes close, and her mouth opens to taste the sound. "This isn't real."

"Hmm. I can list a half dozen legends that weren't supposed be real, not to mention a few love stories and one savvy reincarnation. Why don't you meditate on that and get back to me?"

"Malice?"

"Wonder?"

"Are you a ghost?"

"Not anymore," he says, "as sexy and perverted as that would be. But you can call me a god. Or better yet, call me Hades. I like being called Hades."

It sounds as though he's inches from her. But she won't turn, she can't turn, she'll never turn. If she does, what if this moment vanishes?

What if it doesn't?

And what had he said a second ago? Before she dropped the lupine?

Oxygen stutters from between her lips. "You said that I remembered. What did you mean? What did I remember?"

"To come back," he replies.

She had expected him to say that she'd remembered his name...the name of his present life, not his past one.

But, no. That's not it.

In the library, Wonder had kissed his lifeless mouth and swore to return from the meeting with her classmates. She had vowed to watch him fade, insisting that she would be right back.

But his declaration is wrong, because she hadn't fulfilled that promise, because she ran out of time. Hadn't she?

"I told you not to go anywhere," she accuses.

"I didn't." A sly grin fills his tone. "*He* did."

And it doesn't take skill to know who he's referring to. She has been raised on awe, and musings, and enigmas. She has spent her life meditating and discovering. She has grown up harvesting mysteries and translating secrets.

Oh stars, she knows who he means.

But how has she not considered this? Perhaps she hadn't dared. For once, she hadn't risked hoping for the implausible.

The first time he died, destiny trapped his soul, caging him in between his mortal demise and an immortal's hold. Only when restoring his heart—by valuing himself and embracing love—did he restore the past. And only when perishing for the second time did he truly free himself from it.

Malice hasn't faded. Quill has.

At last, his former self is a genuine memory. At last, the boy named Quill rests in peace.

Finally, he's just Malice. And he's very much alive.

"You disappeared," Wonder testifies. "The table was empty. You were gone."

"Eh. For a little while," he supplies. "I was dreaming of books, and then I heard you whispering to me. You left after that, but you were on your way back, because I heard you. So yeah, you kept your promise. And just when your come-hither footfalls reappeared around the corner, the sound of you dissolved, and I was dreaming again. When I finally blinked awake, the library was vacant, and I was still on the table, alone and groggy as shit. Sort of like a death hangover."

"Dammit, how can you joke about this?"

"Christ, come on. Don't you know me by now?"

In spite of herself, Wonder chuckles weakly.

He was alone because her class had traveled to Stargazer Hill. In her grief, she had come here instead of following them.

And why here? Why this prairie hill from his past life, the environment that still exists unblemished and unchanged? To say good-bye to every place that led to him. Even though he'd been Quill in this setting, that existence had eventually turned him into Malice, the misfit who had shaken her heart and then filled it to overflowing. She had come here to let every piece of him go.

That's why he had known where to look.

"You're...," Wonder trails off. "You're here."

"If that's okay with you," Malice says. "Otherwise, I can't just—"

On a half-sob, half-growl, she spins around.

There he is, looming over her in a black leather sweater that blends into his jeans. He's free of archery and shoes, his bare toes bumping against hers. And there's that crown of mussed, golden waves. The wiry, filthy mouth and cunning chin.

Those manic eyes that are no longer ashen. Rather, they're a silken gray, a mirror of the overcast sky or a subterranean vault. Transfixed by her, the irises glisten with a complex emotion—the most complicated and messy one of all.

He presents the corsage that she'd left with his body and fixes it around her wrist. "Told you I'd give it back eventually." Only this misfit can manage a grin that's equally bittersweet and devious. "By the way? I love you, too."

Wonder launches herself at him. Slamming her fists on his chest, she pounds into him, crying and sputtering—and then flinging her arms around his neck. "Malice," she weeps. "You came back to me."

He crushes her to him, his arms wending around her waist. "Looks like I always will." He seizes her face and lifts her head, their tears fusing as he speaks against her mouth. "You're in my head. You're in my chest, my ribs, my fingertips. You've been there from the beginning, before I laid eyes on you. You've been right there. I'll always come back to you, Wonder. You better believe I'll always come back."

Scarcely finishing that sentence, his mouth tackles hers. And it doesn't matter that he cannot always come back, that he might not be so lucky the next time. It doesn't matter because they're not planning on a third time. He's so alive, and she's so alive, and they're here.

And this is now. Not then, but now.

This is real, with its flawed edges and exquisite detours, with its erudite underworlds and wandering hilltops. That's all she wants, all she needs.

Under this mortal sky, they start over.

Dragging his palms to the back of her head, Malice locks Wonder in place while his teeth nip her mouth, then his lips split her open. They slant into a kiss. He's tart to the palate, like a hard, crimson fruit, and maybe she's sweet like a bud, or maybe they have the same flavor.

Their lips fold, spreading and rolling together. His tongue passes into her, swats into her, the tip riding along her own tongue. They coil, sweeping into a delirious rhythm—a living, sighing, teeming thing.

A moan skitters up her throat, and he catches it. In turn, he emits a guttural noise, the vibration shimmering across her flesh, radiating to the core. She feels that sound flex between her thighs, causing the muscles to tighten.

As his wet tongue strokes into her mouth with a rough tempo, she entwines with him. Her digits climb into his hair, and one of his palms braces around her nape, the other scaling down to her buttocks. Their bodies meld, her ample form snuggling into his angular one as they lunge into the kiss. Teeth scrape, and lips quiver, and tongues probe.

Gasping for air, Malice pulls back to rest his forehead against hers. Those brazen eyes fill her vision as she feels her dress loosen from behind. She reciprocates by fumbling with his leather sweater, which conceals too much of him.

Her belly takes flight, flapping in anticipation, which is odd. They've done this multiple times, from numerous angles, on a variety of surfaces.

Has she ever been nervous with him?

Yes. But never this nervous.

She has never made love to Malice—*only* to Malice.

Wonder whips the sweater over his head, throwing it somewhere, anywhere, elsewhere. The straps of her dress tumble over her shoulders, the garment ready to slip from her completely.

They sink to the grass, her back reclining, the blades of green tickling her elbows and heels. Malice falls into the gap between her thighs, his weight a delicious relief. Her legs hitch around his hips, her knees pitching high as his head dips. And oh Fates, he sucks the pliable flesh of her neck, right where it meets her clavicles.

Wonder mewls, and he hums, increasing the pressure. The result is almost hallucinatory, electrifying her senses.

Dragging down the gown's neckline, he bares a breast, swollen to his view. "What a little pearl," he mumbles. "I need to have that."

His lips find the center, drawing the pert nipple between his ivories. Wonder writhes. His tongue is a torment, tugging her into his mouth, circling and lapping while his talons trace the slumped straps of the gown.

She protests when he changes his mind and inches away,

which only incites a black chuckle. Curse him.

Suspending himself above her, Malice tosses Wonder a wicked, lopsided grin as he enjoys the prickles along her skin. Without warning, those nails give a flick, shearing the threads. Limp, the dress drizzles down her body.

Malice chucks the garment aside and appraises Wonder as though he's never seen her breasts and stomach and thighs, nor the private center of her limbs. The thick, heavy-lidded expression on his face causes that spot to throb. It pulses, growing damp from his stare.

A line of raised tissue runs across his heart, where a lava rock arrow had pierced him through. Her hands map the bumpy pulp of skin there, dulled from an orchid purple to a delphinium pink, while his pulse rams against her fingertips. Then she continues to the contours of his torso, the expanse of muscle, and the taper of hair at his navel.

He's hard and smooth *everywhere*. She sees this when the jeans come off. He leans away to strip the coarse material from his body, kicking the garment aside, exposing himself to her.

Crawling back to Wonder, Malice plants kisses from her ankles, to her ribcage, to her nipples. Then he inhales the flowers around her wrist, the only adornment she's wearing.

Sliding into her arms and limbs, his pelvis settles onto hers, stiffness sinking against moisture. It's heavenly, this glide of skin on skin.

Wonder straps her thighs around his waist, her feet hooking over his backside. She combs through his curls, and he tilts his chin, wanting more. He gazes at her in wild reverence.

"I'm going to watch you," he murmurs. "I'm going to watch everything my body does to yours. I'm going to watch everything you feel."

She bites his upper lip. "Then make me feel."

"I'll study each look, each sound, each movement," he intones. "I'll learn everything, all over again. I'll unravel every secret."

"Then unravel me," she whispers.

They're panting, exchanging haggard breaths. His claws glide over her cheekbones, his hips inching into hers, a subtle grind that pushes a whine out of her, a rumble out of him.

"On one condition," she moans.

"A bargain?" He quirks a brow. "I like bargains."

"Only if I get to conquer you, too."

"Ahh, but you've already done that."

"Then I'll do it again."

"That's my selfish, curvy queen," he quips, his waist strumming into her, pushing her to insanity. "Then make me feel, Wildflower. Unravel me."

She nods, starting with this: "I love you."

Malice's pupils swell. And this: "I love you more."

Not true. In this, the score is equal. She would say so, but then his pelvis swings forward, his length plying into her, filling her to the brim.

Wonder's head thrashes back, her spine snapping. "Uh..."

He gives her no chance to recover, thrusting fully and without reserve. The pace kills their debate, robbing them of logic. Her thighs splay around him, rocking each pass of his body into hers. All sense pivots to where they're joined, and joined, and joined.

They reel over the grass, crushing the blooms, chanting under the sky, exploding beneath the stars. He groans in rapture, and she cries in pleasure.

"Who's inside you?" he entreats. "Who's pumping into you?"

"You are," she moans. "You are, Malice." She clasps his laboring backside. "And who's surrounding you?"

"You are, Wonder. You are."

Who are you?

That question. It's the most vital inquiry they've ever encountered, the most elusive answer they've ever chased.

This is who they are. Wonder and Malice.

She's a goddess of libraries and blossoms, a wandering deity who dabbles in legends and defies the odds. She's a wisher, a muser, a fighter who has gifted her heart to a demon.

He's a god of pages and pomegranates, a scheming deity who dabbles in secrets and curses the odds. He's a plotter, a thinker, an offender who has offered his heart to an archeress.

Together, they're tempters of fate.

Rising high to peer at her, Malice braces himself on his forearms, the fletching-and-quill tattoo straining across his bicep. He moves inside her, and she sheaths him deeply, their bodies whisking in union. And they watch each other, and they study each other, and they disarm each other.

Grabbing one of her limbs, he changes the angle, fucking into her sweetly. Her pulse crests, her voice fluttering to the firmament, about to come undone—to come with him. But it isn't until he steals one of her hands, it isn't until his lips sketch her scars, it isn't until he kisses the starbursts that she actually does.

Exertion produces beads of perspiration. Their bodies tense like springs, then splinter into a thousand fragments of light, the sound of it rattling two realms. Malice's mouth returns to hers, opening with hers as they shout across the hills, shaking the roots and constellations. Clinging naked to him, she bursts to life, and he follows her there.

When the frenzy subsides, they go limp. Malice lands, and she catches him. The breeze stirs petals over the panorama.

He raises his head, a golden sphere against the ink of night. Their stomachs rub as they hunt for air, staring at one another in amazement. That was...that was...

They laugh. He nuzzles her breasts, then kisses her face, then flirts in her ear, muttering intimate puns.

"We've got centuries to make up for. Know what that means?" he asks, propping his cheek in his palm while they're still entangled.

"It means you'd better get comfortable," she says, pecking his lips.

And he agrees, "Because we're not done yet."

And finally, they don't have to be.

EPILOGUE

MALICE

The stars are out.

Sort of like magic, the clouds jet on by, exposing a gang of constellations. The celestials blaze, the lights smirking and beating darkness out of the way. Humans and deities call them different things, which is fine by him. There's plenty of room for every idea.

Anyone who says differently can go to hell, which can't be all that bad. He's heard the weather is fantastic in hell.

It's been months since his second resurrection. Tonight, he sits nude at the top of a hill, with a voluptuous wildflower reclining in his arms. Curling on the grass, she tucks her naked shoulders into his torso and rests her head against his chest. That alone drives him crazy. But then, she's always driven him crazy.

Right from the get-go, she'd affected him. This goddess, with her grit and generosity, her intelligence and resolve. This sprite, with her strong-willed jaw that he'd routinely wanted to lick, her wandering voice that had turned his heart into a battering ram, her competitive streak that had gotten him as hard as a screwdriver, and the marigold hair that he'd constantly had an urge to wind around his finger…sometimes to tug, sometimes to caress.

So easy to push her buttons yet so freaking tough. She'd clashed with him, stared him down, fallen asleep with him. She'd wrung him out and filled him with adrenaline, rivalry, and rage, swamping him with confusion and cravings.

And yeah, desire. And affection.

And then more. A heck of a lot more.

But fuck, right here, right now? This is a new kind of crazy, with a new shape. It's a peaceful, happy crazy.

Why had fate done all this? Why had the stars enabled any of it?

Maybe he'd been reincarnated because of his letter to Wonder, when he'd expressed a desire to know what immortality was like. Maybe the sky had listened. Maybe the constellations had granted him that wish as compensation for what one of their goddesses had done, having cut short his life's path.

And in the Hollow Chamber? He might have released Quill, but he'd still been shot through the heart. So maybe he'd been given this new chance at immortality because of the legend, because he'd only just succeeded in recovering his heart, because he'd only just earned the reward. And maybe fate had wanted to apologize for the ruler who'd struck him down during a ceasefire.

Maybe all of this had happened because of one thing. Or a shitload of things.

Maybe a bunch of stars had aligned.

No matter what, one fact is clear: Destiny had expected this. It had taken crucial steps to unite Malice with Wonder, knowing what they'd mean to each other, knowing he would play his part in the bigger picture, in the balance of fate and free will.

Oh, the irony.

Malice grins. He bows his head, skimming Wonder's nape with his lips, relishing the goosebumps charging across her flesh.

His limbs bend on either side of his library queen, and his arms sling around her. Conjuring a blanket, he wraps them in the material, their cheeks touching as they watch the landscape thrive.

It's only been a few minutes, and already his body simmers. How many hills have they christened so far, since he came back to her for the second time? He's lost count.

He nibbles her shoulder. "Rawrrrr."

She giggles. "Again?"

"Is that a question? I like questions."

"This is dangerous," she gasps when he cups her tits under the blanket and snacks on her neck. "We should prepare."

"Where's the fun in that?" he pouts.

"I can't believe you talked me into this."

"If I recall, you're the one who tore off my sweater. We haven't done much talking since."

Also not true. He usually has a lot to say when they're in the thick of it.

As to their location, sure. She's right about doing this here, of all places. But really, he likes to think of it as a rebel's rite of passage.

Why not bless the battlefield, give it a dose of lovin'?

Malice mumbles as much, earning an aerial laugh that slips right into his abdomen, joy lurching through his blood. It's the best sound in the universe, other than when she's reading aloud or moaning his name.

His name.

"Malice," she says, twisting to receive his greedy kiss.

"Wonder," he says, savoring her tongue.

A throat clears, its high pitch skipping across the summit. By contrast, a less discreet throat blusters, "What the Fates?"

The stormy sound jackhammers through the atmosphere.

Wonder peeps and jerks away. Malice groans, recognizing that thunderstruck voice.

Great. Just when he was about to take his wildflower for a victory lap.

Goddammit, Anger.

The six rebels gather on the hill, thanks to Malice's Asterra Flora. Constellations riot in the backdrop, and cliffs rise like fists behind the troop.

"You're early, mates," Malice mock whines. "What have I told you about being early? Bad, bad deities."

With pink blotting her complexion, Wonder scrambles in his arms. "Dearests! We were just…"

"Please don't clarify," Anger grumbles.

"Speak for yourself," a swanky timbre says. "I want details."

Malice sniggers as a pile of black clothes fly at him. Their group is hardly as condemning toward Wonder, who accepts her pants and blouse, both extended by the dainty hand of Merry, who beams at them.

That she can gush at Malice after everything? That she'd actually accepted his apology when he appeared on Stargazer Hill with Wonder, shocking the fuck out of everyone? It must be the former love goddess in Merry. She's a romantic who puts faith in redemption and shit.

All right, it does lift his mouth and blunt the edges…maybe a little.

The others remain wary. He doesn't blame them considering it's only been a few meager months since the Hollow Chamber's demise, since he joined their celestial band of renegades. Though occasionally he'll crack a joke that'll make one of them snort. Or they'll glance at him for insight while discussing conflict tactics.

To say the least, sex in enemy territory isn't part of the

strategy. But maybe they're getting used to Malice, because at the moment, they don't clamor, just wait in silence as he and Wonder get dressed, which takes all of a millisecond.

Envy ogles the post-coital scene, grinning like an asswipe. He's positioned himself on the opposite end of the line, farthest away from Sorrow, who rolls her eyes at him. It's been this way ever since Wonder shared the latest legend with them. Guess the hot and heavy times are over between those two, so long as they deny what they've been told.

But that's their choice. And it's their story.

Andrew glances away while pressing a fist to his smiling mouth. Beside him, Love taps her foot impatiently, giving Malice her default look—the one that states she'll castrate him if he ever lets Wonder down.

She doesn't have to worry. None of them do.

He's here to stay.

Merry squeezes Anger's hand, preventing him from rushing Malice. Too bad. Fucking with the god is fun, and fun is just so very funny.

All the same, Anger the Angry opens his mouth.

"Ah-ah." Malice flaps his finger, his sharp nail slicing the air. "Don't go there, mate. It'd be the pot calling the kettle black."

"You couldn't wait until you were home?"

Ahh. Their home, away from home, away from home. He and Wonder share an annex in the Celestial City's library, a cozy little retreat that she prefers to the vault.

"We ran out of surfaces—and hills," Malice defends, snatching his hickory bow off the grass and strapping it to his back. "We needed extracurricular options. And don't go telling me the rest of you avoid getting frisky in public. I've seen every one of your afterglows. Besides, who doesn't like to experiment—"

Wonder slaps a palm over his mouth. Playfully, he bites her hand.

It's a good thing her Guide isn't here. If Harmony were, she'd have words for them. Instead, she's back in the mortal realm with their allies, rallying exiles and defectors alike.

Malice collects Wonder's quartz weapons and hands them to her. Joining the archers, they step to the crag's edge, where they gaze at the mountain range carpeted in purple, the misty waterfalls, and the sedate pools of water in the distance. In the valley below, a forest crowds the depths, with the silver dots of young dragonflies speeding through the beeches and willows while their gargantuan parents dwell by the sea.

Shrouded in the dale's woodland is the Archives and the ruins of a forbidden repository. Hopefully, they'll repair the damage someday. They'll remake the Hollow Chamber, because if anything should be immortal, it's books.

Aside from that, he'd left his saddlebag and envelopes there. Does he want them back? Eh. Not necessary anymore.

As Malice glances at Wonder's profile, it's clear that he's got everything he needs.

Besides, they'd managed to save the copy of her first letter to him. That's plenty.

Anyway, they're not heading to the Archives this time around. Nope, they've got a different destination in mind.

Everyone stares, the moment sinking in. They'd agreed to meet on this hill and then forge ahead. Shit's about to get real. Time to put their plan into motion. This isn't a scheme anymore; it's either the beginning or the end.

"Are we making the right choice?" Anger asks.

"We won't know until we try," Merry says. "But how thrilling to have a choice."

"What are we waiting for?" Love demands. "One of us should take the first step."

Malice would volunteer, but he doubts they want him leading the pack.

Andrew speaks up when no one else makes a reply. "You know what I've never understood? Why the hell is love the outcome of only five emotions? If it's the most complex one in existence, shouldn't a bunch of other feelings play a part? We feel a crap ton of things when we're with someone who matters, and I wouldn't break it down to just a handful. And what about happiness? What about confusion? What about *fear*?

"Plus, Merry feels love, and Malice feels it, not just the Infamous Original Five. I mean, we've established that it's possible all deities might feel it and just need convincing, right? All they need are examples that prove it. So maybe…I don't know, but maybe every deity is love itself."

Well, hell. For a mate who can't shut up, he's got something there.

Everyone stalls. They stare at one another, like Andrew's speech had never occurred to any of them. It definitely hadn't to Malice.

Love grins at Andrew. "I suppose we're the core."

"That's why evolution starts here. It's up to us to make the first leap," Wonder adds.

Malice can swallow that. It sounds plausible, if heavy handed.

Andrew nods. "Then I'll do it."

Meaning, he's the first to make a move. Done gawking at the landscape, he limps down the incline while armed with his frost crossbow. Love skips after him, linking their arms together.

Anger and Merry trade sappy glances and follow. The goddess hops on her immortal skateboard and cruises ahead, the wheels shearing smoothly through grass as if on solid ground. The rage god strides next to her, keeping up with the pace while they each balance weapons of neon and iron.

Envy and Sorrow avert their gazes from each other, like that's going to make a damned difference. Until they get their heads out of their asses and give the final legend a try, this class has a contingency plan to act out.

The swaggering god and sour goddess trudge into the forest, marching alongside their class, forming one insurgent line.

Wonder glances at Malice while adjusting the straps of her quartz archery. "Ready?"

"I'm always pumped to raise hell with you," he says. "Oh, and when this is over, we're soooo coming back to this spot."

She throws back her head and chortles, a boisterous sound that he'll never get tired of hearing. "I'm counting on it, Demon," she says.

"Then lead the way, Wildflower," he invites.

Wonder kisses him and threads her fingers with his, her scarred hands clasping his clawed ones. And hell, this female is sexy when she arms herself while also wearing a corsage. His blooming, bookish, badass goddess.

Yeah, he's got it bad. Forever bad.

Malice nips the base of her palm, loving her mirthful flush—loving all of her.

How clever. Here they are, descending into the unknown, returning to deadly terrain. But this time, he's whole. He knows himself, and she knows him, and they're still here.

And now he knows what that feels like.

Thank you for reading Wonder & Malice's story!

Ready for Envy and Sorrow?
Get *Transcend* (Selfish Myths #4)!

Join my mailing list to get exclusive content, advanced updates, and details about new books at www.nataliajaster.com/newsletter

ACKNOWLEDGMENTS

Characters never cease to amaze me. When Malice first made an appearance in Torn, I knew immediately that he was going to play an intense role in this series. His diabolical, eccentric, and volatile personality roared off the pages, giving me a starlit flash of inspiration. Ahh, how I love the challenge of a villainous bad boy.

And then Wonder returned to this world. And I knew exactly where this was headed.

And I could not wait.

Hades and Persephone feels, anyone?

The idea of turning Wonder and Malice's story into an urban fantasy mythology retelling flooded the creative well. This couple shoved me out of my comfort zone, with their rivalry, their harrowing past, and their strong wills. The dynamic between them daunted and fascinated me, from the beginning to the end.

And so here we are. While it's not a direct mirror of the original Greek myth, I drew on bits and pieces of tradition while subverting others, outfitting the tale in a leather jacket and giving it a bibliophile flair. The result is a devilish misfit, a scholarly wildflower, and a magical library underworld.

I loved every moment with these two bookish deities. And I hope you did, too.

As always, I'm blessed in my constellation of supporters.

Thank you to Esther Gwynne for being an editing goddess.

Many hugs to Michelle, Jessa, and Candace for your illustrious beta skills—and more importantly, for your immortal friendship.

Thank to you my family, for brightening my sky.

To Roman, all the kisses for being my soul mate.

And to you celestial readers, who have showered Selfish Myths with love. To my ARC team, the Myth & Tricksters reader group, and each person who has given this series a bookish hug.

I cannot believe we're almost to the end of this universe. Where is this journey headed? Hehe, you'll find out soon.

So now get ready for Envy and Sorrow...

ABOUT NATALIA

Natalia Jaster is the fantasy romance author of the Foolish Kingdoms & Selfish Myths series.

She loves to dream up settings that are realistic yet mystical. She loves when raw angst collides with lyrical beauty, and when sweetness escalates to hotness. And she definitely loves treading the line between YA and NA.

She's also a total fool for first-kiss scenes, fanfiction, libraries, and starry nights.

COME SAY HI!

Join Natalia's mailing list: nataliajaster.com/newsletter
Bookbub: bookbub.com/authors/natalia-jaster
Facebook: facebook.com/NataliaJasterAuthor
Goodreads: goodreads.com/nataliajaster
Instagram: instagram.com/nataliajaster
Tumblr: andshewaits.tumblr.com

See the boards for Natalia's novels on Pinterest:
pinterest.com/andshewaits

Printed in Great Britain
by Amazon